Savor Me

BETH BOLDEN

CHAPTER ONE

WHAT THE FUCK.

Xander Bridges slammed on his brakes half a second before he remembered it was storming, the rain coming down in unrelenting sheets, and the road resembling a creek more than it did an actual swath of asphalt.

It would have been really fucking difficult to make him forget it was raining—the water coming down from the sky had been relentless for his entire drive home from another long day at Terroir, the Michelin-starred restaurant where he worked insane shifts as a *sous chef*. But the sight before him made him forget nearly everything.

To the left, there was a vineyard, which was not the surprising part of the view. There were vineyards everywhere you looked in the Napa Valley, some better, some worse, some merely mediocre. Xander *knew* that the vineyard he was looking at now wasn't any of those. It was one of the first vineyards that had ever been planted by the Hess family, and therefore one of the first vineyards ever planted in Napa. It wasn't just good or great or anything else on that spectrum; essentially, it was priceless.

And there was a man out there, battered by the sheets of rain, yanking up the vines with his bare hands.

It wasn't even close to the smart thing to do. Xander hit the brakes anyway, and skidded along the edge of the road, finally coming to a stop right next to the embankment.

He sat there for a moment, heart thumping with the surge of adrenaline. From the skid he'd taken or the man, who was still ripping up the vines, it was hard to say.

If Wyatt or Miles, his best friends, had been here, they would have told him to keep his ass in the car and drive away. No good could come from him walking into the torrential downpour and confronting someone who was clearly insane. But Wyatt and Miles weren't here—they had moved to LA, leaving Xander behind—and he was riding a rough-edged *fuck it* mindset these days.

The only smart thing he did was to leave his phone in the console, charging, and to pull off the zip-up sweatshirt he'd thrown over the undershirt he generally wore under his chef whites.

It was wet, sure, but it wasn't cold, and he didn't need to be bogged down by extra soaking wet fabric.

He knew it was going to be miserable, but the first blast of moisture to the face still made him gasp as the rain ran down his face. Slamming the car door shut, he struggled through the mud of the embankment, finally making it to the edge of the vineyard. He climbed over the short, pointless wire fence, and started walking toward the man destroying hundreds of thousands of dollars of vines. Maybe even millions.

The man hadn't seen him yet, even though Xander stopped in front of him, only a few yards away. He was completely intent on the vines, hacking away at them with his bare fists, tearing and pulling and grasping, caught up in a rage that Xander recognized, deep down. He'd never acted on it though, had only internalized it, and had developed a finely honed sarcasm to express it safely.

The man wasn't internalizing jack shit.

It occurred to Xander that despite not wanting to ruin his phone, he shouldn't have left it in the car. Now he was completely at this man's mercy, and he didn't seem particularly stable, with a side dish of barely leashed control.

He shouldn't be here. Shouldn't be interfering. But he was here now, increasingly soaked, and so he spoke up.

"What the fuck?" Xander asked.

The man looked up, rain pouring down his face. His hair was dark and cropped close to his head, his face a pale swath under all that water, his eyes a surprisingly light bluish-green. They stared right through Xander, as he held himself motionless.

It was something to behold; all that muscular power being held still. And Xander knew just what was hiding under his soaked flannel shirt because it clung to every inch of him. His jeans, too. Xander shouldn't even be thinking it, but those were definitely the finest thighs he'd ever had the privilege of not seeing.

At least if he died, he'd have a real good view at the end.

"What are you doing here?" the man growled. "You're trespassing."

"And you're basically ripping up money," Xander challenged right back. He really should have called the cops, instead of deciding to confront this guy by himself. What he was doing *was* a crime, wasn't it?

A segment of vine still hanging from the man's hand dropped to the mud with a solid *plop*. "They're mine, I can do whatever I want with them."

"Including being stupid?" Xander asked. Really the only stupid person here was him, but it was in his nature to keep pushing and not let things go. It was how he'd ended up *sous* at Terroir, and also how he'd ended up in this vineyard, past midnight, in the middle of a gigantic storm. It was probably how he was going to end up murdered, he thought darkly.

The empty fist opened and then clenched tightly again. "You don't know what you're talking about."

This was undeniably true. "So why don't you tell me," Xander suggested. Not like they were in the middle of a storm. Instead like they had just met at a local bar, and Xander, completely unlike himself, had approached the built and rugged man everyone kept eyeing nervously and offered to buy him a drink.

There was shock radiating out of those light eyes. Like the last thing he expected Xander to do was to ask. To *care*.

As far as Xander was concerned, that was his ultimate curse. He always, always, *always* cared too much, no matter how much he tried to hide it under layers of sarcasm and bitterness.

"You really want me to tell you." His voice was cautious and a little gentle now, nothing like the fierce growl from only a few minutes ago. As if Xander had managed to calm him despite himself.

"I'm here, aren't I?" Xander spread his arms, the rain continuing to come down around them.

"Hell if I know why," the man grumbled. "Let's get out of the rain first." He jabbed a finger quick and sharp toward a ranch-style house that sat a few hundred yards away.

Xander hesitated, and the man must have sensed it. He extended a muddy, grimy, *bloody* hand. "I'm Damon Hess."

Damon *Hess*. Well, now it was official. Xander felt stupid as shit. Damon probably owned these vines—or his family did. And why he was out here, in the middle of the night, ripping them to shreds, really wasn't any of Xander's business.

Yet when he shook his hand, palm sliding wetly against Damon's, Xander couldn't miss a loneliness he recognized peeking out from behind the wall in his eyes.

Maybe the man really needed someone to talk to, and that was why he'd resorted to the worst-case scenario of pulling up the god damned vines. God knew, Xander hadn't been able to talk his friend Kian out of making an enormous mistake, but maybe he could be an ear for Damon.

"Xander Bridges," Xander said. "Sure, why not. Let's go talk."

The walk to the house was both short and also an eternity. His pants were soaked through, the sodden fabric slapping against his legs, rain dripping down his chest in big, fat rivulets.

He couldn't wait to stop getting poured on, and find a towel. Karma, Xander supposed, for going after Damon, even though there was a god damn storm swirling around them.

It was his whole fucking problem, encapsulated into one single decision. He always thought he could be good for people, could *fix* them, but the truth was, he was just as much of a disaster, if not more of one. His meddling typically made things worse, and at the end, he was always left holding the shit end of the stick.

Damon threw open the back door of the house, glancing back at Xander. Luckily, it was the laundry room, and it was covered in a functional linoleum that they probably couldn't ruin. Probably. Xander stayed on the concrete stoop, pretty sure his shoes and pants were both headed to the trash bin.

"I'll go grab some towels," Damon said. He leaned over, fingers fumbling with the muddy laces of his boots. And Xander, who was a terrible human being, couldn't help but check his ass out.

He felt only a single pulse of guilt; it was a pretty fantastic ass, though not quite as fantastic as Damon's thighs. But then, those were clearly a work of art, deserving of all sorts of worship that Xander would never get to perform.

Damon finally got his boots untied and toed them off. He was only gone a moment, which made sense because it wasn't that big of a house. It certainly wasn't the kind of simple, homey residence that he'd expect a Hess to own, never mind live in. It felt more like a caretaker's house, or a vineyard work-er's house.

When he re-appeared, he was toweling off his head, color back in his cheeks, and Xander nearly took a step back, right back into the mud. Damon, who had looked pretty attractive in the middle of a rainstorm, was crazy hot. Sort of loner, intense hot, with that farmer thing going on. He unbuttoned his plaid shirt and dumped it straight into the open washing machine.

Turning toward Xander, Damon extended a towel. "Feel free to use the washer, if you'd like," he said, and the gruff sort of edge was back in his voice. Like he'd invited Xander here on a whim, and now he was rethinking the whole thing.

Well, that made two of them. But Xander was curious now, too. Why would a Hess live here? Why would a Hess tear up his own vines? Never mind *those* vines?

He wiped his face off, and without a second thought pulled his white tank over his head. He was in decent shape, and despite his own inability to stop checking Damon out, there was very little chance Damon was actually interested in men.

Xander dropped the wet cloth into the washing machine and tried not to look as Damon dumped his own white undershirt in. He was definitely ripped. His muscles practically had muscles. He was tall and big, and since it wasn't that big of a room he took it over.

Damon didn't look over at him as he wrapped the towel around his middle and shed his jeans, the fabric landing with a sodden plop on the floor. Xander copied his movements, shoved the wet pants into the machine, and Damon got it started.

It wasn't until the mechanical whir of the washing machine began that he looked up at Damon again. "Want some coffee?" he asked.

"We've got an hour or so to kill," Xander said wryly. "Sure."

He followed Damon through the house, and it was exactly as he'd imagined. The furniture was worn, and the house was lived in. There were books scattered throughout, a worn blanket tossed thoughtlessly across the back of the leather sofa.

The kitchen was small, but very neat and very clean. Which, considering Xander's profession, was an essential requirement.

A stainless steel espresso machine gleamed on the counter, and a glance at the brand told Xander that it was worth probably more than all the furniture in the house combined.

Damon fired it up, looking like he knew exactly what he was doing. "Espresso okay?" he asked.

"I'll take a cappuccino if you can manage it," Xander said.

Damon gave a rough laugh, and leaned over, grabbing a carton of milk from the fridge, all while holding his towel firmly around his waist.

Xander slipped onto one of the barstools that overlooked the kitchen. "Why don't you tell me what you were doing out there?"

"You're a chef," Damon said, not answering Xander's question.

"I am." Xander wondered what had given him away, then remembered he'd still been wearing half his chef uniform. At least before the distinctive checkered pants had gotten soaked and muddy and had taken a trip to Damon's washing machine.

"A good one?" Damon's voice was deep and rumbling, like a boulder rolling down a hill. Xander liked how he could feel it deep in his chest. If he was being really honest, he liked it a little too much.

"Yes," Xander said shortly. He'd left his jacket with Terroir's emblem embroidered on the pocket in the car, and it seemed like that was for the best. Xander had no intention of sharing that he worked for one of the best restaurants in the world.

"So you're connected," Damon said. He turned back, holding out a solid white enamel mug in one hand, the other still keeping his towel up. Xander wanted to ask him what he was packing in his boxer briefs that had him so protective, but a lot of people didn't understand or appreciate his sense of humor, and Damon was still very much an unknown entity.

Xander took the coffee and took a sip. It was excellent, which either said something about the person who'd made it, or at least about the investment Damon had made in the machine.

"What does that even mean?" Xander questioned. Damon turned back to the espresso machine to make his own cup. "Why does it even matter?"

"I don't want this getting out," Damon said quietly. "People in Napa talk."

"Yeah, it's a surprisingly small community," Xander agreed. The wine and restaurant businesses were particularly intertwined, which was probably why Damon had questioned what kind of chef he was. Definitely good that he hadn't mentioned he worked at Terroir. "I'll keep my mouth shut, but I have to tell you, people are going to notice that you're ripping up your vines. Especially those particular vines."

"You know what they are?" Damon questioned. He'd finished making his own coffee, and from Xander's vantage point, it looked dark and thick as mud.

"I've lived here a long time. I know a lot about this area."

"It's inevitable people will notice the vines are gone. I just don't want them knowing *why*." Damon's jaw tightened and his eyes looked particularly bleak, so light and clear in his tanned face.

"I'm not going to go blabbing around, if that's what you're asking," Xander retorted.

"But you're the kind of guy who pulls over at midnight, and goes tromping out into a muddy vineyard in the middle of a storm to ask me why," Damon said.

"Like I said, I know those vineyards," Xander said, setting his coffee on the countertop with a decisive click. "I don't think I need to tell *you* what they represent."

Damon looked away, his fingers tightening on his own coffee cup. "No, you do not." He hesitated for a long moment, and if Xander's clothes hadn't been in the wash currently, he would have left. There was no point in trying to talk to someone who didn't want to talk. It was like trying to milk solid fucking stone.

Xander didn't know which annoyed him more; this difficulty or Kian, who would actually listen to everything Xander said, and respond all the way up until the point where he flatly refused to change anything he was doing.

"I'm an alcoholic," Damon said finally.

"Wow, that sucks. For a Hess, especially," Xander said. He was definitely surprised, at least at first, but when the confession sunk in properly, he realized it wasn't all that shocking. Damon looked like he'd cornered the market in loner-ism. He was hiding out here, except that the property was surrounded by the very thing he was trying to battle.

In fact, there were miles and miles of it, caging him in entirely. Suddenly, it wasn't a shock that Damon had tried to tear down his vineyard with his bare hands—it was amazing that he hadn't devastated all the vineyards in the Napa Valley.

"For a Hess, yeah. It's definitely not convenient for my family." Damon's voice was bitter. "I'd actually moved away, was doing better, away from all . . . *this*. But then my grandfather died, and they all wanted me to come home so desperately, I guess he thought leaving me one of the original properties was supposed to be an enticement."

"And it wasn't," Xander said.

"It's a fucking jail sentence," Damon gritted out. "I've been sober four years, and this is a test I don't want to fail. But I don't know how to pass either."

"Put that way, I can't blame you for destroying those vines. Have you thought about selling?"

Damon looked mildly shocked. "Selling this property? To who? This has been Hess land as long as there have been Hesses in California. Besides," he added wryly, "one of the stipulations of the will was I had to keep it for at least ten years."

"Does it have to be a vineyard?" Xander asked. His family had always been supportive of him. It hadn't mattered if he wanted to be a chef or if he was gay. They hadn't ever cared, had always loved him no matter what. It was hard hearing about someone who seemed decent who hadn't had that unconditional support system surrounding him.

Damon shrugged. "I don't give a fuck what it is, as long as it's not a vineyard."

"This is still wonderfully fertile land," Xander said. "Why don't you grow something else?"

Damon leaned against the back counter, and Xander had a really difficult time not staring at his bare chest. A dark trail of hair that started just under his belly button disappeared into the towel, accentuating the ripples of his abs. He looked like he worked for a living—or maybe *worked out* for a living.

And even though Xander had sworn off crushes on men who were almost definitely straight long ago, he wanted to lay his palm across the bulk of Damon's pectoral muscle and feel his heart beating underneath.

Xander told himself that he wasn't staring, that he wasn't obvious, but Damon was big in such a small space, and it was nearly impossible to look anywhere else.

A loud *buzz* from the washing machine interrupted the sudden silence, and Damon shot Xander a tiny, lopsided smile. The first smile he'd given Xander since they'd met. It wasn't much but Xander had a feeling that he didn't really have a lot of reasons to smile these days.

"That's the cycle finishing," Damon said apologetically. "I'll go throw the wet things in the dryer, and you'll be on your way in about twenty minutes."

"Twenty minutes?" Xander asked, surprised—and if he was being very honest, disappointed—at the length of time he'd be required to stay here.

"Whether I like it or not, this is still a working farm. If you'd ever worked a farm, you know how vital laundry is," Damon said, as he walked back toward the laundry room. Xander trailed him, not wanting to let him out of his sight. And that was definitely a problem.

"You've been tending the vines?"

Damon threw the clean clothes into the dryer and pressed the start button. He'd used the edges of the towel to tie some sort of complicated, very secure-looking knot around his waist. That towel wasn't going anywhere, no matter how much Xander wished it would. "There's not exactly anybody else."

"Your whole family?" Xander pointed out. Damon looked up swiftly, his light eyes going darker. "I'm sorry," Xander said hurriedly. "I have a terrible habit of being uncomfortably honest."

Damon's eyes went softer as they walked back to the kitchen. Xander resumed his position on the barstool, and to his surprise, Damon picked up his coffee from the kitchen and sat right down next to him. "I bet that doesn't make you very popular sometimes."

This was true, but Xander didn't want to talk about it. Which, he supposed, was pretty hypocritical of him. After all, he'd tromped across a muddy vineyard to demand Damon tell him why he was destroying his vineyard.

"Sometimes," Xander answered vaguely.

"So," Damon said, "what do you think I should plant instead of grapes?"

He hadn't been intending on telling Damon where he worked, but then Damon probably hadn't intended on telling Xander he was an alcoholic, so Xander figured he owed him. "I work at a restaurant named Terroir." He saw the moment the name registered and how familiar Damon was with it. But Xander forged on, anyway. "We source everything we can from local farmers and suppliers. This would be great ground to grow vegetables."

"I didn't know Bastian Aquino was a proponent of the farm-to-table movement," Damon offered wryly.

"Chef Aquino does what is most convenient for Chef Aquino," Xander admitted. "And it makes him look good to try to source stuff locally."

"Yeah, that sounds like him," Damon said casually.

"You've met Chef Aquino?" Xander asked, which was *stupid*, because he was a Hess. The Hess family didn't run the Valley exactly, because there were too many big wine families for anyone to have a monopoly, but they were definitely one of the more important players.

"A couple of times, before I moved away," Damon said. "You must have skin like steel to work for him."

"Yeah, something like that." This was hardly the first time someone had pointed out that Bastian Aquino was an asshole, and it was definitely not going to be the last. "There's a reason he's affectionately known as the Bastard."

"Have you ever thought about leaving?" Damon asked.

Had he ever thought about leaving?

It was tough to consider leaving, when everyone else kept leaving *him*. First, Miles, to his big cooking show career in Los Angeles, and then Wyatt, as a private chef to professional baseball player Ryan Flores.

Only Kian was left out of their original foursome of friends and roommates, and Xander wasn't sure that these days Kian would even consider them close anymore.

That was the problem with trying to give people advice; when they wouldn't listen and you started sounding like a broken, desperate record, your friendship generally suffered.

"I hadn't. I became *sous chef* six months ago, and it's better with some power in the kitchen." This was a terrible lie, but Damon, who had plenty of demons of his own, didn't need a rundown of Xander's.

Especially considering that up until tonight, he'd even been tending the vines he'd eventually be driven to tear down. It must have been a bad night, and Xander was glad he'd intruded if only because Damon had clearly needed a distraction.

"You seem very capable, so I'm not surprised Bastian would promote you," Damon said.

"You've never seen me in a kitchen," Xander pointed out.

Damon flushed, and Xander had a heart-stopping moment where he thought he might be flirting with him. But that wasn't possible.

Because even if by some miracle Damon was interested in guys, he probably wouldn't be interested in Xander. He was a *Hess*. He owned some of the most valuable land in California. He was undoubtedly rich, with a handsome trust fund. Add to that his incredibly good looks, all of which added up to the fact that Xander needed to get out of here before he began thinking there could be some nebulous possibility here, with Damon.

"I'm going to go check the dryer," Xander said, sliding off the barstool before he could get any more wild ideas.

Damon didn't say anything, just stared down into his empty coffee mug.

Maybe he knew Xander was running away, but he definitely didn't know why, and as far as Xander was concerned, that was what mattered.

The clothes in the dryer were still a tiny bit damp, but he pulled them out anyway, tugging his pants on, and pulling on his tank top. He dumped the towel into the washing machine, and walked back out toward the kitchen.

Damon was washing out Xander's mug in the sink.

"Thank you, for coming to talk to me tonight," Damon said before Xander could say goodbye. "I was having a really bad night. Worst night in awhile, if I'm being honest. And you showed up, even though you didn't have to, and kept me company."

It ached that Damon thought Xander had done it for selfless reasons. And there *were* selfless reasons, but selfish ones too. Like the way the muscles in Damon's back bunched as he dried out the mug.

"You're welcome," Xander said quietly. He knew he should ask if he should stay, if Damon would like his phone number if he ever had a bad night again, because it didn't seem like Damon had a lot of people he could talk to. But he didn't do either of those things. Self-preservation, he told himself. "Actually, I should be going. I have an early morning tomorrow."

"Of course you do." Xander told himself that it was okay, that everything was fine, because there was a dark thread of amusement in Damon's deep voice. If he was amused, he couldn't still be struggling so much.

"Thanks for the coffee, and the washing machine, and for not calling the cops on me," Xander said in a rush. He couldn't quite look at Damon's bare back anymore, and Damon hadn't turned around to face him either.

This was better all around, Xander told himself.

"See you around," Damon said.

Then there was nothing left to do except go the way he came, opening the back door to only a weak sprinkle. Xander said a blessing, shoved his feet back in his muddy sneakers, and closed the door behind him.

CHAPTER TWO

ONE YEAR LATER

Xander took the same route to work that he'd been taking for the last year.

He and Kian shared a car sometimes, when Chef Aquino didn't need him ridiculously early in the day, and once Kian had asked why he'd changed his route.

Xander couldn't tell him that he wasn't willing to drive by Damon Hess' vineyard and see him on his land again. It wouldn't have mattered what he was doing, Xander still would have pulled over and demanded to know if the spark he'd felt that night was one-sided.

And if it wasn't, he wanted to know what they were going to do about it.

He didn't drive by, because he already knew it was a mistake to do anything about it. That's why he didn't even give himself the option.

It was sort of a lonely existence—home to work and then back home again. He argued with Kian about his ill-advised crush on their boss. Argued with Nate, their other roommate, about everything he could think of, and entertained himself by rebuffing every sexual offer he made. Nate entertained himself by continuing to make them.

There were some days when Xander would give anything to drive by the vineyard. Some days, ignoring the basic curiosity took all his self-control. Had Damon torn up the rest of the vines? Planted a garden? Sold the property? In the year since that night, Xander had imagined three hundred and sixty-five different possibilities.

Some good, some bad, some made up of plain normal life, but all full of a tantalizing possibility that Xander couldn't seem to forget.

He knew he was romanticizing a single encounter that hadn't even lasted an hour. But when the alternative was resenting the happiness his friends had found in LA, and worrying about Kian's future, most nights Damon looked really damn good. Maybe even better than he had for real.

The memory took on an elastic quality, like it wasn't quite real, and Xander exploited that, tugging it and turning it and manipulating it just a little. A second longer where he'd lingered, staring into Damon's eyes. An undeniable interest in those eyes, instead of the more ambiguous truth.

When his job sucked, like today, it was comforting to pull the memory out, and relive his encounter with Damon the way he wished it would've happened.

"Bridges, what the *fuck* are you doing?"

Xander jerked himself out of the memory and instantly re-focused on the monotonous work in front of him. Naturally it was impossible to tell what was so terrible about his prep work on the eggplants—but that was par for the course with Chef Aquino. Every basic action was a disaster waiting to happen, and inevitably a disaster in his own paranoid mind.

Aquino yelled because he was a notorious sadist who apparently got his rocks off by torturing everyone within hearing distance.

Especially anyone who worked for him.

"Those aren't thin enough," Chef bellowed. His arms were crossed across his broad chest, chef jacket rolled to his elbows, exposing his forearms. They were objectively nice-looking forearms but Xander would have rather crawled into a pit of fire ants naked than find his boss attractive.

Besides, Kian had the market cornered on that kind of insanity.

"I'm using the mandolin," Xander said slowly. Enunciating. Chef was not stupid, but sometimes he threw a hissy fit about the same stuff that he insisted they do every single damn night.

Apparently today was one of those times. To illustrate, Xander pointed to the metal slicer in front of him, clearly set on an eighth of an inch, because preciseness was the cornerstone of every kitchen, and the foundation of Terroir.

"Is that set correctly?" Chef demanded. Xander barely refrained from rolling his eyes, because it was *clearly* set on the correct setting.

Instead of saying anything, Xander leaned over, checked the setting, and exaggeratedly set it a click higher, then returned the dial back to an eighth of an inch.

"All better," he said in a fake relieved voice. It wasn't that convincing, because 1) Xander was not that good of an actor, and 2) he put in zero effort.

Chef's eyes narrowed, like he wanted to call Xander on his attitude in front of the entire kitchen, who was currently watching their exchange with a held breath. It was the beginning of prep. If someone pissed Chef off now, they were in for another eight hours of hell. But he turned away abruptly instead of arguing, and stomped off into his office, calling for Kian as he walked off.

It wasn't something Xander was proud of, but he was relieved that Kian was going to have to deal with the Bastard's passive-aggressive pouting now instead of him.

After all, Kian was the one who acted like he was in love with that monster.

Damon Hess almost never gave a shit. Not anymore, not after he'd been forcibly dragged, demons kicking and screaming, back to the Napa Valley. Today, though, today mattered. Which was why he had given about half a shit, and had made sure his boots weren't muddy, and his jeans didn't have any particularly awful stains or patches.

"Do you have a reservation, sir?" The Terroir hostess was as polished and elegant as the rest of the surroundings. Just casual enough, with her colorful scarf elegantly arranged over her classic little black dress, a pair of designer flats on her feet. There was always a reminder that under all the unstructured relaxation, this was one of the finest dining establishments in America.

"No," Damon said.

"I'm sorry," she said, and she might have been a budding actress, because she sounded genuinely apologetic. "We don't have any tables available."

She did, but she didn't know that he knew that. He also really didn't want to act like his father, walking into places, demanding everything he wanted, just because he was a Hess.

Unfortunately she wasn't leaving him much choice, continuing to stare at him with that pleasant rejection smile on her face.

Damon sighed, considered leaning conspiratorially over the hostess stand, but it looked pretty flimsy, and it wouldn't help his case to destroy the furniture.

"My father is meeting me here," he lied. "I'm sure he's going to be really disappointed that we couldn't get a table at Bastian's restaurant."

She did two double takes. One, at the father comment. The second, that he called Chef Aquino, *Bastian*. Not many people did that and lived to talk about it.

Damon figured that he could have really been an asshole and called him the Bastard, but he still wanted a table, and that might have been a step too far for the hostess.

"And your father is?" she asked, directly yet delicately.

"Nathan Hess." Damon would have rather ingested rocks than used that name, but he also really needed a table, and she'd left him no choice.

Her shoulders straightened. "Of course, right this way, sir."

The *sir* was back, too, despite his too-casual jeans, and Damon hated it because he knew why she was saying it.

He was shown to a table near the floor-to-ceiling windows, allowing diners to look out on the incredible vistas of the Napa Valley, but near the corner, which guaranteed privacy. Damon had only come here with his father a handful of times, but it was enough to remember that this was his regular table.

The hostess waited for him to seat himself, draping the napkin across his lap with an elegant flick of her wrist. "I'm sorry, again, sir. I didn't recognize you. We didn't realize you'd come home."

Damon hadn't realized he'd come home either, so they had that in common. Maybe because home had never felt like a place to him, but a person, and then that had gone to hell. "Of course," he said. "Not an issue."

He was barely settled—pointedly ignoring the temptation of the wine book sitting so innocently in its cognac leather binding—when the waiter arrived to introduce himself.

"Mr. Hess, it's so good to see you, sir," the waiter said. He was Bastian's perfect combination of urbane formality. "I hear Mr. Hess will be joining us."

"He may be running late," Damon said, and the waiter didn't bat an eyelash. Likely he didn't give a shit, as long as he got a good tip. Which Damon fully intended to leave him.

"May I fetch you a glass of wine while you wait?" the waiter asked. He'd told himself to expect the question, because he was a Hess and because this was Napa, so it was easy enough to turn aside.

"I'll have iced tea, unsweetened," Damon said. "And I'd like to speak to a *sous chef* in your kitchen. Xander Bridges."

Damon fully expected to see the panic lights flashing in the waiter's eyes, and he didn't disappoint. One of the tenets of Terroir was that you *never* saw any kitchen staff on the dining room floor, with the illustrious exception of Bastian Aquino himself. That was because Bastian was an egotistical maniac who couldn't bear anyone else taking credit for his creations.

Even though everyone in here knew that Bastian wasn't actually cooking their food.

"I'm not sure that's possible, sir," the waiter said. He had begun to sweat at his temples, and Damon might have felt sorry for him, but this was important.

Damon had learned from a very young age from observing his grandfather and his father that the most effective way to get people to do what you wanted was to keep repeating the request, over and over, without embellishment or explanation, until you simply wore people down.

"I know," Damon said. "But I'd still like to see Xander Bridges." He didn't raise his voice, but made sure he sounded confident and firm.

He actually sounded like his father, which he would have hated and avoided at all costs except that these were extenuating circumstances.

"I'm . . ." The waiter paused, hesitating. "It's really not done, to bring kitchen staff to the dining room."

"If my father was sitting here," Damon said, still staying pleasant, because it wasn't the waiter's fault that Bastian was crazy, "would you tell him that it wasn't done? Or would you go to the kitchen and bring Xander Bridges up here?"

The waiter was definitely sweating now. "Uh," he said, all eloquence momentarily evaporated.

"Listen," Damon said, leaning closer to the waiter and lowering his voice. "I know it's a huge no-no, to do what I'm asking. But I *need* you to go get Xander Bridges."

"It's important?" the waiter hedged.

"I wouldn't ask if it wasn't really important," Damon promised him.

"Okay, I'll see what I can do," he said.

"Thank you," Damon said, and resolved to give him a *very* large tip. And a job, if everything turned out according to plan.

The waiter was back in five minutes. Damon had looked perfunctorily through the menu, and thought, as he gazed at the listed dishes, that Bastian had used to be more innovative.

This didn't feel *tired* exactly, but it lacked the excitement of previous years. Or maybe Damon had just changed, and wanted something wilder, a little less controlled.

"Are you ready to order, sir?" the waiter asked.

Damon knew he wouldn't be staying long; what he really wanted was to grab a burger at the Napa Tavern, but he felt obligated to order something besides the iced tea.

"I'll take the burrata appetizer," Damon said, handing the menu to the waiter. "And what about my request?"

"I'm working on it," he promised, glancing around pointedly at the other diners. "It *is* the middle of the dining hour, and Mr. Bridges is the *sous* in the kitchen."

Damon had come on a Tuesday, deliberately late, for that exact reason. It was almost the end of service. It should be easy for Xander to duck out and see him for five minutes. There was even a better chance Bastian Aquino wouldn't notice Xander breaking the rules.

He wasn't the world's best planner, but he'd been thinking about this for a long time—just over a year, actually—and while he'd initially thought about catching Xander in the staff parking lot after he was finished for the night, he'd eventually decided that this way carried more weight.

It made him look serious, and it should, because Damon was incredibly serious.

"I'll be happy to wait," Damon said.

The waiter beamed. "Very good."

He returned ten minutes later with the appetizer, and Damon was just digging into the soft, creamy cheese with a toast point when Xander slid into the chair opposite his.

"What are you doing?" Xander hissed. He'd taken off his chef jacket, and had thrown on a navy blue sweatshirt. As disguises went, it wasn't great, but it was probably enough.

"I needed to talk to you," Damon said.

Xander's eyebrows nearly hit his hairline. "It's important," Damon tacked on. "Sorry?"

"You practically gave Nico a heart attack," Xander said. "He doesn't usually wait tables, he's subbing tonight, and demanding a kitchen staff member come into the dining room didn't make his night any easier."

"I'm sorry," Damon repeated. "But I really needed to talk to you."

"So, talk." Xander drummed his fingers impatiently on the tablecloth.

"I'd ask if you remember me, but you obviously do."

"Despite what you probably think, I don't go charging onto other people's property every day, demanding they tell me what they're doing," Xander hissed.

"I didn't think so," Damon said, and he grinned in spite of himself. Xander looked good; of course, he'd looked good that night too. If he was being honest, that night in general and Xander specifically had figured in more than one of his dreams. And his fantasies.

"I ripped up the rest of the vines," Damon continued. "And I'm growing a vegetable garden." *Just like you said.*

Damon hadn't exactly gotten up bright and early the next morning to do it, but it had been close. As soon as Xander had said what he should do, everything, which had felt muddy for so long, had suddenly become crystal clear.

"If you're here to become a supplier for Terroir, you're asking the wrong person," Xander said.

"I don't want to supply Terroir," Damon said. "I want to supply my own restaurant."

"You're opening a restaurant?" Xander asked. This time he looked truly surprised.

"I am." Damon leaned across the table, eyes intent on Xander's dark ones. "And I want you to run it."

Xander froze, looking shell-shocked for a single moment, then leaned back and gave out a bark of laughter. "You want me to run your restaurant."

"I want you to be my head chef," Damon said stubbornly. It had felt for the longest time that this was the only deal breaker in the new plan that had taken over his life. He had to have Xander. No matter how crazy it sounded.

"I have a job," Xander said slowly.

"Aren't you sick of being yelled at?" Damon offered. "I don't know if you've noticed, but I'm not exactly the yelling type. Or the extreme control freak type."

"I noticed." Xander's tone was dry.

"Of course, I'll pay you more than you make here. And you'll get total autonomy over the menu. Input into the design of the space. I want a partner, not a slave."

"You've been practicing this pitch," Xander observed.

"This is important to me," Damon admitted. His mouth felt dry at just *how* important and he took a long drink of his iced tea. "It would be dumb of me to leave it all to chance."

"Aren't you worried I'll say no?"

All the time. Constantly. "It's a good job. Freedom, when you haven't had any for a long time. An opportunity to express your point of view as a chef. And even though I might have been shit at growing grapes, I'm good with the earth. My garden is thriving. Anything I don't have, we'll get from some friends of mine."

"You're really serious," Xander said. "You're really here, offering me a job. After a year."

So he did remember. He'd paid attention, and noticed that Damon had never sought him out. And he hadn't only because Damon hadn't been ready to find him again.

"I am," Damon said steadily.

"Let me think about it," Xander said. He hesitated. "Can I come by and see the garden?"

"I was going to offer, but I was afraid it might hold . . . bad memories still." Damon could hear the wryness in his voice. It was ironic that the man he'd met on one of the worst nights of his life might possibly be the tool in his salvation.

"Not at all. Can I come by tonight? After work? I'll be here only an hour or so longer."

"Sure, of course. You remember where it is?" Damon asked, almost not believing how well this conversation had gone. There had been no interruptions by screaming egotistical head chefs, and Xander seemed to be genuinely considering his proposal.

"I could hardly forget," Xander said, his voice low and serious. It did something to the pit of Damon's stomach. The same thing that he'd felt that night, a year ago. Before, he'd only felt it with women; Xander was the first man.

And like he'd known then, he understood that it was a complication. It wasn't that being attracted to a man bothered him, it was that being attracted to Xander bothered him.

Because the one thing he knew better than anything else was that they could never get involved because Xander deserved better than a shell of a man still desperately trying to find his way. Tearing up the vines had helped. The garden had helped. Building something concrete and unassociated with alcohol would help. But he was under no illusions that he would ever be ready to risk someone else's heart.

Especially not someone like Xander.

It was hardly possible for Damon's land to feel more chaotic than it had the first time he'd been there. The land was dark still, but there was a sweet peacefulness to it now, Xander thought as he wandered between the aisles of leafy greens. Damon's pain wasn't overflowing out of it anymore.

"I can't believe you listened to me," Xander admitted, looking up at Damon, who was still watching him warily from the head of the garden.

"Why shouldn't I listen to you?" Damon questioned.

"I don't know—maybe because I was a completely unknown person, bursting into your vineyard in the middle of the night?"

Damon laughed, low and a little wry. It sent an all too familiar spike of heat through him. For weeks—for *months*—after that night, Xander had thought about him and worried. Had wished more than once that he was less of a coward and could be Damon's friend without worrying about wanting more. He could with countless other men, but he was undeniably attracted to Damon, and knew he was eventually going to want more than just friendship.

Now Damon had come back into his life, and this time it was *him* who wanted more.

A business partner. A head chef. And unspoken between them, a *friend*.

Could Xander be those things and not turn into the worst version of himself? The angry, bitter version of himself who couldn't resign himself to not getting everything he wanted?

He didn't know. But he also knew this wasn't an opportunity that came around every day.

"What did your family say?" Xander asked.

Damon just shrugged, big body a dark outline against a darker sky. No, it wasn't really Xander's business what his family thought of him ripping up seventy-year-old vines. What mattered was that they wouldn't show up to interfere, leaving Xander without a job after burning down the bridge he'd spent years building.

Bastian Aquino was not exactly the "forgive and forget" type. If he left Terroir, he was *leaving* Terroir. There would be no going back. Even if Damon's restaurant never made it off the ground.

Was he ready to take that step?

It came as a total surprise that he was. When he'd been promoted to *sous chef* over a year ago, it had been an exciting change, with more responsibility. Only a little, of course, because the kitchen was Chef Aquino's and he never let anybody forget it.

"I'd like to build something," Xander said. "Here. With you."

It should have scared him more that all the parts felt equally important. He did want to build something. He wanted to do it here, in the place where so much of Napa had begun and evolved, now ripe for a new chapter. And he wanted to do it with a man he barely knew.

Despite the episode with the vines and the storm, Damon felt strong and sturdy. Unshakeable. Just the right person that Xander could batter with his own bred-in mistrust.

Damon didn't just look surprised he'd agreed; he looked elated. That was a god damn genuine smile he was wearing on his handsome face.

"Really?" he asked, excitement seeping into that rough-and-tumble voice.

"This is a good start. I like it." Xander leaned down, and picked up a clump of dark brown dirt. It crumbled between his fingers, fertile and rich. God knew his advice wasn't always great—or taken into consideration—but he'd been right about this. From the look of the plants, he'd been dead right. This was a fantastic place for a vegetable garden.

"When should we start?" Damon asked, like he wasn't really in charge. And maybe, Xander thought with astonishment, he didn't think he was. After what felt like a lifetime of bending and scraping and obeying every order, equality and freedom felt like such a heady thing.

But Xander wouldn't be Xander if he didn't test things. "Aren't you the boss? Don't you have a plan?" he asked lightly.

Damon gave a deep bark of laughter. Xander felt it to his bones. He wanted to put his hands all over the man and feel it as he laughed. "I do. But we're supposed to be partners? When do *you* want to start?"

There was nothing for Xander to do then, but be as honest as Damon was being. "As soon as possible."

Smiling, Damon nodded. "Okay. Do you want to discuss your salary or benefits or anything?"

That was the last thing Xander wanted to do but he wasn't stupid. "You said you'd pay me more than Bastian."

"I will." Steady. Confident. *Sure.* "How much do you make now?"

Xander rattled off a number. He was pretty sure it was correct. To be honest, as long as he had money in the bank to pay rent, he didn't worry about money.

"Twenty percent more now, and then consider it doubled when we open," Damon said calmly.

Xander might be *laissez-faire* about money, but that was not an insignificant amount. "Are *you* sure?"

"I'm a Hess, aren't I? We should do something with my god damn trust fund, and paying your salary seems as good a use as any," Damon said.

It was hard for even Xander to argue with that.

This time when Xander left, they exchanged phone numbers, Xander promising to be back in a couple of days, after his time at Terroir was finished. Damon mentioned a contract,

Xander agreed to read and sign it, which normally would have felt foolish to him, but this was Damon. He was like a rock. Unshakeable, even with the addiction. Probably even more so, because of it.

Even though Xander had misjudged people before, he knew he wasn't misjudging now.

When he turned to go to his car, he glanced back, and saw Damon standing there, watching him go. A darker outline in the dark of the night. And it felt right to have his eyes on him still.

So right that Xander gave himself a blistering lecture when he got into his car.

"You will not fall in love with him," he sternly told his reflection in the rearview mirror. "You will not fall for another straight boy who won't love you back. You won't pine or yearn or otherwise ruin your life panting after someone you can't have, like Kian. You *won't*."

God knew if the lecture would stick, but at least Xander knew where the lines were drawn.

"Where did you go last night?" Kian asked as he julienned about a hundred thousand carrots, his knife flashing as it flew through the orange flesh.

Chef Aquino must be in a bad mood. He hadn't forced Kian to prep vegetables for the side sauté they served with some of their main dishes in ages. It was an annoyingly menial job, even though Kian was really good at it.

Probably because he'd been stuck doing it so many times.

"Why are you doing that?" Xander asked, gesturing with a whisk at Kian's mound of carrots instead of answering his question. He still wasn't sure how to break the news. Or if he even should. Was Kian still on his side, still *his* friend, or had he permanently defected to the Aquino camp?

"Steve, one of the new kitchen assistants, quit unexpectedly today."

"Do you even have to add the *unexpectedly* part?" Xander wondered out loud. "It seems a little unnecessary these days."

The meaner Chef got, the faster his new employees departed. And that only wrenched him tighter, leading them all in a vicious cycle. Some days it felt like Kian was the only one who could talk him down.

"We needed him to prep these today," Kian said, not even bothering to answer Xander's question.

"So you're doing it instead." Xander was prepping the sauces, which was his main job every day, along with soup of the day. That, a delicate creamy *vichyssoise*, was already simmering away on the stove in a gigantic pot.

"Someone has to do it, and that's part of my job. To fill in, wherever I'm needed. That's part of the cross-training Chef promised I'd get."

Xander rolled his eyes as he peeled shallots. Three years in, and there was still that note of hero worship in Kian's voice whenever he talked about Bastian Aquino. These days, it was accompanied by a healthy dose of unrequited pining.

That worried Xander enough, but at least it was still unrequited. The day it changed, Xander was going to have to punch the Bastard in the face for taking advantage of a subordinate. For taking advantage of *Kian*. Xander wasn't looking forward to it.

"Oh yeah, you've gotten a really well-rounded education," Xander drawled. "A great opportunity to grow a thicker skin."

Kian's knife didn't even pause. It still flew through the carrot at breakneck speed, each julienned slice perfectly sized. But his voice got harder around the edges. "I don't know why you keep doing this. If you're not happy here, if you don't enjoy working for Chef Aquino, then *leave*. I don't need you to stay here just to protect me. I'm a grown man. I can take care of myself."

"Yeah, that's exactly what I'm worried about," Xander muttered. Kian looked up. "And maybe I will," he said louder. "Maybe that's where I was last night. Maybe someone offered me a really good job."

Kian's eyes went wide. "Did they really? Who is it? Are you leaving?"

"Shhhhhh," Xander snapped. "I'm . . . I haven't told anyone else. Especially Chef."

"Maybe don't do it today. You know, with Steve and all." Kian's tone went wry. He might defend Chef Aquino to the ends of the earth, because he was not very secretly in love with him, but he was also a realist.

Steve hadn't even been around long enough for Xander to remember his name.

"I'll tell him in a few days," Xander said. "We're still finalizing the details." Damon had texted this morning, promising a copy of the contract in his email in a few days. And Xander, while giving his word, was still not stupid enough to quit his job until he'd made sure that everything Damon promised was also in writing.

"Who is it?" Kian whisper-demanded.

"It's a Hess," Xander said, and sue him, he definitely sounded a little smug. "They want to open a farm-to-table restaurant and they approached me for the head chef position."

Kian's already big eyes grew wider. "*Head* chef?" And Xander did understand his surprise. The Hess family was big in Napa, and if they were really going to open a restaurant under the familial auspices, they'd bring in someone well-known to head the kitchen.

They definitely would not be hiring Xander, who had never been head chef before, and who was definitely not well-known.

But Damon Hess wasn't his family, with none of their high-profile obligations, which had opened the door wide for Xander.

Xander thought about telling Kian but he was going to be worked up enough already, being the last of their friend quartet to still work at Terroir—and everyone and their mother knew he wouldn't be leaving anytime soon—so he kept quiet about that important detail.

"Head chef," Xander confirmed.

"Wow." Kian's knife still worked away, reducing the pile of carrots from stupendous to merely numerous.

"Don't you have zucchini to do after that?" Xander asked. He finished chopping his shallots for the wine butter sauce they served with rockfish, and moved onto garlic.

"And the red peppers," Kian said. "Also I think Chef said he wanted to add turnips today too. Said he got some in fresh.

What kind of menu are you thinking of?" As he asked, his knife flew through the last of the carrots.

"I got offered the job last night," Xander retorted. "I haven't signed the contract. How could I have decided on a menu yet?"

Except that he had. He'd spent the last few years of his time in Terroir getting through the worst of Chef Aquino and his temper by clinging to his food imagination. What might he do with this rockfish, if he served it? A sweet corn gastrique, maybe?

Definitely not this tired shallot butter wine reduction that he could make in his sleep.

"You're going to take it, aren't you." Kian said it flatly; a statement, not even a question. Like leaving Terroir was some kind of unspeakable crime.

Xander slammed his knife down onto the board. "Of course I'm going to take it. We're not all like you, in thrall to the Bastard. You wouldn't take another job even if the French Laundry came calling."

"I don't want to work for Thomas Keller," Kian retorted stiffly.

"That's exactly the point I'm trying to make." Somewhere Xander had lost the steam of his temper, and all that was left was regret. Regret that he'd never been able to save Kian from wasting his abilities and all his blood and sweat and tears, sacrificing them to a man who didn't care.

The color rose on Kian's pale cheeks. Pale, despite living in California. Probably because he never left this god damned kitchen.

"You're pissed off that I won't listen to your fucking advice," Kian spat out. His knife had finally stopped, and it trembled, the shining steel flickering under the lights of the kitchen. "Well, not everyone is you, Xander, and you don't know what's right for everyone. Maybe if you did, you could tell yourself, and you wouldn't be so god damned bitter all the time."

If Chef was around, he wouldn't tolerate this argument, never mind a friendly discussion. Work was for work, as he liked to say. It was not social hour. But he wasn't around, probably dealing with the fallout of Steve's departure, and Xander discovered that despite usually not giving a shit, he *really* didn't give a shit today.

He still hadn't picked up his knife. Instead, he leaned over, and flipped the gas off the stove. The shallots that were slowly sautéing in a puddle of melted butter would slowly grow cold and congeal without their heat source.

"What are you doing?" Kian demanded. His flush rose brighter.

"Leaving," Xander said calmly. "You can tell Chef Aquino I'm done."

Kian stared at him wordlessly. No doubt shocked silent.

"You could come with me," Xander said. "You *should* come with me."

"You should at least give your two-week notice," Kian insisted. "It's only fair."

"Why? So Chef Aquino can scream at me and belittle me and act like he's better off without me when I know the truth? That I should have been promoted to *chef de cuisine* forever ago, but that Aquino pretends he doesn't need one, so he doesn't have to? Yeah, no, thanks. I'm done."

He picked up his knife, slid it into the cloth wrap, next to all his other knifes, and rolled it up. He didn't look back as he walked out, but he knew Kian was staring at him the whole way.

There should be guilt at how he was leaving Kian to deal with the Bastard, but wasn't that what Kian wanted anyway? To *deal* with him, all the fucking time?

Instead of guilt, all Xander felt was delicious, intoxicating freedom as he left Terroir behind with one gigantic middle finger to all the shit he'd put up with for far too long.

CHAPTER THREE

"So the rumors are true. You *did* destroy this vineyard."

Damon looked up from his position on his knees in the dirt, where he was carefully weeding around his cabbages.

Bastian Aquino stood tall and arrogant, eyes covered with silver aviators, arms crossed across his chest, his mouth compressed into a tight line.

Damon didn't say a word, didn't move an inch. Sometimes it was good to remember he was a Hess. Not always, but sometimes.

"You tore up all these vines and then stole my *sous chef*," Bastian continued. "I'm still trying to figure out what I ever did to you."

Like most egotistical assholes, Bastian would naturally make Xander's defection about him.

"Nothing," Damon said, finally rising to his feet. It didn't matter to him what position he occupied—he already knew that power had nothing to do with being on your knees, but Bastian clearly hadn't. The only way to face him was to don the trappings of an authority he'd long rejected.

Sort of the way he'd done to trick his way into Terroir.

"I know you lied to get into my dining room," Bastian continued, the edge of his voice cruelly patronizing. "I know you weren't meeting your father. He never would have asked a server to bring a member of the kitchen staff to a table. He never would have ordered a single appetizer and an iced tea and then left."

Nathan Hess wouldn't have. He would have never dreamed of speaking to a staff member unless he needed something. He would have ordered a full meal, several bottles of wine, and then spent the next several hours enjoying what he considered the just fruits of his labor.

"Is your problem with the single appetizer or the iced tea?" Damon asked mildly. He wasn't going to fight with Bastian Aquino about his father. Xander—that was a slightly different story.

Bastian ripped the sunglasses from his face and took a few strides, stopping short of where the garden began, eyes narrowing at the muddy knees of Damon's jeans.

He couldn't help but wonder the last time Bastian had gotten his hands—or anything else—dirty.

"*My problem*," Bastian snarled, "is that you fucking poached my best chef."

"If Xander is your best chef, then you can't be surprised that he left. Isn't that what good chefs are supposed to do? Spread their wings? Develop their own point of view? I thought that was supposed to be something you wanted. The pedigree of a whole stable of famous culinary offspring."

"Generally that's the idea," Bastian said. It looked like it hurt to admit it.

"Then why are you here?" Damon asked, turning away from the man in front of him. He'd already wasted enough breath on Bastian Aquino; he was never going to understand why everyone left him.

"I came to tell you to back off, and that when Xander rethinks his behavior, you're going to encourage him to stay at Terroir."

Damon glanced over from his position by the cabbages. When he'd woken up this morning to Xander's text that he'd walked out in the middle of prep for the night's dinner service, he'd half-dreamed that Xander might show up bright and early in the garden. It turned out Bastian Aquino was not a pleasant substitution for what Damon really wanted.

"He doesn't need to stay at Terroir. He shouldn't stay at Terroir. He doesn't *want* to stay at Terroir." Damon made sure his voice stayed calm, but it was firm. Implacable. His demons were a hell of a lot tougher than Bastian Aquino, and he faced them down every damn day.

"He will if I offer to make him *chef de cuisine*," Bastian said smugly.

Damon didn't know exactly what that particular position entailed, but by the way the chef was referring to it, it was illustrious and there might be some circumstance under which Xander would take it.

He still didn't know Xander well enough to be sure, but he'd gotten an indelible impression of him from just the few times they'd met. Damon knew Xander was loyal and hard-working, and would never walk out on a job just because he got annoyed with something.

The annoyance would have to be long-occurring, far-reaching, and far more serious.

"I think if Xander wanted to keep working at Terroir, then he wouldn't have left," Damon said simply. "I don't think it matters what position you want to dangle in front of him, he's done with you. He's done being treated like a toy you can win back with a prize, after you've mistreated it. Xander deserves to work for—*with*, actually—someone on his side. And that's never going to be you."

"You seem very sure about that," Bastian retorted wryly, a corner of his mouth twitching upwards.

"I am," Damon said. And he was.

"You think you can be that *partner*," Bastian sneered, shoving his sunglasses and covering up his smug, handsome face. "A Hess who isn't even a Hess. A Hess who ripped up his own vineyard."

Better than the drop-dead drunk Hess, Damon desperately wanted to say, but Bastian Aquino had already spent too much time poisoning the place where he'd begun to find peace.

"Get off my land," he said, beginning to rise to his feet again, because if push came to shove, he would literally throw him off of it, if he had to. Bastian Aquino wasn't a small man, but Damon was bigger. And Damon owned a wealth of determination that Aquino couldn't even begin to touch.

But to Damon's surprise, Bastian actually did as he was told, turned and stomped off, and left him wondering what the hell had just happened.

Xander woke to someone pounding on his bedroom door. He opened one eye, saw the mostly empty bottle of cabernet that he'd stolen from Nate the night before on his nightstand, and promptly closed it again. Rolling over, he groaned.

The pounding continued and intensified.

"Xander, I know you're in there," the voice outside the door insisted. It was Kian. It could only be Kian. Though, Xander theorized, it could also be Nate, pissed that he'd nicked one of his better bottles of wine. But Nate knew he'd taken it, and had even offered to drink it with him.

But Xander had been celebrating and hadn't felt like entertaining himself by turning down Nate's sexual offers.

"You're wrong," he croaked, "Xander isn't here."

Kian finally got sick of pounding on the door and opened it. He didn't look amused.

"I need to talk to you," he said, leaning against the doorjamb and doing his best Bastian Aquino impression, which was not very good, because Kian was a marshmallow and couldn't pull off asshole even with extensive training.

"So talk," Xander said, rolling over and burying his face in the pillow. "Clearly nothing is stopping you."

"You walked out last night," Kian began, but Xander interrupted him before he could get the rest out.

"I quit," Xander corrected grimly. "I didn't just walk out. I fucking *quit*. Just in case that wasn't clear."

Kian glared. "Believe me, it was."

"Okay then," Xander said.

"What I keep trying to tell you is that you don't have to. Leave, that is. Chef is here . . . and he wants to talk to you."

There wasn't much Kian could say to get his undivided attention right now. Not with rancid red wine on his tongue and the insistent throbbing in his temples. "Chef is here?" He couldn't help it, he gawked a little. "In *our* house?"

"Yes," Kian said primly.

"What the fuck."

"I suggest," Kian said, his tone of voice much more insistent than a suggestion, "you get cleaned up and get out here before he gets tired of waiting and leaves."

But would that be all that bad, in the scheme of things? Xander wasn't sure. He did know that the last thing he expected was for the Bastard to show up at their house, prepared to beg him to come back to his old job.

He knew what it was like when people quit Terroir. There was usually screaming and yelling and almost always missiles of some sort. When Wyatt had left, Bastian had cleared his whole desk—keyboard, laptop, paperwork, several glasses—with a single sweep of his arm.

As far as Xander knew, there had never been a counteroffer.

And maybe there wasn't one. It was entirely possible that instead of coming here to win him back, Aquino had come here to kill him. But Xander was fairly sure that he wouldn't commit murder in front of Kian—or make him clean up the mess.

Even if he wasn't going to take whatever offer Aquino had come here to make, Xander figured it was probably worth hearing. His curiosity demanded at least that much.

He threw the covers back and staggered upright. Kian glared. "Hurry up," he said, before closing the door behind him. No doubt he was freaking out that their boss—*his* boss, Xander corrected—and the unrequited love of his life was sitting in their living room, probably trying to assess the dubious provenance of their couch.

Dressing was as simple as throwing on a pair of athletic shorts and a shirt that was probably clean. *Mostly* clean, Xander decided as he sniffed it. Good enough. He stopped by the bathroom, brushed his teeth, vaguely tried to neaten his bedhead, and called it good enough again.

As he predicted, Bastian was on the couch in the living room, with Kian hovering within reaching distance, looking an uneasy mixture of anxious and elated.

"Xander," Bastian said to him. He sounded just as arrogant as always, but there was the tiniest bit of contrition layered over it. An apology without the actual words.

Meaningless, basically.

Xander crossed his arms over his chest and didn't sit down. "What do you want?"

"You quit last night."

"I did," Xander said steadily.

"You're not even going to give me the benefit of a two-week notice?" Like there was ever a real two-week notice at Terroir without some benefit to Bastian.

"No."

"Or an opportunity to counter what Damon Hess offered you?"

Xander glanced over at Kian, who had the nerve to look ashamed. "Not much is a secret, is it?" Xander said bitterly.

"Kian is worried about you. Worried you're throwing your career away on someone who can't properly support you. You know, he isn't even really a winemaker. He's not a restauranteur. He's playing at growing a garden. But he's not even a Hess—not like you think."

Xander regarded Bastian steadily. "He's exactly what I think he is."

"So there's nothing I can offer you that might make you change your mind?" Bastian looked sneakier than usual, and considering that Xander had never trusted him on a normal day, this was worrisome. "What if I made you my *chef de cuisine*?"

"You mean the job I've deserved for six months?" Xander demanded. "The one you should already have offered me?"

"I can't apologize for that, Xander," Bastian cut in smoothly. And no, he wouldn't, the bastard. He never apologized for anything.

"I think I'll take my chances with the 'not real' Hess," Xander said, using finger quotes. Kian, out of his field of vision, gave a stricken gasp. He probably couldn't imagine anyone turning down Bastian.

But Xander was sick of his shit, sick of the backhanded manipulations, the hissy fits, and was definitely not interested in continuing to work for someone who didn't feel it was necessary to treat him right until he actually walked out.

"You really mean that." Bastian sounded like he couldn't even believe it. "Hess said you'd say that, but I couldn't believe it. Couldn't believe you'd turn down *chef de cuisine* to work for a part-time gardener whose restaurant is currently a ramshackle shed without a real kitchen."

It had clearly been too long since Aquino had worked in someone else's kitchen, because the idea of creating his own space, shaping his own legacy, sounded incredibly appealing to Xander. Even if it meant a shit ton of work. Even if it meant working in a ramshackle shed without a real kitchen.

It was only after Xander had worked through *that* thought that he had another one.

Damon had talked to Aquino? He'd told him that he'd turn down the promotion?

Xander frowned. "You went and talked to Damon?"

Bastian stood and began pacing in the tiny empty space of their living room. Xander could practically feel Kian's anxiety begin to spike. "He *poached* you. In my own fucking restaurant! What else was I supposed to do?"

Xander crossed his arms across his chest and gave his ex-boss a glare that sang with finality. "Fucking ask *me* if I wanted the job. Not my new partner. Not my friend and my roommate. *Me*. That's your whole problem. That's why I left. You have to control everything, and it fucking sucks." And apparently he really wanted to flush everything down the toilet because the word vomit kept coming. "And that one," he said, pointing in Kian's direction, "is too nice to ever say anything to your face, but you're a psychotic megalomaniac who desperately needs to be checked."

Aquino's expression shuttered hard and fast. He gave Xander one last bitter, angry look and turned and marched away.

"You're an idiot," Kian hissed. "Are you really going to let some guy tell Chef Aquino what you want to do?"

Xander rolled his eyes. "Are we really going to do this? You and me, *really*?"

"I don't know what you mean," Kian said stiffly. He was still glancing over at the door every ten seconds, like Aquino was going to march back through it, throw him over his shoulder and take him with him—and Kian was going to *let* him.

"I mean, are you *really* going to get bent out of shape over my new partner telling Aquino to take a hike when I was going to do that anyway? When you would follow Aquino to the depths of any hell he concocted, just because he asked you to, just because you're too in love with him to ever tell him no?"

Kian opened his mouth and then shut it again. "No," he finally said shortly. "No, I guess we're not."

"Okay then," Xander retorted, the testy edge to his voice growing sharper. "I'm going to go back to bed, contemplate my brief joblessness, and you can go running after Aquino, because I know you're dying to."

Kian looked like he was desperate to argue, but they both knew it would be a lie. Turning, Xander walked back down the hall to his bedroom and tried to ignore it when he heard the door shut behind Kian and the engine turning over on Bastian's Audi R8.

Picking up his phone from the table, he sent Damon a quick text. **The Bastard was just here, I'm assuming you had to deal with him too. We'll talk later tonight. I'll be there around five.**

He lay back down, stared at the ceiling and tried to banish the thought that he'd just made a life-altering mistake. Things would be different, Xander told himself, but they could be *good* different. At the very least, he wouldn't be making the same mistakes over and over again.

Then he remembered how his blood had spiked every single damn time he looked at Damon, and *yes,* maybe he was about to make a mistake, but at least this was a familiar mistake.

✦✦✦✦✦ ✦✦✦✦✦

"What's all this?" Damon asked when he opened the door.

"Dinner," Xander said, hefting one of the grocery bags a little higher on his hip. "I got the impression last time I was here that you were good with that espresso machine but that you don't use your stove that much."

Damon grinned, unexpectedly fierce and bright, and it nearly knocked Xander right back. "Guilty as charged," he admitted, opening the door wider to let Xander come into the house.

It looked much the same as it had that night, a year ago. A little cleaner, perhaps, like Damon had gotten that text and had decided to neaten up in anticipation of Xander coming over.

This is not a date, Xander reminded himself.

He'd had to remind himself of this more than once when he'd been at the grocery store picking up food for tonight. First he'd agonized at the meat counter. When you brought a filet for dinner, what did it *mean*? What about salmon? Shrimp?

Love, marriage, or maybe even eternal devotion? A white picket fence?

Xander had to stop himself before he asked the butcher if the different cuts had deep, secret meanings, like flowers. There was no cut of meat that communicated: "this is just a friendly work dinner, but if you wanted it to be more, I could be convinced. And by the way, do you like men?"

"I decided," Xander told Damon as they walked through the living room toward the kitchen, "that it would be completely stupid for you to hire me if I'd never even cooked for you before."

Damon shrugged, one side of his mouth quirking up a little. It had the side effect of making his bottom lip look very bitable.

Xander set his groceries on the kitchen counter and began to unpack them like they held the secret to world peace. He was attracted to Damon and it was a problem, but their partnership didn't have to be defined by his inconvenient attraction.

"I think I'd like to see you explore what you're interested in," Damon said quietly as he settled in one of the barstools. The same one Xander had occupied a year ago. Xander told himself that meant nothing. After all, there were only three barstools to pick from. Maybe that one was secretly the most comfortable and Xander had just gotten lucky.

It did something to the base of his stomach to think that Damon didn't care; that he just wanted to give Xander the freedom and the space to do what *he* wanted. It had been a very long time since anyone had thought highly enough of him to do that, and Xander told himself not to be fooled into thinking that's what this was.

"You really don't care?" Xander asked in disbelief.

He'd never hired a chef before. Maybe when you hired one, you just naturally assumed you were getting *their* point of view, not your own.

"My point of view is the garden," Damon said. "As long as you use as much of it as you can, I'm good."

And Xander had taken at least that much away from their previous conversations about the restaurant, so he'd bought lots of vegetables, which he spread out across the counter now.

"Someday," he told Damon, "all this will be from your garden."

Damon set his elbows on the counter, forearms rippling with muscle, because even though he was wearing another plaid shirt, of course he'd rolled up the sleeves. But his intent couldn't be to drive Xander crazy; it was just probably more comfortable. Maybe those crazy gorgeous forearms didn't even fit properly into shirts.

Xander swallowed hard and looked away. "I figured I'd make a quick pasta with roasted garlic and sautéed vegetables. I got a nice salmon filet too."

"Salmon's good. I like salmon," Damon said.

It was weird cooking in someone else's kitchen, and it was even weirder doing it with Damon watching him so intently.

All of Damon's pans were hung up on a nice suspended rack in front of the front counter. They weren't the best pans he'd ever worked with, but they were fine for his purposes tonight. He picked one and set it on the stove. After breaking down the head of garlic, he set a few cloves in to roast, and cleared the marble counter to make his fresh pasta.

"So Aquino came to see you," Xander said. He'd figured out quickly that Damon wasn't a big talker, unless you asked him a direct question and expected an answer. And not only was the purpose of tonight's dinner to make sure his cooking didn't disgust his new partner, it was also important to get to know each other better. After all, Xander had come here with every intention of signing the contract, and he knew there was due diligence he needed to exercise first.

"Yeah, this morning. I knew he was a jerk, but wow," Damon muttered darkly.

"And he told you about the job he wanted to offer me," Xander said. He wasn't mad exactly . . . but maybe he was. Maybe he would have taken the *chef de cuisine* position—Damon didn't know him well enough to know either way.

The last thing he wanted was a partner who thought he knew best and would speak for Xander. Of course, Xander didn't really think Damon was like that, but the worry was still there, hidden in the back of his mind.

After all, Xander wouldn't be Xander if he wasn't always expecting the other shoe to drop.

"Yeah," Damon said, and then he laughed self-consciously. "He told you that I said you'd turn it down, didn't he?"

Xander had wondered if Aquino was trying to play them against each other, hoping he'd come out on top if their partnership fell apart before it ever began, but it was extra annoying to discover that he'd been right.

"He did," Xander confirmed.

"I did say that I thought you'd walked out for good reasons that had nothing to do with me. I didn't think you'd take the job back, unless they were extraordinary circumstances."

"It wasn't even extraordinary circumstances that made me walk out," Xander said wryly. He cracked a few eggs in the center of the flour he'd formed into a loose pyramid shape on the marble. "More the straw that broke the camel's back. He pulled one of his stupid ego stunts and I suddenly thought, what the fuck am I still doing here, catering to this asshole?"

Damon nodded. "I didn't mean to speak for you, I just wanted him off my land with his smug attitude, if I'm being honest."

Xander waved a flour-dusted hand. "It's fine, really. He *is* a smug asshole, it's undeniable. He was even smugger when he came by my house today. It felt good to tell him to get the fuck out.

"But," he continued, "I don't want to get things off on the wrong foot. I just left a restaurant where nothing I said mattered. One of the reasons your offer looked so appealing was my opinion counting. And I want it to count."

Damon didn't say a word, just slid a sheaf of papers across the eating counter, until they were precariously balanced over where Xander was mixing his pasta dough.

"It's all there," he said. "You get full say over the menu. Kitchen design. Collaborative input over the design and direction of the dining room and the restaurant itself. I want us to be partners. Don't let Aquino get in the way of that."

"I don't want to," Xander said. "I want this to work out."

The intensity of Damon's gaze told Xander that he was telling the truth. Xander still wasn't sure *why*—specifically why Damon had picked him to be head chef, but maybe that wasn't important. Not nearly as important anyway as having full control over the kitchen spelled out in the contract.

All the rest they could figure out later.

"I don't have a pasta machine," Damon said apologetically just as Xander whipped out a long wooden rolling pin that he'd had forever and that worked beautifully on pasta.

"I guess you don't need one," Damon added, a self-conscious smile on his face.

"I'm adaptable, and I like doing things by hand," Xander said as he steadily rolled out the dough. "This whole process is relaxing for me."

"Is that why you started cooking?"

"I'm not sure why I started," Xander admitted. "Probably because my mom was always teaching in the late afternoons and someone had to make dinner."

"Your mom was a teacher?"

Xander told himself the real interest he was hearing in Damon's voice didn't mean anything. He wasn't sure he entirely believed it.

"Piano," Xander said. He shifted the sheet of dough on the counter, making sure it wouldn't stick. He looked up at Damon. "Pizza wheel?"

"Second drawer to the left of the stove," Damon answered right away, and Xander had to admire a man who was organized enough to know where all his tools were.

"I eat frozen pizzas a lot," he admitted when Xander pulled it out of the drawer.

"Not anymore you don't," Xander retorted. He paused, pizza wheel above the dough, and really thought about Damon's question from earlier. "I guess I started cooking because I had to. I kept going because I was good at it. But I'm ready to figure out again why I still want to."

"I hope you can." Damon looked down at his hands. From where he was standing, Xander could see the nicks and cuts and the sheen of dirt that he couldn't get off no matter how much he washed. They were the hands of someone who worked with them for a living.

Xander began to cut the dough into long, thin strips, demonstrating his own confidence in his hands. Not many people made pasta with only hand tools—but Xander liked the rustic quality it gave the pasta. He also liked relying entirely on himself to get the job done.

"That's amazing," Damon said, sounding awed as Xander, with a few clever flips of his fingers, curled the pasta into several little nests, dotting the countertop. "You're totally going to throw away my frozen pizzas."

"You want pizza, at least let me make it for you," Xander insisted. He ignored the thrill that resounded deep at the idea of feeding Damon for every meal.

He wasn't Damon's personal chef, but maybe he wanted to be. Maybe he wanted to be everything Damon needed.

Definitely everything he wanted.

He pulled out his chef's knife and began decimating the pile of zucchini and squash that he'd bought at the store, and maybe his chopping motion was a little more emphatic than it needed to be, but who could blame him?

It didn't matter that he'd gone down this road before, and it had been epically disastrous. Clearly he hadn't learned, because it didn't feel like falling for Damon was a matter of *if*, more a matter of *when*.

Finishing up with the vegetables, and moving onto the salmon, Xander looked up, surprised at the quiet. Damon wasn't a big talker, but they'd been having a decent conversation, he was taken aback to see that the other man had disappeared.

The seasoning on the salmon was simple—just a squeeze of lemon, a sprig of dill, and some salt and pepper. Despite claiming he didn't cook, Xander noticed that his pepper grinder was high quality, and the salt was the brand Xander himself recommended.

Damon might not cook for himself, but he knew his way around a kitchen. Xander wondered why he'd stopped. He knew it didn't always make sense to go to the trouble just for yourself, but Damon, despite his solitary demeanor, maybe hadn't always been alone.

"Table's set," Damon said, and Xander turned back from the stove, surprised to hear his voice. He'd gotten lost in the quiet, and in the rhythm of prep and cooking.

The salmon sizzled on the stove behind him. "Where are we eating?" Xander asked. "I've got about five more minutes here. The pasta just needs to cook, and then tossed with the vegetable medley."

"Outside," Damon said, gesturing. "I figured we should eat our first meal together as partners in the garden. Found an old table, dragged it out. It's not perfect, but it'll work."

"That's . . ." *Pretty fucking romantic*, Xander didn't want to say. "That's really nice," he rephrased, mentally wincing at how lame that sounded.

A few minutes later he was carrying plates outside, following where Damon had gone through the sliding glass door to the garden. Sure enough, there was a flagstone patio with an old wooden table set with silverware and glasses, and *god damnit*, he'd lit candles and there were several strings of clear Christmas lights crisscrossing the patio, augmenting the mood lighting.

This is not a date, Xander reminded himself for the hundredth time.

Maybe it wasn't him that needed reminding though. *But did Damon even like men?* Xander wondered. He didn't really give off a gay vibe, though Xander had felt some sort of interest directed toward him more than once.

And now there was this.

"I hope iced tea is okay," Damon said. "I brew it myself."

Normally Xander would have begged a nice white or a rosé from Nate to complement the meal, but obviously he wasn't going to drink in front of someone who was a professed alcoholic. Not unless Damon made it explicitly clear that it was okay. And from Damon's offer of tea, Xander took that the opposite was actually true.

It was okay, it was fine. Xander didn't *need* a glass of wine with a meal. It just would have settled the sudden fluttering of the butterflies at the base of his stomach as he set the plates down on the table and slid into a chair.

He watched, trying to be casual and not like he was internally freaking out, as Damon lit the candles, and slid the lighter into his pocket.

"This looks great. Thank you for coming over and cooking," Damon said, and his warm smile made Xander wonder just how lonely he'd been since coming back to Napa.

"It was no trouble. Plus, I figure it's a semi-decent audition." *More* than semi-decent, if Xander was being honest. He cut into his salmon, and was definitely pleased by the slight pinkish tone of the inside. It was *perfect*.

Eat your fucking heart out, Bastian Aquino.

"You don't need to audition," Damon scoffed.

"Because I worked at Terroir?" Xander said, taking a sip of tea. It was well-brewed, with the faintest hint of mint on the tongue. Not too sweet, either. And was that basil in the after-taste? Xander remembered the perfect cappuccino from that night a year ago, and now this tea, clearly crafted with love and skill. An undeniable skill.

Damon inclined his head, twirling pasta on his fork.

That was a non-answer, but Xander wondered if he'd get anything more straightforward out of the man. He was quiet, so much of him buried far under the surface—and he was dying to go digging.

"Obviously, you grew up here," Xander said. "But you mentioned you left for awhile."

The corner of Damon's full mouth quirked up. Like he knew that Xander was digging and *why*. Maybe he did, but then if he knew, why had he set this table with candles?

"I did leave. It turns out that living in Napa sucks for an alcoholic." He took a deep breath. "I left after my divorce. Not only was Napa too small for me and the vines, it was too small for me and Rachel."

It shouldn't have hurt. It was hardly an official statement of his sexuality. Lots of men married women and liked men. Lots of men liked both. It was hardly the end of hope, but the salmon in Xander's mouth turned to ash.

"I didn't know you were divorced," Xander said stupidly, like Damon was an open book, when actually the opposite was true. The truth was, he didn't know what else to say without exposing his own interest in Damon. He'd known it was a bad idea from the first moment, and here was nearly the confirmation he needed to believe it.

"I don't exactly go around talking about it," Damon said with a quiet, wry amusement.

"Right, no, of course not." Xander hesitated. "I've never been married."

"I know," Damon said, and the amusement was a little more pronounced now.

Xander raised an eyebrow.

"You and your friends, all Terroir employees, all living in that rental house. You're not exactly low-key, not in this small town. Lots of people are willing to talk if you ask."

So Damon knew he was gay, *and* he'd asked about him. Xander knew what he'd probably heard: gay orgies and all other sorts of sordid rumors. None of which were actually true, because nobody who worked fourteen-hour days on average, six days a week, had the energy to hold orgies.

"And what did they say?" Xander asked, more than a little bitterly. He couldn't help it. He felt dumb and played, because he'd gotten distracted by an incredible pair of forearms and some soulful gazes.

"That you're hardworking. That you all barely sleep. That you run that restaurant for Bastian Aquino. That you're good guys who work for a shitty boss."

Not what Xander had been expecting him to say.

"That was all I listened to," Damon continued and the kindness in his voice was both galling and a balm to all that bitterness flooding him.

"You could have come and asked me directly. Might have avoided some of the more . . . colorful stories," Xander pointed out.

"I didn't want to approach you before I was ready." Damon ducked his head, flush on his cheeks, almost like he was bashful about this confession. "I sought you out when I was ready. That night we met, I wasn't ready. Not even close. I'm still not as rock steady as I want to be, but the garden helps and this project has kept me going. Even more, I want to be the kind of partner you deserve."

"You are," Xander said, and he knew how god damn earnest he sounded. Like the kid he'd been right out of high school, desperate to prove to everyone how genuine he was. He hadn't been that kid for a long time, but he felt the echo of him tonight, sitting across from Damon.

"We'll see." Damon's smile was wry. "Sorry to be such a downer, on such a great night."

"This is important stuff we should be talking about," Xander said, even though part of him desperately wanted to laugh off this whole conversation. Probably because it struck so deep, and Xander was used to keeping that softer side of himself barricaded with jaded sarcasm. But jaded sarcasm just didn't feel right, at least not at this moment.

Definitely not when Damon was beginning to open himself up.

Chapter Four

Hands down, it was one of the best meals Damon had ever eaten. Even though he'd watched Xander prep it with his own two hands, it was a marvel that he'd done it with *only* those hands. It was a far better meal than any he'd ever had at Terroir, and that was prepared by an entire staff and countless pieces of expensive equipment.

Xander had come to his house with a bag of groceries and a knife, borrowed a pan and a pizza cutter, and had made an astoundingly delicious meal. It was talent and drive, all wrapped up in one package.

A *cute* package.

Damon had been telling himself not to notice—or if he was going to notice, then he should just ignore the attraction. But sitting across from Xander, staring at him in the candlelight, it was much harder than he'd imagined. Especially when he looked relaxed and much more at peace than he had that night a year ago.

At first he'd been too worked up himself to notice the anxiousness that Xander wore like a cloak. Or a very difficult-to-scale wall complete with archers equipped with fiery arrows and soldiers pouring boiling oil.

But tonight his guard had fallen a little, and despite everything, Damon wanted desperately to believe it was more than just quitting a job he'd really hated.

Damon wanted to believe the smile on Xander's face had something to do with him.

"Thank you," Damon said. "If that was an audition, you nailed it."

"I know." He was a little smug, and it was more than a little adorable. The way his nose scrunched up, the eye crinkles, the expressive look in his dark brown eyes.

Damon had imagined he might be in danger, hanging around Xander all the time, especially considering the impression he'd made on him in such a short time, but this was Trouble with a capital *t*.

"You'd better watch yourself. Not sure your head's gonna fit back through the back door," Damon teased.

"You wanted a chef," Xander said, spreading his arms. "You got one."

"They're sort of thick on the ground in Napa," Damon softly insisted, "but it turns out I'm particular."

"Imagine that, a Hess particular." The sarcasm in Xander's voice cut through the dreamy romantic quality of the candlelight and let in a little of the real world. Specifically his family.

He couldn't exactly tell Xander he didn't ever want to talk about his family. After all, this land was their legacy, and his trust fund was making the restaurant a reality. Truth was, he *really* didn't want to talk about them, and it felt like Xander brought them up as some sort of defense mechanism. Damon still didn't understand why, and this was definitely not the first time it had happened.

"What's your deal with the Hesses?" Damon asked. Might as well be honest, at least before Xander walked back in the house and signed the contract that would tie them together for the near future. Of course, that also meant the question had barely made it out of his mouth.

Something ugly churned deep in his stomach, exactly the opposite reaction he should have had after that incredible meal.

What if he changes his mind?

"Nothing," Xander said, but his chin was jutting out again, and his fingers were drumming anxiously against the wood tabletop. It sure didn't look like nothing.

There was a definite voice in his head, begging him to leave it, to make sure he didn't drive Xander away with his insistent questioning. After all, Xander wasn't signing with Hess Vineyards, he was signing with Damon, who stayed as far away from his family as possible.

But Damon's last name was still Hess, and it wasn't going to change.

"Really?" Damon asked.

Xander sighed. "I said it was nothing, and it is. It's stupid."

"I don't want it to interfere," Damon offered. "Not with what we're about to build."

"It won't. I promise. I know you're not your family. And to be honest, that's what it is. I've had a few run-ins with Hess employees. But you're not like them."

The thing Damon had discovered before coming back to Napa, and definitely after returning to the Valley, was that he could run as far and as hard as he could, but his family was still his family. Time and distance couldn't alter his blood, no matter how much he wished otherwise.

"Okay, that's fair." Damon stood, and brushed off his jeans. His best pair, without any mud or holes. Terroir hadn't even gotten that much from him. He leaned over to snuff out the candle, and the scent of beeswax filled his nostrils.

"If you don't mind, I'm going to go read through the contract," Xander said.

"Sure. I'll just clean up." Xander looked like he was about to protest, but Damon held up a hand. "I'm no good in the kitchen, but I can use a sink and a dishwasher."

"If you insist, I'm not going to stop you," Xander conceded with a smile. He'd relaxed again, and Damon found himself hoping that Xander let whatever issue he had with his family go for good this time.

He gathered up the rest of the dishes, and when he let himself in the sliding back door, Xander was at the counter, absorbed in the printed pages of the contract.

"Dry reading?" Damon asked as he flipped on the sink, filling it with hot soapy water.

It was obvious that Xander was a professional cook, because even though he had used a number of pans and utensils to prepare the meal, they were all neatly piled next to the sink, and the counter and stove had all been carefully wiped down.

"It could be more interesting," Xander admitted. "Do you mind if I take this with me?"

"Sure, but if you'd like I can email you an electronic copy to take to a lawyer," Damon said steadily. It was the right thing to do, but his heart had wanted Xander to sign tonight. Before he could figure out that Damon wasn't as good of a bet as he appeared.

"That would be nice, but I'm not taking it to a lawyer. I just want a copy for myself."

Xander had gotten a real nice sear on the salmon filets, and the pan needed to be soaked. Filling it with hot water, Damon set it aside. "I don't want you to look back on this conversation and wish you'd done things differently," he said.

"It's a straightforward contract, and anyway, I trust you."

Damon glanced over, and was surprised to see in Xander's expression that he really meant it. "I know we just met," Xander rambled, "I know we also met under . . . extraordinary circumstances. But I choose to believe that we can make something extraordinary with those circumstances."

It was inevitable that it would happen one day. Damon had known since he was twelve that he was attracted to both sexes. But he'd met his ex-wife so young, there had never been an opportunity to explore that attraction with men.

Until now.

He kept his trembling hands submerged in the sink, holding like a lifeline onto the pot he was scrubbing. He didn't want Xander to see how affected he was—and he definitely wasn't ready to approach Xander yet. If he was ever going to feel ready.

Also just because Xander was gay didn't mean he was interested in Damon. After all, Xander knew he was a recovering alcoholic, and Damon had always imagined that not many people would ever choose to take that sort of burden on in a romantic partner.

Still, the possibility existing at all, even in a nebulous future, made Damon swallow hard.

"That's a lot of trust to give," Damon said, voice raw. He didn't have to add, *to someone who you personally witnessed falling apart only a year ago.*

Xander shot him a quicksilver grin, and went back to reading the contract.

He finished washing and drying the dishes, putting them away, but Damon felt shaken to the core by Xander's words, and his own reaction to them.

Whether Xander acknowledged it or not, he was taking a chance, and there was definitely a part of Damon that didn't feel worthy of it, especially when he heard Xander scrawling his signature on the contract, the pen scratching across the paper.

"There," Xander said with finality. "All it needs is your signature."

He could have slid it over the counter. Damon's hands were still a little damp, but he could have leaned over the prep counter and signed.

Instead, Xander left it next to him. *Right* next to him. Like he was inviting Damon into his personal bubble.

Damon hesitated, almost definitely for a second too long, because Xander chuckled, low and a little rough, and it did all sorts of things to Damon's stomach.

The truth was, Xander had a supernatural effect on Damon's stomach. He fed it incredible food while giving it the sort of nervous, hungry butterflies Damon hadn't felt since he was a teenager.

"Come on, I don't bite," Xander said, flashing another one of those bright smiles. "Hard."

There was nothing else to do but walk out of the kitchen to where Xander was sitting, until their shoulders were brushing up against each other.

It was the closest they'd ever been. Damon could feel the warmth of Xander's skin through the cotton of his t-shirt, and his fingers trembled so hard he had to clench them tightly together.

Xander *had* to know he was prodding the bear, but he offered the pen up anyway, dangling it in front of Damon's face. "You ready to sign?" he asked.

It was blatant flirting—even Damon knew what it was, and he was clueless about most romantic behavior.

He plucked the pen out of Xander's hand, gave himself a pat on the back for not succumbing to his *very* base desire and signed the contract, right above where Xander had.

"It's settled then," Xander said. Damon took a step back, back out of Xander's space. No matter how much he wanted to stay, wanted to see what else Xander might invite, this was a slippery slope and Damon wasn't sure he was ready to tackle it yet.

Honestly he wasn't sure he would ever be ready and he wasn't willing to subject Xander to the same thing he'd already done to the rest of his friends and family, but mostly his ex-wife.

"You want to see the restaurant?" Damon asked.

Xander raised an eyebrow. "Maybe instead of auditioning, I should have been looking at the space."

It was difficult for Damon not to flush bright red. Xander might not have seen the evidence under his farmer's tan, but its existence flustered him regardless. He *should* have shown Xander the restaurant first thing.

"It's not much," Damon warned as they walked out the back door and he took Xander through the edges of the garden. "There's a lot of work to be done."

It was difficult to see Xander's face in the growing dusk, but Damon glanced over anyway—an instinctual reaction he was finding it tougher and tougher to resist. For so long he'd stood out in the fields with just himself and the vegetables for company, and imagined what Xander might say to him. It was surreal to have him actually here, and Damon had to keep reminding himself that he was in fact real and not a figment of his imagination.

Damon brought them to the old barrel house on the property, long abandoned by the Hess family. Even as this vineyard had remained a jewel in the crown of their legacy, wine production had been brought into the twenty-first century by his father, increasing capacity and ensuring consistency of quality. Places like this one had faded away, some remaining ramshackle buildings on the Hess properties, others torn down to make way for more vines.

When he'd inherited this property, Damon had fully expected that this barrel house would have gone the way of so many others, but to his surprise, it had still stood. Weathered and not in the best of conditions, but still existing, a testament to a time long gone.

"This is the restaurant," Xander stated, and when Damon glanced over, he was gaping. And not in a good way. "This is a *shack.*"

"I told you it needed some work," he retorted defensively. "Think of it like a blank canvas. We can do whatever we want with it. And the history . . ." Even if it wasn't history that

Damon always appreciated, it remained important, and it was important to Damon for Xander to recognize that.

This was what was left of his legacy, and the only part of it he still felt comfortable embracing.

Xander took a deep breath. "A blank canvas, falling apart around our ears."

"It's not going to be falling apart. When I left Napa, I did construction for awhile." Damon was all too aware of how defensive—and desperate—he sounded. "I can fix it."

Xander's expression was incredulous. "You worked in construction?"

It was unsaid hanging between them. *But you're a Hess. Your family practically runs this valley. You have a huge trust fund.*

All of that was true. And for a while, none of it had mattered to Damon, and it was all he could do to get away and do something, *anything*, else. Working with his hands had been soothing somehow. Creating something with his own two hands. Building something, instead of tearing it down.

But that was stuff he barely even felt comfortable sharing with his sponsor still. He couldn't tell Xander. No matter how attracted to him he was, he was still almost a stranger. They'd agreed tentatively to trust each other, but that didn't mean sharing every personal feeling.

"I enjoyed it," Damon retorted shortly. "Anyway, it's going to come in handy, because now I can help fix the building. Our restaurant."

"Do you have a name yet? I noticed there wasn't a clause in the contract providing me approval or denial on the restaurant name."

"The Barrel House." Damon told himself Xander's opinion of the name meant little, but maybe it would also help him to understand the complex association Damon had with his own history.

Xander was quiet for a long moment. He tilted his head, eyes skimming the building from top to bottom again, taking in every broken board, every sagging eave. It still had good lines, and Damon knew he could bring them out again. "It suits the building." He hesitated. "It suits *you*."

He would have to be in a lot more denial to think he hadn't been waiting with bated breath for Xander's opinion. "I think so," Damon said quietly. It was a relief to imagine that at least Xander might be beginning to understand.

"Can we go inside?" Xander asked. "Without being in mortal danger, anyway?"

"Of course. It's all superficial damage. Easily fixed. *Restored*. That's what I plan to do with it anyway. It's not going to be fancy or polished, but it's going to be what it was before."

Damon led the way into the house, opening the door on hinges he'd kept continually oiled in the last year. He'd spent a lot of time in this building, making plans.

"Kitchen would go over there," Damon said. "I want it to be open. Want diners to see their food being prepared."

"Glass panels," Xander said. "Floor to ceiling."

Damon had never considered glass walls. At first he might have rejected the idea as far too Terroir-like for their restaurant, but the more he thought about it, the more he liked the idea of the high end merged with the more rustic originality of the building.

"That could be really cool," Damon said. He had his phone out of his pocket, and was making notations. People he would need to call.

"Tables over here, then," Xander continued, waving an arm. "Hostess stand here. Refinished wood. A little glass for contrast. Simple, classic earth tones."

"No barrels," Damon said.

Xander looked over, and there was a concerned wrinkle between his dark brows. "Barrels?"

"It's called the Barrel House, but I don't want any barrels in here. I want the history but not the strong association with the winery," Damon insisted.

Xander's face softened. "I understand."

He probably thought he did; most people who didn't struggle with something as basic as a drink menu sitting innocuously on a table on a restaurant thought they knew what it would be like. They didn't.

Alcohol, especially here in Napa, was *everywhere*.

"I don't want to serve it. No wine. No beer. No booze."

Damon told himself that Xander couldn't possibly be surprised; after all, he'd *just* said he didn't want old wine barrels decorating their restaurant which was named after them. How could he want alcohol on their menu?

"But this is a restaurant in Napa," Xander said slowly. The wrinkle had reappeared as quickly as it had disappeared the first time. "People would expect they can get a glass of wine with dinner."

"No." It didn't make sense to add any additional arguments, because this wasn't an argument Damon intended to have. It was his one line in the sand. Still, he braced himself for an explosion out of Xander.

Instead, Xander did something he did not expect. He reached over and wrapped him in a tight, not-very-quick hug. He lingered, his hands, insanely capable and talented, lingering over Damon's shoulders. And when he finally moved away, Damon wanted to grab him back and tell him never to stop.

"It'll be a challenge," Xander said, and his voice was very matter-of-fact, nothing like the sudden tenderness of the hug he'd just given Damon. "And nobody can say that I'm not up for a challenge."

"You seem very sure of all of this, no matter how many obstacles I keep throwing your way," Damon said incredulously. He'd planned on confessing this particular wrinkle at some later date. Not the first night. Definitely not the night they'd signed the contract, when it would be so easy for Xander to walk back to the house and rip it up.

But it had felt wrong *not* to tell Xander. Not exactly a lie, but something akin to it.

"I'm a very determined person. And I'm determined to make this work," Xander said.

"Something we have in common," Damon pointed out.

"So . . ." Xander hesitated. "Where do we begin here?"

There were old broken-down barrels, fragments of the wooden racks that had used to hold them, and other random crap scattered around the enormous room. "Clean this up first," Damon said. "I'm planning on starting tomorrow."

"I suppose since I don't have any other plans, I'll be here," Xander said wryly.

In his head, it was a simple answer. *Yes.* This was never something Damon had wanted to build alone; he'd always wanted a partner. And simply, he needed the help. But something else entirely came out of his mouth.

"If you want. You're not obligated to help. Not with this part of the process."

Damon didn't imagine the incredulous look Xander shot his way. Damon felt like shooting an even stronger look at himself. Why did he keep self-sabotaging this way? If Xander was less *Xander*—less determined, less stubborn, less committed—then he would have been out of here, running as fast as his legs would carry him.

"I'll be here anyway," was all Xander said. "What time?"

"Eight. Is that too early?"

"You remember that my boss used to be Bastian Aquino, right? That guy that showed up here today, in all his manipulative *fuck you* glory? Eight is nothing."

"Even when you were working an evening shift?'

Xander gave a short laugh. "Like that ever mattered to him."

"Well, it matters to me." Damon meant it. He just hoped, even with all the stupid shit he'd said tonight, that Xander believed him.

Xander patted him on the arm. It was a far cry from both his earlier embrace and the ambiguous invitation into his personal space. Damon fought the instinct to reach out and grab his hand back.

"If I'm going to be back here at eight, I'd better get home," Xander said. "I'll see you tomorrow."

It wasn't a date, but as Damon watched Xander walk out to his car, he realized that he felt gypped that he hadn't gotten a goodnight kiss.

"You're home at a weird time," Nate said when Xander walked into the kitchen to get a glass of water.

Nate was leaning against the far counter, a glass of rich red wine dangling from his fingers.

Xander switched directions and grabbed a glass from the cupboard and poured himself a few inches of wine from the bottle on the counter. It was Nate's wine, which meant it was really good wine. Also, his stomach was still jittery from butterflies and water wasn't going to settle them enough for him to sleep.

"I can't believe you missed the hot gossip. I quit last night." Xander took a sip of wine, glancing over at the bottle. "This is good."

"Don't sound so surprised," Nate grumbled.

Xander shouldn't have been surprised. Nate was a certified sommelier, and worked at one of the more prestigious wine tasting rooms in the county. He also moonlighted at a smaller, very exclusive late night wine bar. He was also his friend Wyatt's ex-boyfriend, and certifiably obnoxious. His access to very good wine was one of the only reasons Xander had agreed to let him move in as his and Kian's other roommate.

Also, it was a little flattering and more than a little entertaining when Nate would hit on him. Xander had never been tempted to give in to more, but quitting had him feeling freer than he had in a long time.

And it was undeniable that Damon, with his soft, hesitant, but fiery looks under his lashes as he'd eaten Xander's food had set him on fire. He was worked up with no place to go, except to his own bedroom with his own hand, and nothing about that sounded particularly appealing.

Frankly Nate, despite his model features and slim build, had never appealed to him either, but maybe . . . *maybe*.

"So you finally left Terroir. I guess it was only a matter of time," Nate said, taking another long drink of wine. "I bet Kian's freaking out."

"Kian is mad as fuck," Xander said.

Nate laughed. "Where is he, anyway? He's not home yet either."

"Feeling lonely?" Xander said, and he knew he was baiting Nate. It wasn't right. It wasn't good. But somehow it felt satisfying.

"Are we going to do this again?" Nate questioned.

"Do what?"

"You taunt me into flirting with you, then shut me down. What are you, frigid? A virgin?"

"Neither," Xander said. He finished his wine and sauntered back close to where Nate was standing, and picked the bottle up off the counter. "Do you mind if I finish this?"

"Nothing I say would probably stop you," Nate grumbled.

"True," Xander said. He finished filling his glass and tilted it toward Nate. "Cheers. What should we toast to?"

Nate rolled his eyes. "I want to believe this sudden *friendliness* is you turning over a new leaf, but you never do anything without about ten ulterior motives."

"I do not," Xander retorted. "You're . . . my roommate. We can share a glass of wine and toast to something pleasant. It wouldn't kill you."

"It wouldn't kill you," Nate said, voice very steady as he gazed right into Xander's eyes. His eyes were a nice innocuous brown. Perfectly nice, if you liked brown eyes. Xander usually didn't have an opinion, but maybe he should. Maybe instead of throwing his heart away to someone who—per usual—did not appreciate it, he should give someone a try who could actually be interested in him.

He never would have picked Nate for that option, but Nate was also convenient.

Setting his wine on the counter, Xander gave a nod. "You're right; it won't kill me."

He leaned in, telegraphing his intentions a mile away, and brushed his lips against Nate's.

Xander wanted to believe that he had every intention of giving this . . . experiment . . . a real shot at success. But the instant his lips touched Nate's, he instantly knew it was a failure. Nate wasn't who he wanted. He already knew who he wanted; he'd been desperately trying to get him out of his mind for a year now, and Damon was still as firmly as entrenched as ever.

All tonight's "business meeting" had done was make Xander want Damon even more. And this experiment? It was a hot fucking mess.

"Well," Nate said, after Xander had pulled away. The truth must have been written all over his face because it was clear Nate knew. "That could've gone better."

"It could have," Xander admitted with a sigh. He leaned back against the counter and picked up his wine again. "That was a terrible idea."

"Kissing me when you're actually thinking about someone else? Yeah, I could have told you that."

Xander digested this. "How did you know I was thinking about someone else?"

"You had that *gung-ho, I'm going to do this despite everything I really want* sort of thing written all over you. Also, you've never been even the slightest bit interested in kissing me before tonight. You let me flirt with you because you're bored."

It was not a particularly flattering list of reasons. Even Xander could admit that. "I'm sorry," he said. "And I'm sorry I keep drinking your wine."

"It's okay," Nate said, and he actually sounded like he meant it. "It's better than drinking alone. After all, your ex-boyfriend didn't end up hooking up with a rich baseball player and then falling in love with him."

"I don't have an ex-boyfriend," Xander said, and the wine must have loosened his tongue because he normally never would have admitted that. Especially to Nate.

"Really?" Nate didn't sound all that surprised. "I guess that makes sense. You keep falling for the wrong guys. So is this new one going to end up like Miles?"

"I wasn't in love with Miles," Xander said stiffly. "He was my friend."

"Right, okay, you just keep telling yourself that," Nate said. "So, this new guy?"

Xander sighed. Swirled his wine in his glass. "Almost definitely straight."

"Almost definitely? Sounds like there's some room for movement there."

"He looks like he's interested, sometimes. There's something between us, for sure. But he was married to a woman."

Nate smacked him hard across the arm. "So he could be bisexual or pansexual or maybe he didn't even *know* he liked men. Lots of gay men marry women at some point in their lives."

Xander raised an eyebrow. "All I'm saying," Nate continued, "is that you keep falling for these guys and then never doing anything about it. Almost like you're scared they're going to like you back."

"I am not scared."

But Nate's gaze was gallingly truthful. Like he could see right into all of Xander's soft, mushy bits inside and knew what was really going on: that he was scared shitless a good portion of the time. Especially when it came to relationships.

"Then give this guy a chance to open up his horizons. You deserve that, at least." Nate drained his wine, and tipped his empty glass jauntily toward Xander. "Cheers. To new beginnings."

Chapter Five

The alarm went off at 7 a.m., and instead of getting up like he always did, Xander hit the snooze button once, and then twice.

There was part of him that was excited to go to Damon's, and help jumpstart the beginning of his new career. There was another part of him that felt absolute dread.

Dread *and* guilt.

It had been so stupid to kiss Nate last night. Stupid, petty, and childish. The ultimate move when you were holding so tightly to your blinders that you couldn't see even a fraction of the truth in yourself. But just because Xander knew why he'd done it, that didn't magically erase any of the guilt.

Of course, he should feel the most embarrassed over facing Nate, but the thought of running into him in the kitchen, sleepy-eyed and grumpy, pouring himself a cup of coffee, didn't keep him in the bedroom. It didn't matter that Damon would never find out what he'd done. *Xander* knew, and that was bad enough.

Finally, when he couldn't possibly avoid it anymore, he got out of bed and slunk down the hall to take a fast shower. He threw on jeans and an old t-shirt he liked to jog in, and because he had at least an inkling of the sort of work they'd be doing today, tied on a pair of work boots that he hadn't worn in years. Not a lot of call for construction work for a chef. But Xander's stepdad was a general contractor, and had always believed in having a pair of good work boots handy.

His stepdad would love Damon, and his determination to build something out of nothing. Especially out of the ashes. But that didn't matter, Xander reminded himself, Frank was never going to meet Damon. At least not in the context of him approving and becoming friendly with him—becoming part of the family.

Xander could hear Frank's no-nonsense voice in his head now: *You can't let the past define your future, kid. You've got to give it a fresh chance.*

It sounded way too much like Nate's, *you keep falling for these guys and doing nothing about it.*

He grabbed two pieces of brioche bread, and slathered on some of the apple butter Wyatt had sent them in his last care package—like Xander and Kian, who were both chefs, were somehow starving without him feeding them. Frankly, Wyatt was probably bored, sitting around the mansion he lived in with his professional baseball player boyfriend. Making apple butter for Xander and Kian was probably keeping him from climbing the walls.

The time on the clock in his car was 8:03 when he pulled into Damon's gravel driveway.

"Cappuccino?" Damon asked distractedly when he opened the door. His hair was still damp and he was wearing another one of those damn flannel shirts, already turned up to the elbow, exposing way too much muscular forearm for just after eight in the morning. Xander felt dizzy with it.

A little forearm skin was enough to make him fluttery. If he ever saw Damon naked, he'd probably keel over dead.

"I'm not going to turn down your coffee, pretty much ever," Xander said, following him to the kitchen. In the morning light, away from the dusk and the dark of the night before, the atmosphere felt slightly less charged. But the electrical zing when Damon handed Xander his cup and their fingers brushed for a split second was still there. It was just fresher and more innocent in the morning than it had been the evening before. Full of more serious possibilities than a fling, or a single night that Damon would probably regret.

The fact that he was even considering serious or possibilities at all were enough to have Xander turning toward the back sliding door, staring out at the blue sky over the garden. Better to look there than straight at the person he had trouble looking away from.

Better to stave off the inevitable and eventual feelings as long as possible.

"You ready to get started?" Damon asked. He had his own cup of coffee, thick and rich and dark—Xander could smell it even though he stood a few feet away. It made him want to crowd into Damon's space, take the cup from his hand, and taste all that richness right off his tongue.

Yeah, kissing Nate had definitely not made him forget about wanting to kiss Damon. He looked down at his watch. It was seven minutes after eight. He'd been in Damon's presence for four minutes, and he'd already felt it again.

What he should really do was bring up Damon's ex-wife again, and pry a little, no matter how incredibly rude it would be. Maybe then he'd find some unassailable evidence that Damon was straight and his heart would stop wishing for shit it couldn't ever have.

But even Xander, who had a reputation for being blunt as fuck, couldn't figure out a way to bring up Damon's ex-wife without torturing them both. So instead he nodded, and said, "Sure, let's get started while we still have the day."

"My granddad used to say that all the time," Damon admitted as they trudged through the morning dew toward the barrel house.

"Funny, that's a favorite saying of my stepdad, Frank," Xander said.

"Let me guess, he thinks it's awesome to get up early," Damon said. "It's still dark out and he's chomping at the bit to get going."

Xander shared a commiserating smile. "Basically."

"God, *morning people*," Damon said with a bright, blinding grin.

And Xander, who might have lumped himself in with that group until this morning, when guilt had weighed him down so much he'd had trouble getting his ass out of bed, simply nodded. Just to see that smile again.

"You're not a morning person but you're up this morning. Eager to get started?"

Damon unlocked the door to the barrel house, clipping the keys to his belt. "I've already started. I've been up early every morning since I started the garden. I've found it's a lot easier to work in the mornings."

"I guess I didn't think of it that way," Xander admitted. Damon had already been committed to this project for a year. Because without a garden, there would be no garden-to-table restaurant.

"It's okay, I get it. This building is the beginning for you. First," Damon said, gesturing around at all the broken-down crap piled in the corners, "we've got to get all this out of here."

Xander sighed. "I was afraid of that."

"Afraid to get your hands dirty?" Damon asked, shooting him a quick, slanted look. Xander felt it along his skin, in the blood in his veins. It was difficult to see this project and this partnership as a mistake that was only going to lead to a broken heart, but when he stood here, on this land, looking at the walls of this old, still majestic building, it was impossible to see himself anywhere else.

Some things, Xander decided, were inevitable, and some fates unavoidable.

And this was his. It had been crystal clear the moment he'd kissed Nate, but the truth was, he'd known it for a lot longer than that. He'd known it, deep down, the first moment he'd seen Damon's figure through the pouring rain. Why else feel so compelled to stop?

"No," Xander said. A lot more than his hands were going to get dirty on this project.

Some of the debris had to be broken down into smaller pieces of wood. Damon produced a pair of gloves for himself, and then surprisingly, a pair for Xander that fit him perfectly.

Xander flushed as he pulled them on, trying not to think that Damon had sized up his hands, and then gone and bought gloves to fit.

Damon must have seen, because he explained, sounding nearly the most self-conscious that Xander had ever heard him. "Your hands . . . you might put them through hell," Damon said. "But I'm not going to let you get a splinter on my watch."

"You realize I get worse than a splinter all the time," Xander had responded, and hiding the fondness in his tone had been impossible. Maybe they couldn't ever be *in* love, but Damon clearly cared what happened to him.

"Burns, cuts, scratches, right?" Damon asked and Xander nodded.

"Don't care," he concluded. "No splinters, not if I can help it."

They'd gotten to work then, Xander trying to focus on the pile he was breaking down and lugging outside to the spot Damon had designated. It was harder than he'd imagined it would be. Not the work—that was easy. The wood was old and soft. Easily broken down so it could be carried outside in armfuls. No, the problem was Damon, and the flex of his biceps as he used a crowbar to pry the metal ring off some old wine barrels. The problem was the little grunt he let out when he pried each one off.

Xander tried not to think about how Damon might sound as he fucked, that little grunt louder as he bottomed out every time. He totally failed.

"Something really interesting in that wall?" Damon asked, totally catching Xander in the middle of a really good, really explicit fantasy. The other problem was that it had been so long since he'd had sex, and it didn't look like that streak was getting any shorter, considering how the kissing experiment with Nate had gone.

Xander blushed bright red. The wall in question was the wall right behind Damon. "Uh no, just . . . thinking of a new dish."

"What is it?" Damon asked, because *of course*.

"Uh, uh, it's . . ." Xander was usually a lot quicker, even with a lie, but not much of his blood was in his brain at the moment.

"Sounds really good," Damon said solemnly.

Xander resembled the color of the radishes Damon was growing outside. "Really good," he managed to agree.

Damon laughed. "Whatever it is, I think I want some."

The culmination of all of Xander's problems: Damon probably didn't want any, and probably wasn't ever going to want any.

"Yeah, yeah," Xander grumbled, turning back to his own pile and getting back to work before his inconvenient erection could be any more obvious.

The work wasn't particularly hard, but it was time-consuming. There was a lot of crap tucked into the corners of the barrel house. Xander was pretty certain it hadn't been cleaned out after it had stopped being used. They'd just kept everything in here, a mausoleum to the old-fashioned method of winemaking. Over time, it had rotted and broken down and then finally fallen apart.

"I'm hungry," Damon said after a few hours of work. "I'll go grab us some sandwiches from the corner market."

Xander considered protesting, and saying he'd make lunch instead, but his arms and legs were streaked with dirt and grime. He'd have to shower to feel ready to enter a kitchen. And he knew the "corner market" was actually a pretty high-end country store that catered to tourists who wanted a picnic to take with them on their wine tasting tours.

"Sure."

"Any preference?" Damon said, removing his gloves and setting them on one of the barrels in a long line he was breaking down.

"Anything that looks good. I'm not picky."

Damon looked surprised.

"Don't look so shocked," Xander teased. "We're not all Gordon Ramsay."

"Gordon Ramsey isn't picky," Damon protested. "He wants to eat food that's edible that wasn't prepared in a kitchen that looks like a garbage dump. He doesn't want food poisoning. Can you really call that picky?"

Xander burst out laughing. "Are you in the Gordon Ramsay fan club?"

"I actually watch a lot of bad reality television," Damon admitted in a quiet voice, like he was almost ashamed to admit it, but not enough to change the subject. "Gordon is pretty cool."

Xander raised an eyebrow. "He is?"

"He's good to kids. He tries to help people that don't always know how to help themselves," Damon defended.

"He also yells a lot, which, as you can imagine, I'm not a fan of," Xander said. "That was all I knew about him."

"You should watch *Kitchen Nightmares* sometime," Damon said. "I have pretty much the whole show saved on my DVR."

"Do you watch *Real Housewives* too?" Xander asked in a teasing voice. "Orange County or Atlanta?"

"I used to, but I got into food shows in the last year or so," Damon said, and he sounded self-conscious again. "*Chopped* and *Food Network Star* and *Holiday Baking Championship*. Even watched *Kitchen Wars* on-demand."

Xander definitely did not ask if the sudden interest in food was because Damon had decided to open a restaurant or if it was meeting him. "I keep trying to get my friend Miles on *Holiday Baking Championship*. He'd do so great. Right now he hosts a show on *Five Points*. But he could do a lot bigger things, if he wanted."

"You're friends with Miles Costa?" Damon asked. Undeniably starstruck. "I never miss his show." He hesitated. "Duh, of course, he worked at Terroir with you."

"He was one of my roommates, before he left for LA," Xander explained.

"I'm going to need to meet him sometime," Damon said. "Okay, I'm off to the corner market."

It was only after Damon walked away that Xander realized they'd had an extensive conversation about bad reality TV. And it wasn't like he didn't have those conversations with straight guys sometimes, but wow, he could still feel the echo of it, the same as he'd had with Kian or Nate or any of his other gay friends.

Instead of asking about *Real Housewives*, he should have asked about *RuPaul's Drag Race* instead.

This particular fact wouldn't have told Xander what he wanted to know, but it might have given him a clearer idea if he even had a chance.

Fifteen minutes later, Damon returned with a plastic bag full of sandwiches.

"What is all this?" Xander asked as he dug through the bag. "There must be six sandwiches in here."

"I wasn't sure what you wanted. Bonus points: anything we don't eat today, I can have for dinner."

Xander glanced up. "You eat cold sandwiches from the corner deli for dinner?"

"Long days," Damon said, and he sounded almost apologetic. "I don't have the energy or the inclination most days to make a dinner for one."

Xander tried to remember the last time he'd made a meal for just himself. Even in the mornings when he and Kian were rushing to get to Terroir and Nate was headed to the winery, he'd often make a big scramble with whatever was left in the fridge.

And at Terroir, there was the big meal they all shared before the dinner service started.

In fact, Xander couldn't even remember the last time he'd truly eaten a meal alone. Suddenly it made a lot of sense why loneliness seemed to emanate from Damon. Every single time Xander had been over to his house, there'd been zero evidence of any other visitor.

It made Xander's heart hurt for him. Divorced, estranged from his family, and dealing with the sort of demons that haunted men, Damon needed a friend, badly.

A little voice deep inside Xander told him that Damon needed a partner—and not just in his business ventures. Xander just wasn't sure that was him. Even if Damon was genuinely interested, Xander had never even had a boyfriend before. And if Nate was to be believed, that was because Xander couldn't put himself out there enough to make it happen. If he couldn't even convince a guy to date him, how could he be the sort of rock that Damon might need?

"It's pretty sad, isn't it?" Damon scoffed, and there wasn't even bitterness in his voice. Simply resignation.

"It's not, it's really not. Not sad anyway. I was thinking that I couldn't remember the last time I ate alone. You don't do it much in my world. You tend to eat in packs. Either at our house or at the restaurant."

"That sounds really . . . nice." Damon sounded plain wistful now.

"You need to come over to our place," Xander said, picking at the label of the roast beef and Havarti he'd selected. "It's not fancy, but we can make a mean meal." And, unspoken was the fact that Damon wouldn't be alone.

"You don't have to do that," Damon said, picking out a turkey with cranberry cream cheese. Xander's second choice. Damon, whether he realized it or not, had good taste.

After all, he'd picked Xander to be his head chef, hadn't he?

"I want to," Xander insisted.

"I guess you're going to have to do a lot of recipe testing," Damon suggested hesitantly. "I guess you have to feed the possibilities to someone."

"Exactly," Xander said, shooting Damon a quick grin.

"I'm going to go wash my hands," Xander said. "I'm gross."

He stood, leaving the wrapped sandwich on the wine barrel that was serving as their impromptu table.

"You're dirty, not gross," Damon corrected, and this time when he smiled, even his dimples came out. Xander got the briefest, most tantalizing peek of what a younger Damon, less lonely and less tormented, might have been like. And even though he was already hooked, it felt like that single moment was enough to reel him right in.

"House is unlocked," Damon continued when Xander hesitated. Torn between going to wash his hands and telling Damon very firmly that he could not say that sort of thing to him because he might get ideas and he already had enough of those swirling around his head.

"Great," Xander said shortly, and turned toward the house.

He washed his hands quickly and efficiently, forcing away any and all of his curiosity to poke and prod around Damon's very clean hall bathroom. Xander didn't even think Damon used it, but the temptation was stronger than it should have been.

Clearly, Xander wanted to know more about him, but he wasn't sure Damon would open up if he asked.

He returned to the barrel house, to find that Damon had waited for him to start eating. Xander didn't point that out, but it was hard not to feel, *again*, that Damon was that real deal he'd kept telling himself he was waiting for. Someone kind and thoughtful. Someone who put Xander first.

They ate their lunch and then continued working, mostly in silence, which was something Xander was fine with. Unnecessary chattering was heavily frowned upon at Terroir, and at pretty much every other restaurant he'd ever worked at, so he'd long ago killed that need inside him to fill up emptiness with words.

Xander figured that if Damon had something important to say, he'd say it, and assumed that Damon understood the opposite was also true.

Four rolled around, and Xander looked up as he wiped a dirty forearm across a forehead that was damp with sweat.

"You about finished?" Damon asked.

"Yeah, I just have the remains of this pile."

"I just broke down the last wine barrel. I think . . ." Damon let out a short, almost incredulous laugh. "I think we might almost be done lugging out all the shit in here."

"A miracle," Xander said dryly. He'd known this would be hot, heavy, unpleasant work. He wouldn't have been caught dead doing it, if this wasn't going to be partly his place too. And, Xander figured, he had done far worse things with a far worse view, all in the name of culinary advancement.

"As soon as we're cleared for burning, I'll have a big bonfire with this pile," Damon said.

"A bonfire?" Despite his own best intentions, that sounded fun. And maybe even a little romantic.

"Maybe tomorrow night. Maybe the night after. You wanna come and hang out, watch it all burn?"

Xander wondered if Damon realized he'd been leading him into the invitation. If he'd wanted to invite him anyway. But in the end, it didn't matter, because he'd been asked, and he was definitely not going to turn it down. "Sure. Sounds like fun."

"I have a schedule," Damon said next. "Next on it is refinishing the floors, which I plan on doing next week. You want to help with that too?"

Xander knew, from his stepdad's work in construction, that refinishing floors was back-breaking, unpleasant and messy. He still nodded.

"I'll let you know about the bonfire," Damon said. "But in the meantime, I'll be tending the garden. Thinking about clearing some more land, maybe put in an orchard. It won't be ready right away, maybe not even for a few years, but eventually, we'll have fruit."

An orchard. Xander shaded his eyes and looked the way Damon was pointing, far in the distance. Yeah, he could see apple trees there. "Can you text me a list of vegetables that you'll be ready to harvest for the restaurant opening?" Xander asked. "I'm going to spend the time in recipe development."

"Yeah, sure. And I almost forgot." Damon dug in his back pocket and pulled out his wallet. Handed a plastic card to Xander. When he took it, it was still warm from his body. Xander curled his fingers around it, the edges biting into his palm.

"That's a debit card to the bank account I've set up for the restaurant. Feel free to charge any purchases to the account. There's plenty of money in it."

Xander remembered Bastian Aquino demanding a receipt for some strawberries he'd been asked to pick up at the farm stand. He remembered his honesty over the dollar amount being questioned without one. And here Damon was, just handing him the key to a whole bank account.

This must be what being trusted felt like.

The next day, Damon felt stupid that he hadn't invited Xander to see what a day in the garden was like. He didn't need his help, but he'd discovered that even though it had taken months to get used to the silence, it only took a few evenings and a day together to remember how much it sucked.

It took him the entire morning to go through the garden, checking plants, pulling encroaching weeds, spraying everything with his homemade bug repellent that he'd invented after too many evenings scouring the internet for something non-chemical and organic.

Then Damon looked over at the big pile of wood and garbage that he and Xander had spent the last day dragging out of the barrel house. Really, he needed another day to sort through it, and get the bonfire ready. He didn't want to wait another day, but there was no point of having the fire if he couldn't do it properly. Also, the forecast called for some rain tonight, and if he tarped the pile, the surrounding ground would be damp enough that the burning restriction for the county would probably lift.

He worked the rest of the afternoon, sweating through his shirt and sorting out the garbage he'd have to take to the dump. By five, he was halfway through, and felt good about confirming the bonfire tomorrow night. Maybe he should even get marshmallows and graham crackers at the store, make it a s'mores party.

Grabbing his phone from his counter, he shed his filthy clothes right into the washing machine and texted Xander on the way to a much-needed shower.

He typed in: **Bonfire + s'mores tomorrow night?** and hit the send button.

It was a difficult decision between a cold shower and a hot one, but the boiling temps, barely counteracted by the old air conditioner in this house, made the decision for him.

He'd soothe his aching muscles by swallowing a few painkillers with dinner. There was a time when he'd have wanted to drink a beer or two or six to drown out the pain. And that had always been the problem with him and alcohol. There was no safe middle ground of a handful of beers. There was only no beer or a whole six-pack and then whatever other booze he could scrounge up in the house.

Cold water sluiced over his overheated skin and he leaned back against the tile wall and tried to think of nothing, because the alternative was thinking of Xander, and Damon knew he'd already crossed too many lines thinking of Xander.

He didn't need to cross this one. But he couldn't seem to stop his own hand, as it drifted down his chest, his stomach and settled low at his groin, wrapping around his half-hard cock. The water was cool and refreshing and his dick hadn't seemed to get the memo that he wasn't supposed to be thinking about this.

He'd tried thinking of Rachel. He'd tried thinking of other women. The hot checker at the grocery store who always gave him appreciative looks whenever he bought food. But none of them did it for him anymore. His body knew what he wanted, and it wasn't so much a shock that it was a man, as it was a surprise that it was Xander.

Since realizing and acknowledging he was bisexual in junior high, he'd never gotten a chance to try anything with a guy. Rachel had asked him once how he could even know, if he'd never even kissed a guy. He'd asked her how she knew she liked guys before she'd kissed him, when they were fourteen and snuck into one of the big winery parties his family threw.

She'd responded that she'd just *known*, and before he could even point out the double standard, she'd laughed, a little self-consciously and pointed it out herself.

That was the first and only conversation they'd ever had about it, but when she'd left him, she'd told him that some-day he'd meet someone who wouldn't mind wrestling with his demons.

The *someone* had reminded him that now that he and Rachel were over, and when he finally got clean, there was always the chance that when he found himself attracted to someone again, that person wouldn't necessarily be a woman.

And now it had happened, and it was definitely not a woman.

Damon gave his cock a half-hearted tug. His body was definitely all-in, interest piqued like it hadn't in years, but his mind was still freaking out. Not over the fact that Xander was a man, though that was a little intimidating considering how little experience he had, but over the chance that he could fuck it all up again.

Rachel had been bad enough, and she'd gotten away before he'd truly been able to ruin her life. But what if he ruined Xander's? He wanted Xander to be part of his personal life, but he was already part of his professional one. What if he couldn't keep it together? What if the Barrel House pushed him back into old and destructive habits? Damon still wasn't certain he trusted himself.

He definitely didn't trust himself enough to drag someone else into his hot mess.

The problem was his body was hearing, but not really listening, to the arguments his brain kept setting out. It knew exactly what it wanted—a firm mouth, stubble scraping against his cheek as they kissed; a muscular shoulder he could brace his hands against. But mostly he wanted those scarred, talented hands, so delicate but so tough, wrapped around his cock right now.

Damon had a lot of self-control these days. He'd spent years developing and cultivating it. Which was the only reason he'd managed to keep his thoughts of Xander PG-rated until now. But after spending some quality time with the man, his control washed away like a dirt road in a flash flood.

He tipped his face back, felt the water wash over him in a cool rush, and stroked himself with certainty this time. An embarrassingly short time later, he was watching the result wash down the drain.

"Damn," Damon said to himself.

A quick wash later, he got out of the shower, wrapped a towel around his waist, and because he apparently couldn't help himself at all, checked his phone.

There was already a text from Xander. *Three* texts from Xander, in fact.

Damon groaned out loud. He was so fucked. Especially if Xander was as drawn to Damon as Damon was to him.

We're on.

S'mores sound really good. I'll bring homemade marshmallows.

Don't argue. They're so much better than the ones at the store. Will prove it tomorrow night.

Damon wasn't going to argue, and if he had, he only intended to put up a token protest. He was more than ready to let Xander prove the marshmallows, and just about anything else, tomorrow night.

Chapter Six

"WHAT THE FUCK ARE you doing?"

Xander glanced up from the candy thermometer he was carefully monitoring to see Kian standing in the doorway. It was four in the afternoon on a Thursday, and Kian wasn't at Terroir.

There must have been a disruption in the Force, or maybe the Bastard finally grew a single heart molecule.

"I could ask you the same question," Xander retorted steadily. He and Kian hadn't seen each other since their fight almost a week ago, and every time he thought about the way Kian had sided with Aquino, something in his stomach burned.

He would've sworn it was indigestion, but after dealing with it for a few days and swearing off all spicy food, it remained, persistent and annoying. Making him, who was completely the innocent and wronged party in this scenario, feel *guilty*. It wasn't right, and Xander wasn't happy about it.

"I cut myself pretty badly, had to go to the ER," Kian said. "Chef told me to take the night off."

This time Xander really looked at his friend, and it turned out the large, white bandage on his hand was tough to miss. If you were looking for it, anyway.

"Are you okay?" he found himself asking, because no matter how pissed off he felt, Kian was still somebody he cared about.

"Twelve stitches," Kian said nonchalantly and even for a chef, who regularly cut themselves, that was bad.

"Actually, twenty-four," Kian added. "They had to stitch the inner too."

Xander kept his eyes glued to the candy thermometer and the hot sugar boiling away, but he said, "Must've been deep then."

"I could see the tendon," Kian said. "It's that damn Japanese mandolin."

Even for an experienced chef, the Japanese mandolin with its wickedly sharp and completely unprotected blade had scared the shit out of Xander. He'd always worn the special Kevlar gloves with it, no matter how much Aquino baited him by calling him a pussy.

He was fine being a pussy, as long as he was a pussy who wasn't missing any fingers.

"You weren't wearing the gloves, were you," Xander said. He didn't really need to ask. There was no way Kian would wear them, not if he was trying to impress Aquino. Even if Aquino never would have used it without them.

Actually, as far as Xander was concerned, Aquino hired people so he didn't *have* to use the Japanese mandolin. Talk about pussy moves.

"Of course I wasn't wearing the gloves," Kian said. "They slow you down big-time."

Xander raised an eyebrow. "And a bisected finger doesn't?"

Kian shrugged, like the injury wasn't a big deal. The truth was, they'd probably given him some good pain meds, the kind of meds that made you not care about a single damn thing. When Kian woke up in the morning, and *felt* the twenty-four stitches, it was definitely going to be a slightly bigger deal.

"You didn't tell me what *you* were doing," Kian said, wandering over, smelling like a hospital and also like eggplant, which made sense, because Terroir had a dish of paper-thin eggplant slices roasted, and then layered together with whipped goat cheese and fresh herbs. It was delectable, and also dangerous.

"Making marshmallows," Xander said.

"Isn't this normally Miles' sort of thing?" Kian asked, referring to their friend who was a famous pastry chef. "Is that Hess guy making you work pastry too?"

"Yes, and no," Xander retorted.

"Then why the marshmallows?" It seemed that Kian on pain meds was also an inquisitive Kian.

"Because I wanted to expand my culinary repertoire," Xander explained, not very patiently. "And I'm going over to Damon's tonight. We're building a bonfire of all the crap we lugged out of the building that's eventually going to be the restaurant. And I thought s'mores with homemade marshmallows would be fun."

"Fun." Kian tested the word, rolling it around in his mouth like a savory treat. Like he couldn't quite remember what it tasted like. And frankly, working himself to death for Bastian Aquino probably meant that he didn't.

Of course Kian was also clearly masochistic and maybe working for Aquino qualified as fun.

"Yeah, fun. Do you even remember what that is?"

"Very funny," Kian scoffed. "You're such a fucking comedian. You should quit your job . . . oh wait, you already did."

"For a *better* one," Xander retorted. Normally he didn't stay so patient, and Kian had probably expected that the result of his baiting would be another argument. Clearly, he was spoiling for one. But Xander didn't *want* to fight. The sick feeling in the bottom of his stomach had made that clear enough.

"If you weren't injured," he continued, voice still mild, with only a hint of bite to it, "you could bloom that gelatin for me."

"Or if I knew what that was. I'm not a pastry chef," Kian said sulkily.

"You know what gelatin is." Xander rolled his eyes and pointed to the small glass measuring cup. "Just pour the packet into that cup of water and stir it a bit. It'll get thick."

The rising temperature on the candy thermometer stole his attention away and when he looked back, Kian had reverted to regular form, pouring in and stirring the gelatin conscientiously. Maybe even a little too conscientiously, considering the relative simplicity of the task and the focus Kian was giving it.

"Once it's bloomed," Xander said, "pour it in that big stainless steel bowl there."

"Really going to miss Miles' professional stand mixer, aren't you?" Kian asked, eyeing the small-ish hand mixer Miles had left them, all the while making pointed comments that they wouldn't even need that because baking was foreign to them.

Xander was totally going to send him pics of these killer marshmallows when they were done. He could do pastry, he just chose not to.

"I think it'll be fine," Xander said confidently.

Kian gave him a dubious look. "You won't mind if I stand over here? I already had twenty-four stitches today, I don't need any third-degree burns on top of that."

"Nobody's going back to the emergency room." The candy thermometer hit the right temperature and he pulled it off the heat, re-adjusting his oven mitt on his hand. "Now or never," he said to Kian or maybe to himself.

Carefully, he poured the boiling hot sugar into the bowl, re-dissolving the gelatin, and switched from the oven mitt to the hand mixer.

"See?" he said, switching on the mixer, carefully keeping the beaters submerged in the hot mixture. "No big deal."

Kian nodded, but still stayed on the other side of the kitchen, which considering he'd already had to go to the hospital today, was probably safer.

A few minutes later, even with his hand-mixer handicap Xander had beautiful snowy white mounds of marshmallow.

Kian even looked impressed as Xander poured it into the prepared pan, dusted liberally with cornstarch and powdered sugar. "And now they just set up?" he asked.

"Yeah, for a few hours. Then just cut into squares."

"If I knew this was so easy, maybe I would have tried it before now." Kian had a sweet tooth and a somewhat disparaging opinion of pastry chefs, their friend Miles withstanding, which didn't make much sense.

"No, you wouldn't have," Xander said, laughing. But that feeling in the pit of his stomach had finally began to recede, and Kian had softened during their time together in the kitchen. It could be just the pain medication he was on, but Xander didn't think so. Kian was wound so tight because Bastian was wound so tight. They were each other's mirrors and as a result, each other's worst nightmare.

"Come with me tonight," Xander offered suddenly. "Like I said, it'll be fun."

He probably should have asked Damon before inviting anyone over to his house, but he had a feeling that the man would probably enjoy meeting Kian. Maybe he should even invite Nate. He wasn't sure he was working tonight.

"Are you sure? You don't want to be alone with Mr. Wine Big Shot?" Kian questioned.

Xander definitely wanted to be alone with Damon, which meant he absolutely shouldn't be.

The hesitation was enough to tell Kian everything he needed to know, especially because he knew too much about Xander's romantic history. "You've got another unrequited crush, don't you?" He sighed.

"It might not be unrequited," Xander defended. Even if it wasn't, it was still a bad idea.

"He's probably straight. Did he tell you he wasn't straight?"

Trust Kian to figure out the crux of the issue immediately, like an arrow straight to the heart. "He was married to a woman before," Xander admitted.

Kian's sympathetic expression was like death. Xander could feel the bell tolling for all his hopes, even as he tried to remind himself Damon had looked interested more than once—or at least *intrigued*. "That doesn't mean he's straight," Kian rallied.

"Doesn't mean he's not." Xander knew how bitter he sounded. "Just like old times, right?"

"Miles wasn't straight," Kian said. "Not that him being gay really helped."

"Not exactly." He hadn't been in love with their friend, but he'd crushed on him forever, always hoping for more, and assuming it wouldn't happen. And in the end, of course it hadn't. Miles had only ever seen him as his friend, and then had proceeded to move to Los Angeles for work and fall in love with his producer.

And that was all well and good for them, living in their happy LA bubble of love and success, but where had it left Xander?

Alone. Like always.

"I think you should try, Xander," Kian said. "I know the chances of him reciprocating are small, but you can't just keep letting these chances to find somebody pass you by. Sometime you're going to have to take a leap of faith."

That sounded like vintage Kian, all hope and sweetness and light. Before Bastian had gotten his talons into him.

It also sounded unpleasantly like what Nate had just told him the other night.

Xander rolled his eyes. "If I tell you I'm considering it, would you leave me alone?"

"Yes and no." Kian grinned. "I want to meet him. So instead of giving you some time alone, I'm going with you. I can do reconnaissance."

"Reconnaissance?"

"You know," Kian said impatiently, sounding higher by the second, or maybe just more manic, "reconnaissance to find out if he's interested in guys."

"Oh god," Xander said. "No, you will not. You absolutely will not."

Kian grinned wildly. "Oh, but it'll be fun!"

Of course, the marshmallows were not amazing or incredible or even the tiniest bit transcendental.

Kian peered over the side of the pan and poked at the goopy mess with an offset spatula. "What's wrong with them?"

"I don't know," Xander snapped. "God, Kian, it's like you expect me to be Miles or something."

"They *were* supposed to set up, right?" Kian asked.

"Of course they were." Xander grabbed for his phone. "I'm calling Miles."

"I'm going to go take a shower," Kian announced lazily.

"Wrap your hand!" Xander called after him after dialing. He hoped that Miles wasn't filming today, but it felt like Miles filmed a lot of days now.

"Wrap my hand?" Miles answered, voice puzzled. "Did I hurt my hand?"

"Oh, that was for Kian," Xander said. "He cut his finger pretty badly today. Twenty-four-stitches badly."

"That explains why he's not at Terroir right now," Miles said. "And I know you're not there because you quit, you smug bastard. I'm still wondering why all I got was a text message to our group chat."

"Because you're a busy and important man and I like to respect your time?" Xander asked meekly.

Miles laughed. "No. I get it. The days after I quit all I wanted to do was sleep and constantly fist pump because the torture was finally over."

"You barely spent any time with the Bastard," Xander pointed out.

"And yet, my job still sucked." Miles paused. "So what's the emergency?"

"How did you know?"

"You always text. You never call. Wyatt's the actual phone-conversation friend in our group. You just send terse texts."

"They're not terse, they're to the point," Xander grumbled.

"What's the emergency?" Miles repeated. "Apparently we're going to some fancy LA restaurant tonight and I need to look presentable. Evan's picking out shirts and I'm going to end up in one that's mandarin orange if I'm not careful."

Awhile ago, Xander would have been unavoidably jealous of the casual affection and undeniable love in Miles' voice as he talked about his boyfriend and producing partner. Now, all Xander felt was relief that he'd never actually done anything about his crush on Miles. They were so much better as friends.

"I was making marshmallows and they didn't set up."

"You were . . . what?" Miles questioned. "Marshmallows? You're not the pastry chef at this new restaurant, are you? Because I'm guessing that's not going to work very well for any-one."

Xander paced across the kitchen, not even bothering to glance over at his sad pan of marshmallows. "No. I'm not insane. I'm going to a bonfire tonight, it's a new work thing, and I wanted to bring something fun. S'mores always seem fun."

"Fun? Xander Bridges looking for something fun? You've got a crush."

"Why do you have to make that sound so accusatory?" Xander objected. "What if I do have a crush? Why is that a prob-lem?"

A year ago, he might have believed that Miles was jealous, but he knew better now. Miles was afraid he'd end up miserable and alone.

Sometimes Xander was worried about that too. Then he'd met Damon and then met him again a year later, and during the last week, that particular fear didn't feel so pressing.

"It's not a problem. It's cute. You're making marshmallows for a crush. Who is it? You said it was a work thing? Oh," Miles said, realization clearly dawning, "it's the Hess guy, isn't it? Your new partner?"

"Did Kian tell you?"

"It was a lucky guess," Miles said, but he was a terrible liar. Kian had totally texted him.

"So how do I fix them?"

"What happened to them?"

"They didn't set up. They're just . . . mush."

"Sounds like you didn't whip the sugar enough with the gelatin," Miles speculated. "Especially if you're using that pathetic little hand mixer I left you instead of my professional stand mixer."

"Kian totally texted you," Xander retorted, a little outraged and a little touched.

"Kian cares about you," Miles argued. "Kian is worried you're going to do the same thing with Damon as you did with all those other guys. You can't just stand back on the sidelines forever, even if it means you're protecting yourself."

"Did Kian write that out for you?" Xander asked bitterly. "If I call Wyatt will I get a similar but different version of the same lecture?"

"Kian cares about you," Miles repeated, a lot more gently this time. "And he's right."

"I don't even know if he likes men. Or if he does, if he likes me."

"Believe it or not," Miles reminded him dryly, "you're fairly likable. Plus you'll never know if you do nothing. Relationships require a certain amount of *fuck it* to work. That means giving up control. And I know you're not good at that."

Xander leaned back against the counter. "I'm not."

"If you called up Wyatt you'd probably get a similar version of this speech because he knows that just as well as I do," Miles said. "You've got to take a chance."

Xander was quiet for a long moment. "Sometimes I think I like unobtainable people because that means I never have to do that."

That was what his crush on Miles had really been about. Someone safe he could like from a romantic distance, even as they'd become closer friends. An excuse to never actually do anything. An easy way to protect his heart.

"There's nothing to be gained without the potential of loss," Miles said.

"How did you get so damn smart?"

"It's not me. It's all Evan." Miles' voice grew a bit hushed, almost reverent. And Xander *was* jealous then—jealous because he'd never talked about anyone that way before, and all he wanted was the chance. He wanted it, and he definitely wanted it with Damon. Maybe even more than he was afraid.

"So I need to whip the marshmallows more."

"I think so," Miles said. "Let me know how they turn out. I'm going to do an orange-shirt intervention."

"Good luck," Xander said and hung up.

They both knew he was going to end up wearing the orange shirt and liking it.

⁂

"So what did Miles say?" Kian asked as they walked to the car a few hours later.

Xander rolled his eyes. "You already know what he said. You can rest easy, knowing you called your ringer in and he gave his best effort."

"The real question is," Kian said, "was he successful?"

"I guess you'll have to see," Xander said, but he was grinning, a little effervescent from the realization that he had every intention of letting his walls down. Maybe not tonight, necessarily, but soon.

"Are you telling me reconnaissance is no longer required?" Kian asked archly. "Because I was definitely looking forward to asking Damon all sorts of uncomfortable questions like, *do you like cock?* And *how do you feel about dick?*"

"Don't you dare," Xander said. His heart accelerated at the thought that Kian could and might and that Damon could say yes. And then he would have zero excuses left.

"I won't need to, if you do your part," Kian said, but he sounded so satisfied there was no question that he had already known how Xander would decide. Maybe he'd even known before Xander did.

Xander was still trying to figure out how people with the most troubled love lives were often the ones who saw other people's the most clearly when they pulled up to Damon's house.

Then he saw Damon's face, smiling as he walked over to the car, and Xander realized knowing why was irrelevant. The only thing that mattered—just like the first awful batch of marshmallows buried in the trash at home and the second, perfect batch, bagged in the back seat of the car—was the result.

Chapter Seven

DAMON HAD BEEN TELLING himself all afternoon not to get his hopes up but he was still inevitably crushed when Xander texted him about five to say he was coming over in a few hours and that he was bringing his friend and roommate, Kian.

Of course, he'd responded in the affirmative, confirming that Xander was free to bring whoever he wished, but Damon couldn't help but think that Xander was bringing a friend to make sure the atmosphere didn't feel too date-like.

Damon reminded himself that the dinner they'd shared the other night had felt plenty date-like and Xander had barely batted an eyelash, but then, besides practically inviting him to sit on his lap to sign the contract, he'd not exactly made any overtures either.

This would all be a little easier—and a little harder, too—if Xander wasn't interested in him.

But then Xander's car pulled up to the house, and he stepped out. His grin was wide, and it took a second, but Damon realized that smile was for *him*.

It wasn't for Kian, who must be the guy getting out of the passenger side of the car. Or food. Or a job offer. Or the Barrel House. It was for *Damon*.

Xander slung an arm around his shoulders, pulling him into a half hug. "Wait until you taste these marshmallows I made," he said. "I think pastry might be my second calling. Maybe we won't even need to hire a pastry chef."

Damon snorted, soft and amused, both from Xander's clear affection and also from his ego. "If you want to work yourself to death, that's on you."

"It's ambition. Just ambition," Xander said, laughing. "By the way, this is my friend, Kian. Kian, this is my new partner, Damon Hess."

As he shook Kian's hand, there was definitely a part of him that liked Xander's introduction. Partner sounded so much better than boss. Probably to Xander too, after so long under Bastian Aquino's thumb.

Kian was a few inches shorter than Xander, and had that look like he was just coming into his adult muscles. Still slender and a bit slight, with a mop of blond hair and a pair of baby blue eyes.

Damon nearly made the crack about Aquino out loud, but then he remembered that Xander had mentioned the other day that his friend had an unfortunate crush on the man.

He hadn't been lying. It was definitely unfortunate. Bastian looked like he could eat Kian for lunch and then spit him back out again for dinner.

"So you still work at Terroir?" Damon asked, as they headed back toward where he'd set up the wood and debris for the bonfire.

"I do," Kian said, and shooting Xander sort of a half-hearted glare. "But I got the night off."

"What he means to tell you," Xander said conspiratorially, "is that he nearly chopped his finger off with a Japanese mandolin."

Damon glanced down at Kian's hand, and sure enough, it was wrapped in a thick white bandage. He'd been so busy staring at Xander, appreciating the tan of his skin against his white t-shirt, that he'd barely spared Kian a glance.

"That sounds . . . dangerous," Damon said.

They stopped in front of the enormous pile they were about to set on fire.

"This also looks dangerous," Xander said, with a gleam in his eye that Damon *knew* meant both terrible and wonderful things.

"You say that with such relish," Kian complained. "You're going to make Damon think you're a sort of pyro creep."

Damon definitely did not think Xander was a pyro creep. Far from it, in fact. But the problem was to explain this without sounding like he had a real serious crush. Which he definitely did.

"Uh, um," Damon hesitated.

"See?" Kian said triumphantly, and Xander frowned.

"No," Damon said firmly. "Definitely not a creep. Nothing like a creep." If anything was creepy, it was probably his own smile as he gazed longingly over at Xander, trying to communicate just how wrong Kian was.

The frown disappeared, which wasn't all Damon wanted, but he'd take it. "So where are these fantastic marshmallows?" Damon asked, trying to change the subject and very aware that he was doing so clunkily.

Xander pulled a Tupperware container out of the paper bag he was carrying. "Right here. I thought it wouldn't do to get too gourmet, and stopped by the store for regular old graham crackers and Hershey's milk chocolate bars to go with them."

"Should have gone for the Valrhona," Kian muttered.

"Don't mind him," Xander said, leaning closer to Damon, his shoulder brushing Damon's arm and making his heart skitter like a teenager again, "his pain meds are wearing off, and he can't take any more until tomorrow morning."

"Should he be here? With his injury?" Damon asked in a low voice, hopefully out of Kian's hearing. He was also hoping his question looked like friendly concern and not annoyance that Kian was crashing their non-date.

"Socializing is good for him." Xander tipped his head up toward Damon's, grinning, and his stomach fluttered. "He's never able to leave that damn restaurant."

"Is socializing good for you too?" Damon asked. He kept his tone even, but it didn't matter how it sounded, the question still sounded flirtatious.

But Xander just nodded, and didn't move away. "I'm not . . . I'm not always good at it," he confessed. "Maybe you can help me practice."

Damon remembered very well the last person who'd asked him for help "practicing" in this area—he'd eventually married her. If Kian hadn't been standing only a few feet away, maybe he even would have thrown rational thought to the wind, and kissed Xander. All in the name of practice, of course.

Maybe it was better that Kian was here. It kept Damon from doing anything he couldn't take back tomorrow.

"I'm not either," Damon admitted. "Maybe we can practice together?" It was hard to even say it without blushing, and he wasn't sure he quite managed it.

If the way Xander glanced over at his friend, and then back to Damon, and then down to Damon's lips, not even being very subtle about it, was any indication, then he thought he'd just been given the green light.

Of course there was still the problem of Kian. He'd walked over to the other side of the big pile of debris, but he was still present.

"Are you two going to stop flirting so we can burn this down?" Kian asked.

Yep. Definitely still present.

Xander blushed a really cute shade of red, but he didn't deny it. And neither did Damon, which he hoped Xander noticed.

"Yeah, let's get this fire started," Damon said, and blushed himself at the double entendre he'd accidentally used. Kian laughed, and when Damon found the courage to glance over at Xander, he was smiling too. He figured that the nervous determination on Xander's face was probably reflected in his own.

"How can I help?" Xander asked.

"Um, you could find some sticks to toast the marshmallows," Damon suggested. "I'm going to go grab the matches from the house."

⚘⚘⚘

"Well," Kian said as Xander pulled some long sticks from the pile in front of them, "he sure seems interested from where I'm standing. No reconnaissance required."

"Shhh," Xander hissed at his friend. "He's going to hear you."

"And know he's interested? Yeah, I think he knows that already."

Xander yanked a stick out, examined and then threw it back in. "It's not that simple. We're business partners. Technically he pays my salary. This restaurant is something we both need. I don't want to fuck that up."

"You don't know it will," Kian said, his tone at odds with the optimism of his words. "Now you're just making excuses."

"I don't know it won't," Xander countered. "I'm just trying to be cautious here and make a good decision."

"Are you? Or are you just afraid of something good happening?"

Xander finally found a pair of sticks he liked, and set them aside. "Something good *is* happening. We're opening a restaurant. I'm going to be head chef of my own place, finally. I don't have to get yelled at anymore. If anyone's yelling, it's going to be me. That feels pretty damn good."

Kian opened his mouth, probably to argue that Bastian was a wonderful person under all his verbal abuse, but Xander didn't want to hear it. "I don't care," was all he said. "I know you and I are always going to disagree on this, but he's a shithead."

"Who's a shithead?"

Damon had come back with the matches, and once he spotted Xander's sticks, pulled a pocket knife out, and opened it, passing it to him handle-first. Like the credit card from a few days ago, the metal of the knife was also warm from his body heat. It was old too, well-used, with nicks and scratches. Xander absently rubbed the warm steel with his thumb as he started to trim the sticks and whittle the ends to a point.

"Aquino is a shithead," Xander said shortly.

"No argument from me," Damon said cautiously. Like he knew, even without being told, that this was a delicate subject between the two of them. "You got that okay?" he asked, gesturing to the sticks Xander was prepping.

Just as he asked, the knife slipped, and poked him right in the thumb. Like all of Damon's equipment, it was well-used but also well taken care of and the edge was sharp. Blood welled from the tiny wound. Xander stuck it in his mouth and sucked it. "I *was* fine," he teased. "You just had to go and ask."

Damon was by his side in a second, a hand on his back—warm and heavy and reassuring. "Sorry. It's sharp."

"It's fine, I'll live," Xander said with a chuckle. "At least it doesn't need twenty-four stitches."

Still, Damon reached over and eased the knife from Xander's grip. "I'll just finish these up real quick," he said apologetically. Like he'd fucked up by keeping his knife sharp and lending it to Xander.

The sticks were almost ready anyway, and it only took Damon a few more expertly aimed swipes of the knife to finish them off.

"I'll start the fire now," Damon said, handing the sticks over to Xander and pocketing the knife.

From the way he lit the fire, Xander could tell he'd done it before. Knew exactly where to get the kindling set and in only a few minutes, there was a roaring bonfire in their midst, chasing away the evening chill in the air.

Xander dug out the container of marshmallows and stuck two on the end of the sticks, handed one to Kian.

"They look delicious," Damon said when he wandered back over. He reached down and popped one from the container at Xander's feet into his mouth. "Taste delicious too," he said through a mouthful of marshmallow.

"I proved it to you. What do I get in return?" he teased, all too aware that Damon was standing close, much nearer than he needed to, only a few inches away, their shoulders practically touching. He leaned in closer.

"Anything you want," Damon said quietly, eyes flicking to Xander's, and then over to where Kian was standing, prepping his own s'mores. Xander felt a single brush on his hand and glanced down to see Damon extending a finger to graze the back of his hand.

It felt more tremendous and shattering than a hundred other, far more intimate touches.

"I'm not good at this," Xander repeated from earlier.

Damon smiled, a bittersweet story written in his eyes Xander hoped he might hear one day. "Me either. But I'm running out of reasons why we shouldn't try anyway."

"Me too." Xander kept his voice low, hoping that Kian, who was pointedly turned away from them, nearly around the other side of the bonfire, wouldn't hear them. It had been the right thing to do to bring Kian, considering their recent problems, but he also regretted bringing him along. Anticipation filled him, all too aware that something was going to happen between him and Damon, but not entirely sure when.

Xander reached back and looped their fingers together. He hoped Damon understood. Felt it when he saw Damon's quiet, satisfied smile. Sometimes Xander felt like he'd made a career out of falling for the wrong men; never before had he started anything with anybody feeling like it wasn't going to eventually end in disaster. But this felt fated. Like he'd come here in the middle of a rainstorm not because he needed to stop Damon, but because he'd needed to meet him instead.

"Let's make some s'mores," he said after a minute. "We can't let Kian have all the fun."

He reluctantly detached their fingers and held the stick with the marshmallow closer to the flames.

"Can you get the chocolate and the graham crackers ready?" Xander asked distractedly, trying to rotate the stick so the marshmallow didn't spontaneously burst into flames. The fire was hot, and burning even hotter every second. "This is going to go pretty quick."

When he glanced back, Damon was there, the requested items already unpackaged and waiting. "Oh," Xander said.

"I have made s'mores before," Damon said, amused. "I might not be your culinary equal, but I can help."

Was it any wonder that Xander, despite all the reasons to be afraid of this, and to approach it more carefully, more cautiously, kept wanting to throw all his worries to the wind and make Damon his?

Xander carefully deposited his marshmallow on the upturned chocolate and cracker and left Damon happily munching away as he went to go check on Kian.

"Didn't Nate say he wasn't working tonight?" Xander asked his friend, hoping he wouldn't immediately understand what he was *really* asking.

"You mean, can't Nate come get me so you can make out with sexy farmer over there?" Kian asked archly.

"No, yes, um, I mean . . ." Xander stumbled. He and Kian might not have been as close as they once were, and he wasn't quite as familiar with this more pointed Kian. Kian with all his soft edges beginning to harden and sharpen. Xander wasn't sure he liked it, but he definitely knew who was to blame for it.

"I took care of it," Kian said.

"You took care of it?" Xander questioned.

"He should be here in a few minutes," was all Kian would say.

"You didn't ask Nate?"

Kian turned to face him. He didn't look happy. "Nate told me what you did. That wasn't cool, Xander."

"I thought maybe . . . I don't know. I thought maybe I should be trying the easy way for once, not just fruitlessly pursuing the hard way."

"Nate is a person, he's not an experiment," Kian argued. "And it doesn't really look fruitless from over here."

"I didn't . . . I wasn't sure. I didn't know." They were all bad excuses, and Xander already knew he was going to have to make a groveling apology to Nate at some point, but he hadn't known he was going to be called out by Kian for not doing it yet.

"Not all of us are good at this," Xander continued after taking a short, clearing breath. "I'm trying." He took another breath, trying to say the right thing for once. "I think what I'm trying to say is that not all of us are as sure as you."

Kian looked surprised. It made sense, because Xander had surprised even himself. "What, no more warnings?" He looked up, like he saw something in the distance and gave a little wave.

Must be the person Kian had called to pick him up.

Then the person walked closer, and his shadowy form cleared into the recognizable bulk of Bastian Aquino.

"He texted me to check on how I was doing after service," Kian said, and Xander knew the defensive tone he was using was all his own fault. Was Bastian the right person for Kian? Maybe it was only for Kian to say. "I told him he could come and check on me in person. We'll get out of your hair in a minute."

"No warnings," Xander answered Kian's earlier question with certainty. "You're an adult. You know what you're doing."

Kian sighed. "Not really. But maybe. Maybe soon."

Damon watched as Bastian and Kian left. Xander walked over, a partially eaten s'more in his hand.

"Was that Aquino?" he asked, even though he already knew the answer. Somehow being alone with Xander had been easier with the added protection of Kian's presence. Now they were alone and his nerves were flaring. Did he have the right to do this? Even with the warning to Xander that he was bad at this? Still, Xander couldn't say that he hadn't been as upfront and honest as he could be. He knew Damon was an alcoholic. Sober and recovering, but still an alcoholic. Rachel hadn't known when they'd started dating, but that was high school and even Damon hadn't known what the future held.

"Yeah." Xander stared out at the retreating figures, and Damon had a feeling more than just their burgeoning relationship was on his mind.

"You okay?"

Xander finished his s'more and nodded. "I keep trying to save him from a big mistake with Aquino but maybe it's not a mistake. Maybe I'm wrong. Who's to say I'm right?"

"Probably everyone else who knows Aquino?" Damon suggested. It occurred to him that if Xander's friends knew about his alcoholism, and what had happened with Rachel, they might be warning Xander off him. The same way Xander had warned Kian off Bastian Aquino.

"The truth is," Damon continued with a heavy sigh. "None of us have a perfect track record with relationships. All we can do is make the effort to do better."

Xander's dark eyes were very serious. "Is that what you want?"

Damon wanted all sorts of things. He wanted to be good, to be a better man—both for himself and for Xander—and he also wanted to be very, very bad.

He reached out and took Xander's whole hand this time, lacing their fingers together. Maybe this was supposed to be hard, but he'd known since Rachel walked out that eventually he'd date again, and it might not be a woman. Wrapping his head around dating again was really the tough part, not the fact that Xander was male. "I want you."

Damon didn't know how Xander could still look surprised, but he did. It was a happy sort of surprise, like winning a lottery you hadn't entered, but Damon had to ask.

"You look . . ."

"Surprised?" Xander answered wryly. "Well, you *did* say you were married before. To a woman."

It had never occurred to Damon before that this could be a problem. He'd heard vague rumblings of the gay community underappreciating bisexuality, but he never would have pegged Xander with that sort of prejudice.

"Is that a problem?"

"No, no, of course not," Xander reassured him, gripping his hand tighter, and tugging him closer. He slid a hand around Damon's waist, and it felt so good that he had to hold back the pleasurable shudder. It had been so long since anybody had touched him. But it wasn't just that; it was Xander. Only Xander. "I hoped. I hoped even though I've been let down before. The truth is, I couldn't help myself."

"I didn't think I was very subtle," Damon said with a wry laugh.

"I told you I wasn't good at this. I'm . . . it's hard for me to open up for people. But I want to try."

"And I want you to," Damon said. Resting his hand on Xander's shoulder, and pulling him into an embrace felt as natural as breathing.

He'd thought about it before, but now he knew for sure. If Xander tipped his head back just a fraction, their lips would meet.

Damon had just about gathered enough courage. He knew Xander wanted this. He knew *he* wanted this. But then Xander spoke again.

"Did you know this would happen when you came to Terroir?" he asked softly.

"I didn't know. But I sure hoped," Damon admitted. "I knew the way I felt—the way I *could* feel—and I hoped you felt a little of what I did."

Xander's eyes were so soft. Damon admitted that he didn't know him that well, but he'd never seen Xander look at anything—or anyone—like that before. It was incredibly humbling, and more than a little enthralling, that it was him on the receiving end of that look.

"I looked for you for months," Xander said. "I wanted to do this. Even back then. Even if it seemed like a terrible idea."

He moved so slow that it felt an eternity before Xander's lips met Damon's. So slow that he would have lots of time to change his mind. He had a feeling that was Xander's whole plan. And that was before Xander even knew this was his first kiss with a man.

Damon didn't think of how different it felt because it was a man, only that it was different because it was Xander. It was slow and sweet and gentle, just the softest brush of his lips over Damon's. Once, then twice, and then he held a little longer the third time.

"Was that your first kiss with a man?" Xander asked, a shy grin on his mouth. Damon couldn't wait to kiss it again. He hadn't realized how much he'd missed just kissing, and he had a lot of lost time to make up for.

"Yes. And I'm glad it was with you."

"I have to say," Xander said, "I keep expecting you to freak out but you seem fairly calm about all this."

"Freak out because I'm interested in a guy? I've known I was bisexual since I was in junior high. I just met my ex-wife young and never really had a chance to experiment. Even if experimenting was my type of thing."

"It's not?" The question was coy and a little flirtatious. Damon knew this was an important conversation—but he also wanted to know why they were still talking when they could be kissing.

"You. You're my type of thing. I don't need to sleep with a bunch of people to know what I like."

Xander seemed really pleased at this answer. "So I don't need to ask if you're sure?"

"Have I seemed not sure during any of this?" Damon asked archly.

He pondered this for a moment and then answered. "No. Actually no. You're good."

Damon grinned. "Let me prove to you just how good I am."

It turned out that it was both very much the same and also very different kissing Xander than it had been kissing Rachel. Then Xander shifted his mouth to a different angle, slanting it much more purposefully against Damon's, and his mind dissolved into perfectly white static. His hands gripped Xander's shoulders, sliding down his sides to grasp his hips and pull him closer.

Kissing was good. Kissing was great. Making out was fantastic. Xander tasted like spun sugar, and his tongue was clever, twisting Damon into knots of pleasure, his cock hard against the zipper of his jeans. He didn't even know he wanted to be touched until Xander did, sliding a palm against it and laughing into Damon's mouth as it twitched in surprise and in an overload of feeling.

Damon broke the kiss, panting embarrassingly, wanting to devour Xander all over again when he saw how red and wet his mouth looked in the remnants of the fire.

It felt like there were two roads. One led to easy, uncomplicated pleasure, and maybe a more complicated journey to figuring out what they wanted from each other. It would be so easy to take that road now, to take Xander's hand and lead him back to the house. To even lead him to the barrel house, which was so much closer, and to let them both take the quick, easy pleasure that they both clearly wanted.

Or they could wait. They could take the road slower. Make it deeper. Make it feel more meaningful when Xander finally came to his bed.

Damon already knew he was going to be happier and also way more disappointed by the choice he was going to suggest. And also that that particular path was probably going to lead to blue balls tonight and more nights in the future.

"Can we take this slow?" he asked, and hearing it out loud, he remembered all too well the awkward teenager he'd been and laughed.

But Xander didn't look embarrassed or disappointed. He looked like he was happy to do whatever made Damon happy. "Sure, of course. I'm happy to go at your pace. This is all new to you."

Damon tugged him close again, making sure he could feel how much he wanted him—though Xander had to know, it was important that he didn't think this had anything to do with him.

"I'm going to enjoy having you show me everything. Every single thing you want," Damon whispered in his ear, pressing a single kiss against his neck. He tasted like smoky sugar, and Damon was never going to eat a marshmallow again without getting hard.

And if he kept Xander around, and Xander kept making him marshmallows, then that might work out well for both of them.

Chapter Eight

It was an unexpectedly hot day for fall in Northern California, and the Barrel House didn't have air-conditioning yet. Xander wiped off his forehead as surreptitiously as he could, hoping that Damon hadn't seen him sweat.

It was silly and childish, but he knew he was walking on eggshells around him. A few kisses, a few promises, and he was a lovesick teenager, terrified of saying or doing the wrong thing.

He knew he was supposed to trust Damon more, but deliberately opening himself up to anybody was new for him. It had been hard enough to make the initial decision to do so, and then he'd realized it was a continuing choice every day.

Each day when he woke up, he chose Damon and all the risk he came with instead of protecting his soft, vulnerable heart. Right now the decision was hard, but ultimately lopsided. Damon won out every single time, no doubt about it. Xander wasn't naïve enough to believe that would always be the case.

"Are you okay?" Damon asked. Xander jerked in surprise. He'd been so sure that Damon was absorbed in listening to the contractor talk about the plans for the restaurant remodel, which were currently spread over the temporary job site office—a pair of sawhorses and an old door Damon had taken off the hinges.

"Fine, I'm fine," Xander said.

Damon smiled. "Sorry, it's boring."

"Just a whole different language," Xander said apologetically. "If we're talking menus, I'm here with bells on."

When Damon had mentioned he was meeting the contractor today, and had offered for Xander to join them, he'd thought it was a good idea.

Okay, he'd actually thought it was a chance to see Damon again after they'd both been busy over the last few days. What he'd been hoping for was more making out and less mind-numbing, nitty-gritty construction details.

David, the contractor, grinned. "I'd be happy to come back to discuss menus. I really admire the work you did at Terroir."

David was shorter than Damon, and all compact muscle, but they were in almost a similar uniform of jeans, work boots, and a plaid shirt. Damon's was autumnal orange tones and David's was red and blue. Still, he had a nice smile, and seemed to know what he was doing. Plus, Damon had known him for a long time, and Xander trusted Damon's judgement on this sort of thing.

Now, menus? That was a whole different ballgame.

"Maybe you'd just like to come back for the tasting sessions," Xander offered. "Once the kitchen is in."

"Yeah, the kitchen," David said, like Xander's words had reminded him of something else to discuss. "Do you have a list of kitchen equipment that you need?"

There was not going to be a large amount of space in the Barrel House kitchen. Not like the gigantic Terroir kitchens that housed every wet dream professional kitchen appliance Bastian Aquino could get his hands on, times two.

Xander was going to need to be careful and conservative, and only put in exactly what he needed.

He'd been working with his hand-drawn kitchen diagrams and appliance dimensions for a few days now, in anticipation of this request, and he still hadn't finalized everything.

"I'm still working on it," he admitted. "The space is tricky."

"I told you that you could have more space, if you needed it," Damon inserted, looking worried.

Xander might have a crush but he was still determined to make this restaurant a success. "And take away from table space? No way. I can manage."

"We might be able to build a small addition in the back for the refrigerated units," David said, pulling out a pencil from a pocket and beginning to sketch directly on the plans. "That would give you a little more work room in the kitchen itself."

Xander leaned over the table, looking at David's scribbles, and tried not to jump out of his skin when Damon placed a steadying hand on his back as he leaned in too.

Tried not to internally freak out when Damon kept his hand there after they were upright again. That was definitely something not "just partners" would do, and if David didn't know they were involved—or getting involved—before, he probably knew now. But he didn't even act like he'd noticed.

"It might add a little more to the budget," David said. "And we'll have to alter the permits, but I think I can charm their way through. They're not much different than the originals."

Damon waved a hand, completely dismissing the extra expense as they walked outside—like somehow he'd known Xander was hot and a little miserable. "I don't want Xander in a cramped kitchen. He's an artist. He needs space to work his magic."

Xander was in the middle of basking in this sweet compliment when he noticed Damon's face change abruptly. His mouth compressed into a grim line, and his eyes hardened unmistakably.

He looked up and followed Damon's sightline to an older man getting out of a silver Mercedes sedan. He had dark hair, touched with a little silver at the temples, and could be Damon's twin, if not for the additional lines around his eyes and mouth.

This must be Damon's father. The famous patriarch of the Hess family.

Damon, who'd had zero issue putting his hands on Xander in front of their contractor, dropped his hand from Xander's back like it had suddenly caught fire.

He didn't want to listen, but as the older man strode toward them, it was impossible not to hear the tiny, niggling voice that the last few days had just begun to silence.

This is just a phase. Damon doesn't really want you. It's just convenient. This isn't for real.

Xander tried silencing the annoying voice by reminding himself that while Damon might be comfortable with bisexuality, that didn't mean he was out to his father.

"David," Damon said, reaching out to shake the contractor's hand, "thanks for meeting with us today. Will you get me a new quote with the changes? Go ahead and start the revised permitting process though. I know it takes a long time to push through and we're in a rush."

Xander hadn't really thought about whether they were in a hurry or not—though he understood that a business' purpose was to make money and all they were doing now was spending it. They couldn't begin to recoup that loss until the restaurant opened.

Still, it was strange that Damon hadn't said anything to him about opening quickly. Or about his dad not knowing about his bisexuality.

"I'll send it over tomorrow," David said, shaking Damon's hand briskly and then moving onto Xander's.

When David started to walk toward the driveway, Damon's father had just reached them.

"Xander," Damon said, his voice mechanical and nearly un-recognizable. "I'll talk to you later."

Xander wasn't stupid. He knew he was being dismissed. It was inevitable that despite understanding the generic reason why, it would still sting. What really bothered him was that he didn't *really* know why. Couldn't he stand here and be a business partner? Wasn't that still his most important function in Damon's life? Why couldn't he meet Damon's father under that circumstance? Damon's sexuality didn't even need to come into the picture.

He'd grown up a lot since high school, since that terrible, awful crush that had decimated his heart when he'd finally realized that he was always going to be Dustin's ugly secret. He'd had years to separate himself from that pain, years to build a wall to prevent him from ever feeling that pain again. And now, today, Xander realized as he turned and walked away that he hadn't just let Damon wiggle under the fence. He'd torn down a part and practically invited him to waltz inside.

Even as he came up with a half dozen very practical, very logical reasons why Damon might not want to introduce him to his father, Xander couldn't help but think this was why he'd stopped letting people in.

Because they inevitably disappointed you, and worse.

❧ ❧

Damon watched as Xander walked away. He knew he wasn't happy with Damon's decision to summarily dismiss him, and he couldn't blame him. But he couldn't let his father dig his poisonous claws into Xander. He'd never done anything to deserve that sort of pain. Damon was used to it; he'd been dealing with its side effects his entire damn life.

"Not going to say hello to your father?" Nathan asked. Passive-aggressive had always been his favorite language, and clearly nothing had changed, despite Damon avoiding him as best he could the last year and a half since he'd moved back to Napa.

"I have nothing to say to you," Damon said shortly.

"But you so politely dismissed your friends so we could talk," Nathan pointed out. "It would be a shame not to take advantage."

"Lots of people think you're important and that your opinion matters. Go talk to them."

"Maybe," Nathan threw out, "I want to see the wreck of our family's oldest vineyard. Are there even any grapes left, Damon, or did you destroy them all?"

This old argument again. Nathan had, of course, come to see him after that night a year ago, livid that he would dare to destroy something so precious. Damon could only retort that maybe his father should care that the vines had been destroying *him*.

Nathan had just shaken his head, disappointed and hurt, which was so much worse than his cutting anger, because it came with a healthy dose of guilt and that had always been tougher for Damon to shake. "Always such a drama queen," he'd said.

Yes, Damon was definitely being overdramatic with his alcoholism. According to his father, alcohol was the golden calf that had always been so good to their family, and anyone who rejected it was rejecting the Hess name.

The day Damon went to rehab, his father had texted him to remind him that alcohol was "always a choice." Like he'd ever had a choice in being an alcoholic.

"There's still some left," Damon said. "Though they won't be around for much longer. Should go check them out before I burn those too. Gonna plant a really nice orchard. Apples, I think."

Nathan's lip curled into a disgusted sneer. He still managed to look handsome, because that was another of the Hess family gifts—or curses. All depending on your angle.

"What are you even doing here?" Damon demanded. "You're not here to see my garden or my land. If you're just here to remind me what a terrible Hess I am, you've succeeded. Now, leave."

Crossing his arms across his chest, Nathan actually had the nerve to look concerned. "I played a round of golf with Walter last week. He mentioned to me how happy he was that you were investing your trust in the family business."

"It's my trust," Damon argued. "I can do whatever the hell I want to with it."

"Including throwing it away on a pipe dream? Starting a restaurant? In that old shack?"

"Why does it matter to you?" Damon was struggling. It wasn't like his horrible, overachieving, critical father was the only reason why he'd become an alcoholic—but he sure hadn't helped.

"It matters," Nathan enunciated each word carefully and slowly, like Damon was an idiot who needed help understanding, "because when you burn through your trust starting a business in a field you have no experience in, in a highly competitive market like Napa, with one of Aquino's rejects, you'll be back on my doorstep, begging to join us again."

"I wouldn't beg, and I certainly wouldn't beg you," Damon said. "I'm capable of working. I've done it before. I can do it again. I know manual labor isn't something your highly privileged brain comprehends, but I'm good at it."

That was the whole root of this disconnect with his father. He didn't *get* Damon, and had long since given up trying.

"You're a Hess," Nathan said. "You're not meant to be working the fields. You're meant to own them."

Damon wanted to tell his father that he could do both, that he was enjoying doing both now. But it had always been useless to argue with Nathan Hess, and nothing had changed in years.

"Thank you for the unsolicited advice." Damon paused. "Now since you're so eager for me to exercise my rights as a land *owner*, get the fuck off my land."

Nathan threw his hands up, his expression making it perfectly clear that he hadn't wanted to come here and argue, but that he'd done it because he'd felt obligated. Not out of fatherly love or familial concern, but fear of financial waste.

Damon watched him walk away and told himself that he'd reconciled himself to a shitty father years ago. But if that was true, why did every encounter feel like razor blades slashing at his composure, at his sense of self? When would he *finally* feel like he wasn't obligated to fulfill the duties of being a Hess? He'd left the family. He'd left the business. He kept to himself, and did his own thing.

The money and the land still tied him to them though, and if it had been any other land, and money from anyone else but his grandfather, he might have rejected both. But his grandfather had *cared* about this land, about what it had meant. Had felt an obligation and a responsibility that far eclipsed his father's *noblesse oblige* bullshit. And when Damon walked it, early in the morning, the sun creeping over the hills, he remembered the only person in his family who hadn't been a total waste of his time.

He'd come here and taken back his land first for his grandfather, and then he'd discovered, especially after that horrible night, a purpose of his own.

John Hess would have been proud of him—no matter what he'd done to the vines. If Damon closed his eyes, he could almost hear his deep, gritty voice. *It's your land*, he'd have said, *you can do whatever the hell you want with it. They're just vines.*

Damon shoved his hands in his pockets, because the urge was strong to call Xander, because he couldn't have a conversation with a ghost. Xander might be one of the few who'd understand besides his grandfather. But their relationship was so new, so fresh, so tentative, and he didn't want to crush it with all his personal baggage. Xander didn't need to hear all of that, definitely not yet, no matter how much Damon wanted to tell him.

He knew some of what Damon struggled with, but he definitely didn't need to know the whole of it. Rachel, who'd practically known him his whole life, had gotten sick of it and left. That had hurt badly, but he'd persevered, and he'd even felt cautiously optimistic about his chances with Xander.

His father showing up had re-opened old wounds, reminding Damon of their existence when he'd been trying so hard to pretend he wasn't fucked up.

That being a Hess carried with it a whole load of ridiculous expectations and that it was bad enough being born into it. Anyone sane didn't *choose* it.

After being dismissed by Damon, Xander went to the grocery store, randomly wandering the aisles, picking up vegetables, and then putting them down again. He finally managed to fill half a cart with ingredients he thought he could use to work on recipes for the restaurant. He went back home, put the food away, and went on a grueling, punishing run.

The truth was Xander really wanted to be pissed, but after exhausting himself, all he felt was empty and directionless. Instead of cooking anything, he grabbed carrots and a tub of hummus and plopped down on the couch.

It was easy enough to feel certain of Damon and Damon's feelings when they were together, but it turned out it was also easy enough for doubt to creep in. No matter how much Xander wanted to trust him completely, he didn't know him completely. *Couldn't* know him completely, not yet anyway.

He stewed all night as he sat on the couch, laptop in hand, as he researched some recipes he wanted to try for the restaurant. He was sure he'd enjoy the quiet, but it turned out the quiet was actually way too quiet—especially when he was upset and wanted someone to vent to. He never thought he'd miss the ambient noise of Nate and Kian being in the house, but it turned out he did.

He almost texted his friend Wyatt, but remembered that this was one of the nights he and his brother ran their food truck near Venice Beach, so he'd be way too busy to listen to or comment on Xander's bad mood.

Calling Miles again was out of the question, as was calling Kian.

Xander impatiently tapped his fingers on the laptop keyboard. Everything he was thinking now was total crap, and he hated how much sense that made. For him, food came from a place of care and love. He cooked because he wanted to share with someone. And right now, what he wanted was to share with Damon.

He glanced at his phone, sitting so innocently on the coffee table. Wouldn't it be better if he found out now that this was normal behavior for Damon? Wouldn't it be better to know now if Damon wasn't worth the trust he wanted so badly to place in him?

The truth, no matter how painful, was always better than a lie. And if Xander was lying to himself, then he needed to know.

He could've just texted—Damon had always answered texts quickly, even quickly enough for Xander's natural impatience—but he dialed his number instead.

Xander's heart thumped in his chest, loud enough that he could hear it even over Alton Brown's muted voice on the TV. He didn't have to wait in suspense very long; Damon picked up on the second ring.

Like he'd been waiting too, trying to decide whether he should call Xander.

Xander pushed that thought aside. He was doing it again: his hopeful heart making up the best possible scenario for him to believe, instead of the truth.

He needed the truth.

"Xander," Damon said breathlessly. Exactly as breathless as Xander felt.

He'd considered playing all his cards close to his chest, acting like everything was okay, and waiting for Damon to say something about earlier this afternoon. But when faced with Damon's voice, Xander discovered that was total bullshit.

He wasn't the kind of guy who prevaricated. He wasn't the person who let shit go for a half-hearted explanation. He'd done it when he was much younger, and after that flaming disaster of a relationship, he'd sworn to himself that he wouldn't let himself be manipulated again. After that, he'd always been straight, to the point of making guys uncomfortable. It was why he'd stopped seeking relationships. He wanted a level of honesty that nobody was quite prepared to give. The initial shock of his attraction to Damon and discovering that it was mutual had thrown him off-balance enough that he'd forgotten who he was. Who he'd become, out of necessity.

"What the hell was with that today?" Xander demanded.

Silence.

Damon didn't know the truth-seeking missile that had been Xander. He'd met him briefly that one night, a year ago, but even then the shock of attraction had melted his rough edges away almost immediately.

Damon didn't know the guy that Miles and Wyatt and Kian did. And it was time he did.

"That was my father," Damon said. "You didn't want to meet him."

"You're right," Xander admitted, and he didn't want to be an asshole, though he knew he got mistaken for one sometimes, "I didn't want to meet him. But I also didn't want to be shoved aside like some sort of toy you're ashamed of."

More silence.

This might be the end of their relationship, personal *and* professional, if Damon didn't understand what Xander was trying to say. He tried again, a little less abrasive this time. Miles had told him for years that wanting honesty didn't necessarily mean being a dick, and Xander had never felt that particular piece of advice had much merit. But he did now.

"You could have explained that to me," Xander added. "Instead of just telling me to leave, like David. You hired him."

"I hired you," Damon said, sounding perplexed, and it was only the confusion in his voice that prevented Xander from exploding into a rage of flames.

Yes, he had technically hired Xander. *Yes,* he was paying him a salary. But they were partners, Damon had made that clear, and they were trying to be even more.

Reducing him to a mere underling hired to be at his convenience smacked of everything that Xander had joyfully left behind at Terroir. He'd done that because he'd believed that Damon would be a far better boss than Bastian Aquino had ever been.

"Can you just . . . let me in?" Damon asked.

Xander nearly dropped the phone. "You're here?" He ran a hand through his hair, messy after a quick shower, and left to dry however it wanted. He glanced down at his old pair of jogging shorts he'd shrugged on. He looked like hell, but maybe that was okay.

Honesty, right? In all things. Including his appearance.

"I wanted to say I was sorry," Damon said, and he did genuinely sound apologetic. "I wasn't expecting . . ."

It was clear what Damon hadn't been expecting. He hadn't been expecting Xander to come at him like a runaway freight train on fire with rage—justified or not.

Xander set his laptop aside, and went to the front door, opening it. Damon stood on the front porch, phone to his ear and a pizza box in his hands. His mouth twisted in a wry, apologetic smile. "You are here."

"I said I was," Damon said. "I'm not going to lie to you."

Damon couldn't possibly know about the fears lurking in the back of Xander's brain, and buried deep, like unexploded mines, in his heart. He still set them to rest. He extended the pizza box. "I thought you might be hungry, and my mother said never to go to someone's house empty-handed."

Popping open the box, Xander took in the scent of fresh dough, tomatoes and grease. "Pepperoni and mushroom?"

Damon shrugged, and looked embarrassed. "Is it terribly self-serving of me to admit that it's *my* favorite?"

Xander just stared at him.

"I thought if you didn't want it, I might as well get something I would eat," Damon said. He stopped, glancing around. "Are you just going to leave me on the porch, rambling about pizza?"

Xander had considered it. It might be an excessive punishment for Damon's crime but he was still mad—or afraid, he'd lost track of what each felt like. "I don't know," he said slowly.

"You don't know." Damon looked like he wanted to grab the pizza back and go back to his car and stress eat the whole thing. Xander understood the impulse all too well.

"I need to tell you something about me first," Xander said, shifting his feet. It was one thing to preach honesty, and to demand it at every turn, but it turned out it was totally different to demand your own honesty when it came to someone you cared about.

"I don't date because I'm not good at it. I need . . . a measure of transparency that most people aren't willing to give," Xander admitted. "I can be a real asshole about it."

"And you don't think I can give it?" Damon asked. Calculatingly, a bit harder than Xander expected.

"I don't know . . . I thought you could. I wanted you to be able to. I wouldn't have started this otherwise. But this afternoon . . ."

"Made you doubt," Damon finished for him. Which was good because Xander hadn't been exactly sure what this afternoon had made him feel.

But he knew the truth, and he wondered if he would ever have the courage to say it out loud. Or if Damon would just say it for him.

This afternoon had made him feel vulnerable again, and he'd sworn that he'd never feel that again. Taking down that wall that separated him from the rest of the world had initially felt good and right, especially when it was Damon he was letting in. But he'd been caught up in the rightness of it, the first initial swoon of realizing that his crush was mutual.

Damon was going to screw things up, he'd admitted that much to Xander before they'd even kissed. And *anyone* would and could. Nobody was perfect.

Xander pushed down the natural fear that bubbled up inside him. "A little, yeah."

"I'm sorry," Damon said, sounding genuinely contrite. "I'm sorry I made you doubt. My dad . . . he fucks me up bad. I can't say he's the reason I'm an alcoholic, but if one person was actually at fault, he would be. I didn't want you to be poisoned by his shit, or watch me as I tried to avoid it."

And looking back, Xander could see that. He'd seen the fear in Damon's eyes, the reluctance as his father had walked toward them.

He understood trying to protect people you cared about from terrible things. He'd been trying to protect Kian for what felt like forever.

This wasn't all that different.

Xander turned and walked into the house, gesturing for Damon to follow him.

He settled back down on the couch, and Damon wavered, unsure, in the doorway to the living room. "Come sit," Xander said, patting the spot next to him, "let's eat our feelings."

Damon walked over, a grateful look in his eyes as he sat down.

They'd each unapologetically devoured two pieces when Xander spoke. "Was it bad today?"

Sighing, Damon leaned back on the couch, crossing his hands across his stomach. He looked younger and more vulnerable than Xander had ever seen him. "Yes."

"Why did you come back to Napa, if he was so awful?" Xander couldn't help but ask. "You could've stayed away? Don't get me wrong, I'm selfishly happy you're here, but wouldn't you have been better off someplace else?"

"My grandfather left me that land when he died about a year and a half ago," Damon said softly. "And I loved him. I wanted to make him proud. I wanted to prove to him that I could be more than just a guy who loved booze."

"You can, you *are*," Xander argued, suddenly feeling irrationally and fiercely angry that anybody could shit on their own family like this—especially for a disease that nobody could prevent. "You're doing an incredible thing. Brave and important."

Damon shot Xander a lazy, soft glance. "I know. Doesn't make it very easy."

"Easy things aren't worth doing," Xander scoffed, and then grinned. "Besides, I'm here, I can help."

His glance slid away, and Xander felt the pizza, greasy and heavy, settling nauseously in his stomach. "You can, you have. But I take more than I give. Today was a good example of that."

"We both have . . . baggage," Xander pointed out. "But I know we can work through this. I want to work through this. I called you even though I was angry with you. But I still called. And you weren't sure if I'd open the door, but you came here anyway."

Damon reached up and cradled the side of Xander's face with his palm. "I want better for you than to have to deal with my baggage."

Xander had had a feeling this was where this conversation was going, and there was no way he was going to let Damon push him away selflessly when he'd already faced his own demons and told them off. "No way. You don't get to make that choice."

"You sure about that?"

"You try to take my personal autonomy away, I'll kick your ass," Xander said.

Damon burst out laughing, and Xander patted himself on the back for lightening his mood. "I'd like to see you try."

"Admittedly, it would probably end up being a lot more homoerotic, and would almost definitely devolve into sex, but the point remains. This is my decision, and I'm not going any-where."

Damon raised an eyebrow. "Homoerotic? Think I can get a demonstration?"

Leaning closer, Xander kissed him firmly on the mouth. He tasted like spicy tomatoes and the earthy musk of mushrooms. Normally he might not like it, but he loved it now. He deepened the kiss a little, Damon's other hand reaching up to pull him closer. It was good, soft but hot, a reaffirmation of everything they'd both admitted they felt. But before it could get too hot, Xander pulled back.

Damon's bottom lip jutted out, and he pouted. "We're still taking things slowly?"

Xander had to nod. He was Damon's first time with a guy. He didn't want to rush him, no matter if he wanted to rush himself.

There was too much at stake here—Xander's heart for one, the restaurant for another.

"Fine," Damon grumbled. "It's probably the right call, but for the record, it sucks."

Xander plopped back against the couch. "Yes, it does. And not even in the good way."

CHAPTER NINE

XANDER WAS FUSSING WITH a ravioli filling—simple but essential that it be absolutely perfect—when his phone rang.

He picked it up gingerly with flour-dusted fingertips and set it between his shoulder and ear as he continued to stir some caramelized onions on the stove.

"What's up?" he asked Damon.

His heart still accelerated a little whenever Damon called him or texted him or otherwise acknowledged his existence. At first Xander had been embarrassed by it, but then he'd caught Damon's fingers trembling the other night as they'd sat on the couch, watching a movie. Damon's cheeks had flushed bright red, and all Xander could do was confess his own crush symptoms.

They were still taking it slow, because Xander was still irrationally worried that Damon might change his mind, and also because neither of them really knew how to just *date* someone. Damon had been married forever, and other than few meaningless hookups, Xander had been celibate and alone. They were still figuring it all out, and they had a mostly unspoken agreement that sex complicated a brand-new relationship that was already complicated enough.

"Good news," Damon said. There was the sound of wind on his side of the line, like he was driving with the window open. Which made sense, because they were having a surprisingly hot spell. Xander was personally sweating his ass off in his un-air-conditioned kitchen.

"Did the permits come through?" Xander asked, continuing to stir his onions. He was looking for a jam-like texture, after the onions had started to really break down and grow caramel in color. The result was not quite there, but he was regretting deciding that today was the day he was going to perfect his ravioli recipe.

"Yeah, they're in. David's starting construction tomorrow. And good news, the HVAC people are going to be in pretty soon, installing the new air-conditioning."

"If the building wasn't going to be a mess of dust and dirt, I would seriously consider packing up and moving recipe testing there," Xander complained. "It's hot as hell in here, and for some reason I thought it'd be a great idea to hunch over a stove all day."

"The ravioli recipe?" Damon sounded sympathetic.

Xander hummed in agreement, reaching down to grab a taste with a fingertip. Close, but not quite. He plucked his bottle of balsamic vinegar from the counter and added a splash, tasted again, and then splashed in some more.

"It needs pepper," Damon said, his teasing tone light and happy. So far from the wounded despondency of a few days ago when his father had visited him. Xander wanted to believe he had something to do with Damon's attitude bouncing back, but it was easy to doubt himself. Too easy.

"You think everything needs pepper," Xander scoffed. "If you tell me this dish needs pepper, I'm going to throttle you."

"Okay, no pepper. Does that mean we aren't having the waiters come to your table with a pepper grinder for your salad?"

Xander made a wounded noise over the phone. "You're physically hurting me. Of course not. Like I would ever make a dish that needs to be liberally coated with fresh ground pepper! That's only for food that has no flavor and they're trying to hide it by ruining your taste buds up front."

"Huh." Damon sounded thoughtful. "I never thought of it that way before."

"That's why you hired me," Xander said, and this time he could say it without even a hiccup, had been practicing saying it and acknowledging it for the last few days. Damon *had* hired him. He was technically Damon's employee. Yes, he was also more—they both believed that—but he couldn't let himself forget that one fundamental fact. He'd started this by pretending facts weren't facts, and that wasn't going to get either of them anywhere. If he was going to commit to this relationship, he wasn't going to let himself forget who he was, or where he'd been. Honesty—and *self-honesty*—was vital.

"It's true," Damon said casually.

"What else are you doing today?" Xander asked, finally pulling the onions off the heat. They looked perfect, and after taking another taste, also had perfect flavor.

"Weeding. Watering, at least after the sun goes down." He sounded as eager for it as Xander felt.

Just as Xander was thinking of how much he'd pay for a dunking that wasn't just a cold shower, Damon suggested, "You could come over, if you wanted. I'll have the sprinklers out. We could run through them like kids. It's not much but it's something."

Xander wiped the sweat from his forehead. Imagined Damon in a white tank, soaked through, outlining every one of his incredible muscles. It was not a tough decision to make.

"Count me in."

"Dusk is about nine," Damon said. "I can't water until then."

"I'll be over then." Xander paused. "I can bring over some of these ravioli. You can try them, but there's one important condition."

"I can't say it needs pepper?"

Xander laughed. "That *and* you don't complain that they're hot. Or warm. Unfortunately they're not meant to be eaten cold."

"You could make a cold ravioli salad," Damon suggested.

Xander couldn't help it—he laughed again. "Pasta salad? With ravioli?"

"That's weird, isn't it?"

"It's . . . different. But different could be good." Xander had an idea, and then three more, just in the quick pause before Damon answered. They weren't really high-end ideas, but every time he had that thought, Xander shoved the snooty voice of Bastian Aquino right out of his head, and did whatever the fuck he wanted.

So far that had seemed to work well for him. Whether that would work once the Barrel House opened and critics showed up, that remained to be seen. But nothing was more freeing than forcing himself not to care what other people thought.

"I like different," Damon said loyally. "Especially your different."

It was taking time, but Xander was finally beginning to believe he deserved that hushed, reverent note in Damon's voice.

"Yours is pretty great too," Xander admitted.

Silence stretched between them, full of things that Xander knew neither of them had the nerve to say just yet. *I miss you. I'm craving you. I want you so badly it hurts.*

Xander was left wondering how long this self-enforced celibacy could continue lasting. Probably not much further, if he was being honest with himself.

"I'll see you tonight?" Damon finally said.

"Yeah, of course. About nine," Xander said, repeating himself because he wanted to linger on the phone, just to hear Damon's voice, even though what he really needed was to finish up the ravioli, get out of this boiling hot kitchen, and take a very cold shower—and not just because it was a hundred degrees outside.

"See you then," Damon said, and finally clicked off.

Xander sighed as he set the phone back on the counter. It was now liberally smeared with flour, like just about every other surface in the kitchen, including his arms and probably his face.

Turning his attention back to the caramelized onions, he tested them with his fingertips, making sure they'd cooled down enough to incorporate them into the rest of his mixture, but they weren't nearly ready yet.

He picked up the pan and hauled it over to the fridge, stuck it on a shelf and stood there for a good minute just letting the cool air billow over him.

"You'd better be paying a higher fraction of the electric bill this month," Nate said from behind him.

Xander didn't budge or even turn around. He still felt a shaft of embarrassment deep inside at how he'd treated his friend. Using him while he'd only ever wanted to kiss Damon. "It's hot as balls."

"And somehow you're still in this kitchen, sweating them off." Nate sounded amused, and it helped break the ice between them. Xander relaxed a fraction, and once he did, found it was easier to let the embarrassment go.

"I have work to do," Xander retorted.

"What, working in the kitchen is work? I thought your new career was all about working Damon Hess?"

"That would be nice, but it's not in the job description," Xander said. He'd do it. He *wanted* to do it. Was slowly dying that he hadn't yet. He was no stranger to celibacy but waiting for Damon to be ready to take things up a notch was giving him an epic case of blue balls.

"Yet."

Xander turned around, bringing out his pan of onions, and this time when he touched them with a finger, they were cool enough. He shut the fridge and walked back over to the prep counter.

"What is that supposed to mean?" he asked.

"That means that Nathan Hess is talking. About you and his son."

"Fuck," Xander swore. "I don't like that guy. I wish he'd leave Damon alone." *And me*, Xander thought.

Nate raised an eyebrow. "It doesn't sound like nothing's going on," he pointed out.

"We're taking things slow," Xander said, hoping that he wouldn't regret confiding in Nate. He had a real ear for good gossip, and this was sweet stuff. Nathan Hess' son hooking up with his new employee and an ex-Terroir chef? It had all the trademarks of a real juicy rumor.

"I can't believe you're not climbing that like a tree," Nate offered.

"Me either," Xander muttered. "Wait, how do you even know it's Damon Hess? And what he looks like?"

"Kian told me. And after your aborted little experiment, I looked him up," Nate pointed out, reaching in the bowl of filling and pulling out a bite before Xander could smack his hand. "But you don't need me to tell you he's hot."

Xander definitely did not.

"He's also technically your boss," Nate continued. Xander was beginning to remember why they hadn't ever really been friends. Why he had disliked Nate the moment Wyatt had brought him home the first time. "I bet you don't feel hypocritical at all, especially after the way you've been trying to get Kian to stop panting over Aquino."

Xander gritted his teeth. "I don't feel that way, no. Bastian Aquino is an asshole who emotionally manipulates people. Especially his employees. Damon couldn't do that even if he wanted to. He doesn't have it in him."

"His father is Nathan Hess." Nate's expression was incredulous. "You clearly know a little of what he's like. I know Damon doesn't like him much, but I'd worry, if I were you."

"Well, it's a good thing you aren't," Xander said. "If I save you some leftovers will you leave me alone to finish this in peace?"

"The truth hurts, sometimes, doesn't it?"

"You sound like a smarmy Bond villain," Xander pointed out. "If I give you some ravioli, will that serve as an apology for how I used you terribly?"

Nate chuckled. "It might, if it was a real apology?"

"Just so we're clear, I'm not apologizing for the kiss. I'm apologizing for . . ." Xander tried to find a reason that made sense that *wasn't* about the kiss, and his sluggish brain wouldn't respond.

"The kiss." Nate rolled his eyes. "Yeah, I get it. Apology accepted."

The first thing Damon smelled when he stepped outside was the rich scent of the earth after baking all afternoon in the hot sun.

It was one of his favorite scents, especially when the land he was smelling was his own.

His father might show up and issue threats, but this land was still Damon's, and as far as he was concerned, it was going to stay his as long as he was in one piece.

He dragged the hose and sprinklers over to the first set of plants. A more professional garden might have in-bed sprinklers, and there were some nights when Damon wished he had them, but he'd also discovered there was a soothing peace to each night's work, tending his garden in the dusk.

If the restaurant failed, yes, he might have to work another job to pay the property taxes on it—the property taxes Damon's grandfather had ensured would always be paid by gifting him a trust upon his death. Grandpa might not be very happy that Damon was spending all that nice, safe property tax money on a restaurant, but he'd also always wanted Damon to fulfill his dreams.

He might be back to construction again, but Damon had made his peace with that possibility. If the worst came to pass, and the Barrel House wasn't a success, the only thing that worried him was Xander.

Xander was depending on him—and on himself—to carve out a niche for now and for a long time to come. Damon was going to do everything he could to make that dream a reality.

"You haven't started yet."

Damon glanced up and Xander was standing there, fists on his hips, dressed in a white tank top and a pair of running shorts. There was a lot of firm, tanned, muscled skin on display, and Damon swallowed hard. He knew what he wanted; he just wanted Xander to trust that he wanted it. To stop questioning whether he'd change his mind.

He wasn't going to. He'd known embarrassingly early in their high school courtship that he was going to marry Rachel. And he'd known from the first moment they'd met that Xander was going to be important to him.

Damon definitely wasn't ready for Xander to know just how important yet. Here Xander was, terrified that Damon was going to get cold feet about having a guy for a partner, when in reality, Damon was afraid he was going to move too fast or demonstrate too much commitment.

It was an ironic situation that might have been funnier if it was a little cooler outside and he didn't want Xander quite so much.

Stop thinking so much, he told himself, and before he could question his own decision, stripped off his worn t-shirt, and couldn't help but watch as Xander's eyes grew big. Damon knew he looked good; he'd started working out in earnest after rehab because he'd always liked to drink in the evenings and if his arms were too tired to even pick up a bottle, then there was a little less temptation.

"Are you okay?" Xander asked carefully.

Instead of answering, Damon turned the hose on him instead of on his carrots.

As the cold water hit him, Xander yelped, throwing his hands up. "I take it back, I take it back," Xander said, moving out of the way to try to dodge the spray after that first, frozen moment. Damon might have been worried, but he was laughing so hard it was hard for him to avoid the stream of water from the hose.

"I thought you were hot," Damon teased.

Xander slipped on a patch of muddy ground, and nearly lost his balance, but his recovery was excellent. He moved with the grace of an athlete—or a dancer—and Damon never wanted to stop watching.

He only realized too late that Xander wasn't just trying to move out of the way of the water. He was actively moving toward where Damon had plugged in one of his sprinklers. He leaned down for a second, his wet running shorts plastered to his ass like a second skin, and Damon lost track of what it was he was supposed to be avoiding. That incredible butt, toned and shapely and essentially begging for Damon to do terrible, wonderful things to it?

A cold spray of water to the face from the hose Xander had unhooked from the sprinkler had him gasping, but his thoughts hadn't gotten any cleaner.

"You're playing dirty," Damon gasped through another burst of water to the face. He wasn't going to tell Xander this, but it felt damn good after sweating all day.

Xander's eyes narrowed, a bright smile blooming across his handsome face. "You love it," he shot back.

He really did, and he never wanted Xander to stop. He loved every sneaky part of him, every achingly blunt part of his personality. Damon wanted it all, if only Xander would let him.

Damon turned the hose on himself, water cascading over his head. "I love *this*," he teased. "But you could lean over again. Could use another firsthand bit of evidence to prove how much I love it."

Following suit with his own, Xander turned his hose on himself, drenching every inch in water. His tank clung to every lean, muscular curve of his body, and Damon wanted to drop to his knees in the mud and *beg*.

I want to prove myself but I want to prove it to you first. Please let me touch you.

"Yeah," Damon ground out, voice gruff and low, his erection growing despite the cold water he was pouring over himself, "yeah, I love that."

Xander's eyes sparkled with impudence as he sidled closer, letting Damon get a good look. He placed a cool palm on Damon's bare chest, right where his heart beat hard and fast. "I love it too," he said.

The hose dropped to the ground as Damon reached out and gripped Xander by his hips, dragging him those last few inches until they were plastered together.

"Is this what you want?" Damon demanded. "Tell me if it's not because I can't . . . I can't. I'm not going to change my mind. I promise."

Xander stared at him, mouth open, for a long moment. He must have felt Damon's hard-on through his paper-thin shorts and Damon's jeans—completely soaked and plastered to his thighs.

"You promise," Xander stuttered back.

"I promise I'm not going to change my mind," Damon vowed. "Because I don't know about you, but I'm feeling pretty damn gay right now."

Laughing, Xander ran his hands down Damon's chest, tracing the trail of dark hair that led to his fly. "You know what? Me too."

Damon decided that was all the agreement he needed, and bent his head down, kissing Xander fiercely. Refusing to hold back anymore, he kissed him with all the desire that had been building inside him without a single outlet. He hadn't wanted to scare him away with all he was feeling, but the time for that had passed. Xander had claimed he wanted honesty, so Damon was going to give him all the honesty he could handle.

Breaking the kiss, Xander panted into Damon's neck, his breath hot against his skin. "Do you mean to tell me that we could have been doing that this whole time?"

Damon shrugged, feeling a little bashful about how much he wanted Xander—but not ashamed. He'd gotten over that in high school. He knew what he'd like, even if he'd never indulged in it before.

"I feel stupid," Xander said, cradling his palms across Damon's cheeks, stroking his beard, his neck, his ears, each pass of his fingers a graceful arc. His hands finally curled around Damon's neck, thumbs rubbing the top of his spine.

Damon thought he looked like he wanted to say more, and decided that while they certainly hadn't finished talking things through—not by a long shot—he was done talking for the night.

"Come on," he said gruffly, reaching up and curling his hand around Xander's bicep, tugging his hands away. "Let's go inside."

It felt like déjà vu, walking to the back door of the house, soaking wet, clumsily untying his boots while balancing against the doorjamb. But before, he hadn't done it with a throbbing erection and he hadn't dreamed about putting his hands all over the man next to him. Yet.

If he'd been thinking straight a year ago, he might have pushed Xander impatiently against the washing machine, but he fixed that mistake by doing exactly what he'd been dreaming of. Xander laughed brightly in between hot, un-relenting kisses, as he tried to shed his soaked tank top.

Then suddenly they were pressed together, damp skin to damp skin, nothing separating them, not even an excuse for why they should stop.

Damon half-expected Xander to produce one, but instead, his fingers trailed downwards, pausing at the top of his fly. He sucked in a hard breath, and Xander tucked in a fingertip, just stroking the skin of his lower abs.

"Please," Damon whispered, as he touched his forehead briefly to Xander's.

He flipped them, forcing Damon against the washing machine with a show of strength that somehow made him even harder. Xander opened the button with a flick of his fingers, and trailed them down his fly, fingers teasing and stroking along his hard length.

He'd always known Xander was good with his hands. Damon had always watched them in the habit of regular tasks—chopping and whisking and mixing—but now he watched Xander's hands with a whole different fascination as he tugged down his jeans partway and then his boxer briefs. Then those hands, so capable and so beautiful, wrapped around his cock, thumb reaching up to give a teasing little swipe to the damp head.

"God," Damon uttered in a gravelly voice, his eyelids slipping shut so he could enjoy the pleasure already spinning through him, "just like that."

Except that Xander didn't do it "just like that." He stopped moving his hand and his fingers completely, trapping Damon's length in his hot, wet palm.

"Look at me," Xander demanded, voice strained. Damon had imagined lots of times—more times than he should ever admit to—what Xander's sex voice might sound like. He'd imagined it in his ear, as Xander pleaded for Damon to give him more, to give him everything. And every single time Damon had done it. At least in his mind.

"What?" Damon asked stupidly, opening his eyes.

Xander rewarded him with an experimental twist of his fingers. "That's better," he crooned. "I want you to watch me. I want you to watch me jerk you off."

"Better. Yes. Now." Damon felt like he was beyond words as he glanced down, and took in the full image of Xander's hand wrapped around him. Then he glimpsed Xander's face. Lips tight with concentration, eyes teasing and burning with the exact same desire Damon felt.

"Feels good, huh?" Xander said, giving another stroke, a tiny bit faster this time.

Damon didn't even need to answer, the expression of bliss on his face probably gave him away. Or maybe his own hands, white-knuckled on the edge of the dryer.

Still, he'd learned his lesson. He kept his eyes open and watched as Xander slowly and inexorably pushed him toward the edge, one tantalizing stroke at a time.

"You like it like this?" Xander asked, even though it was probably very clear how much Damon liked it. "Or harder, and faster, like this?" He sped up, his hand motion making his bicep flex, and Damon bit back an oath.

"You keep that up," Damon gritted out, "and it's going to be over really soon."

"That would really be a shame," Xander crooned, glancing down at his hands. "You've got a beautiful cock."

Xander's words were fizzing in his veins, each syllable a tiny bubble of pleasure exploding.

"What?" Xander continued, expression going sly, his hand slowing down infinitesimally. "You like it when I talk dirty? You want to hear how many ways I want this cock? I want you to hold me down and fuck me so hard I cry. I want my mouth on it. I want to suck you until you come, and then I want to keep you in my mouth until you can't help but get hard again."

It was too much. Damon tried to hold on, but it had been a long, lonely time for him the last few years, and the visuals of Xander's words and the rough edge of his voice as he told Damon all his fantasies was too much for him to handle.

He tensed, and then exploded, Xander stroking him through it with a very satisfied grin on his face. Just like he was the cat who'd finally gotten all the cream he wanted.

"Fuck," Damon groaned as Xander lifted his hand and gave his finger an experimental lick. "You're going to kill me."

"Oh, but the trip is going to be fantastic," Xander said with a sharp, feral grin. "Return the favor?"

Damon opened his mouth to agree, but to also remind Xander that he'd never done this before.

"It's okay," he soothed, edges softening as he guessed at Damon's insecurity. "You've jerked yourself off before, right?"

Damon had practically worn off his skin jerking off thinking of Xander in the last few weeks. He nodded slowly.

"Then you're fine," Xander said. "Just do what you think you'd like."

"What about what you like?" Damon asked.

"We'll figure it out," Xander promised. "Now *please* do something before I get tired of waiting and do it myself."

That was something Damon really wanted to see—but *someday*. Not today. Today he wanted to give Xander at least a little taste of the pleasure he'd just received.

He cautiously reached down, loosening the tie on Xander's shorts. He knew he wasn't as graceful about it as Xander, and it was definitely more awkward than it looked to push down

Xander's wet, clingy shorts. He should be thankful he hadn't been wearing jeans, like Damon was.

Xander was wearing tight black briefs with little chili peppers dotted all over them. Damon knew he must be staring, both at the cute underwear that totally personified him, but also at the pretty impressive hard-on.

Blushing, Xander gave a little aborted shrug as Damon reached out and stroked him once through the damp cotton. "I like fun underwear," he admitted, and Damon thought this was a facet of Xander that he could get used to. Really, really fast.

"I like them," Damon admitted. "They're sexy as hell."

"I hoped you might think so," Xander said, and blushed again. Harder this time.

With minimum difficulty, Damon managed to push them down, letting them fall to the floor with Xander's running shorts, his cock springing up fully hard and definitely ready to go.

Damon wrapped his hand around it gently, and it was him that swore, not Xander. It felt so different from touching himself—so much better than he'd imagined. He'd always been a giver, and he knew from the first feel of Xander's cock that he was going to want to give all the time.

"Ahhh," Xander exhaled as Damon began to pump him slowly. "Don't have to be so gentle."

Damon knew his smile grew wicked. "Like it rough, do you?"

Xander panted. "Maybe."

Damon had already decided that he was down for giving Xander whatever he wanted. Both inside and outside the bedroom—or as this case might be, inside the laundry room. So he jerked him harder, sliding his thumb around the wet head, gathering pre-come to help ease his way a little better.

Xander was right; he did know what to do. His other hand gripped Xander's hip, and held him tight and fast as he gave him what he'd asked for. A little rough, with no quarter. Xander came with Damon's name on his breath and a wide-eyed incredulous look, like he'd just been smacked by a freight train.

"Wow," he exhaled shakily. "Wow."

"Good for a first time?" Damon asked self-consciously. He didn't feel quite as confident as Xander about tasting the stripes of come on his fingers, but he wanted to. Maybe next time. Maybe next time he might even feel confident enough to offer a blowjob.

Licking his lips, Xander smiled bright. "Uh, yeah. Definitely no complaints." He paused. "Did you know I wanted you for the first time in this room, a year ago?"

Damon laughed. "What if I told you that I wanted you before that?"

"Even looking like a drowned rat?"

Reaching up with his clean hand, Damon stroked Xander's cheek. "Even in the pouring rain, standing in a mud pit, you had so much passion and fire in your eyes. I wanted some of that fight for myself. I wanted you to share it with me." He hesitated. "And you did. You *do*, every day. Thank you."

Xander's laugh was shaky, unsure. Even more unsure than he'd been about to get Damon's first hand job. "You're welcome."

Damon reached down, picked up his t-shirt, wiped his hand. Pulled Xander's hand into his own, and wiped it too. He didn't know the etiquette for these kinds of things—not yet anyway—but he knew he always wanted to do the right thing.

From Xander's damp eyes that he guessed had nothing to do with the sprinkler fight they'd had, Damon hoped he'd managed it, despite the lack of experience.

Chapter Ten

The next morning, Xander was in the kitchen, taking advantage of the cool morning by baking a few practice batches of focaccia, when Kian wandered in.

"How's your hand?" Xander asked. He hadn't seen Kian much the last few days, and while he could still see a bandage, it was of the Band-Aid variety and covered in tiny My Little Ponies.

"Better," Kian grumbled, pouring himself a cup of coffee. "But still annoying. I hate having to wear gloves at work."

"It's the worst," Xander agreed, whipping off the damp cloth covering his dough and testing its rise with a fingertip. "I'm thinking about doing a rosemary and sun-dried tomato topping for this focaccia. Thoughts?"

Kian dumped sugar in his coffee and pursed his lips as he thought about it. "You're serving focaccia? I thought you weren't doing an Italian bent."

Xander had spent the last two weeks telling himself he wasn't trying to turn the Barrel House into an Italian restaurant, or even a restaurant with Italian influences. He'd tested a lot of recipes in the last weeks, but the ones that always ended up being the best were inspired by some of Xander's favorite rustic Italian food.

This morning, lying in bed, desperately trying to tamp down his rising feelings for Damon, Xander had wondered why he was fighting his own natural inclinations so hard? Did he want to make his life harder? More complicated?

He liked cooking Italian food. He liked Damon. Why did he spend so much effort trying to deny himself things he liked?

Xander had a feeling he could go to years of therapy and never quite understand that particular idiosyncrasy.

"Things change," Xander told Kian. The Kian of last year, even, would have probably left it at that. But this new Kian, the one who seemed to be actively pursuing Bastian instead of waiting in the shadows, hoarding the little scraps of attention the chef would throw him, was a Kian that Xander didn't really understand.

Somehow his good friend had grown up and Xander knew it wasn't fair to say he liked the other version better—but he'd *understood* that version better. Xander liked what he could reason and quantify, and Kian wasn't one of those things anymore.

"I knew you'd do it," Kian muttered. "It was inevitable. Just like you hooking up with Damon."

"How do you know we're hooking up?"

Kian laughed. "You look about a hundred times more relaxed this morning than you looked a week ago. You've got the *Xander got some* dreamy expression down pat."

Xander really wanted to tell him that in all the years they'd known each other—three at his last count—Kian couldn't know this was his post-sex expression because he'd been celibate the whole time. But telling Kian that would open him up for all sorts of questions that Xander did not want to answer. Most importantly, why he had decided that Damon was different, even though Damon still represented a lot of things that scared the shit out of him.

He couldn't answer the question himself, so he could hardly explain it to Kian.

"Okay, that's fair," was all Xander said.

"But to answer your question, I like the idea of the sun-dried tomatoes. But what about sort of a sun-dried tomato pesto on top? The topping is really the best part of focaccia, so why skimp? Coat that bitch."

It was a really good idea, which didn't surprise Xander at all because Kian had been a special chef even back in culinary school. It wasn't exactly a mystery why Aquino had taken one look at his naïve, sunny disposition and boundless talent and had coveted all those things for himself.

"You can dedicate your first Michelin star to me," was all Kian said breezily. Like receiving one was inevitable, but Xander didn't really have the heart to tell him that the Barrel House, at least in the iteration that he and Damon were creating now, wasn't the type of place that Michelin sought out.

It was the kind of place you took a first date if you wanted good food and not a lot of pretension, or a good spot to soak up a long day of wine tasting.

Xander was good with that, but he hadn't found a way to tell Kian that it was not Terroir-lite. It wasn't because he was ashamed of what he and Damon were creating, more that he couldn't find an explanation *why* he was okay with it. He'd known as early as culinary school that he was meant for bigger, brighter things. It had taken an association with the bigger and brighter to realize those things weren't always in line with what kind of food he wanted to serve people.

Sometimes it was really about the image and not the food, and Xander was done with that sort of subterfuge. But Kian wasn't. He was still guzzling the Kool-Aid as fast as Bastian Aquino could mix it up.

"Knock, knock," a voice said, as the front door opened. "I heard you were baking this morning and decided I needed a coffee refill and something more substantial than a banana."

Damon walked into the kitchen, and Xander went hot and cold all over remembering the things they'd done—not exactly groundbreaking—and what he'd said—groundbreaking for him, and if Damon's reaction had been anything to go by, him as well.

But they'd both enjoyed it, Damon especially hadn't been able to stop marveling at how much he'd loved it. He hadn't specifically said the part where Xander let all his inner raunchy fantasies out, but his meaning had been clear enough.

"Good morning," Xander said, because that was the only G-rated thing in his brain right now.

"Good morning," Damon replied, leaning down and giving him a kiss that wasn't brief by any means.

If Kian hadn't known they were hooking up before, he definitely knew now, and Xander was torn between wanting to tell him how amazing it was, to finally find someone he wanted to trust, and warning him that Bastian wouldn't be this kind or understanding or giving.

But Xander had forced himself to quit his Kian-must-be-saved quest, and that meant sticking to it.

Kian made a low whistling noise as Damon's lips left Xander's. Xander let his eyes open when Damon was still close, and the heat in his greenish-blue gaze nearly singed his eyebrows. Yes, they were going to need a repeat of last night, but this time, Xander was going to be aware he was doing it, and he wasn't going to half-ass it like an afterthought.

"Did you sleep well?" Damon asked lowly. By the time Xander had finally driven home last night it was late and he'd been floating along on a river of endorphins. He'd known he'd sleep like a baby, and had mentioned that much to Damon as they were saying goodbye.

He *hadn't* said just how much he wanted to stay, and just fall asleep on Damon's couch, pressed up close against him. He definitely hadn't said how much he really, secretly, wanted Damon to invite him to his bed.

Those things could all still happen, Xander had reminded himself. They were still new at this, and still figuring things out. Someday, Xander wouldn't have to pry himself off the couch and head back to his own separate, very lonely bed.

"Like a baby," Xander said, pasting a bright smile on. Once he was wearing it, he discovered it didn't feel forced.

"I didn't want you to go last night," Damon confessed softly, echoing exactly what Xander had been thinking.

"Funny," Xander said, ignoring Kian's fake vomiting sounds, "I didn't want to either."

"Next time," Damon promised, and it felt like a vow.

A vow that Xander was absolutely going to hold him to.

"I actually came by to show you something," Damon said, leaning his hip against the kitchen counter, cozying right back into Xander's personal space.

"This sounds like the beginning of a really bad porn," Kian announced loudly, "and that means it's my cue to leave."

"I don't know, I thought it sounded like a pretty good porn," Xander defended with a raised eyebrow. "I think we'd enjoy it anyway."

Damon's hand curled possessively around Xander's hip. "I think you're probably right."

They stood there for a single moment, staring at each other. Xander was absolutely thinking about last night, and the way Damon was looking back, there was no way he wasn't thinking about the same damn thing.

"Are you thinking what I'm thinking?" Xander asked, his lowered voice barely a gasp. He felt breathless and lightheaded, his cock thickening beneath his sweatpants.

Damon flushed. "It was so good, it's hard to think of anything else."

"So you don't regret it?" Xander teased. He had to do something to break this moment, or they were going to end up on the kitchen floor, making out and probably coming in their pants. Which . . . might not be a terrible thing, he realized, except that Kian was definitely home, and Nate probably was too.

He didn't want to do anything with Damon if they had an audience. Especially if he was going to try out more of the talk he'd used the night before.

"I told you last night. I don't regret a thing." Damon sounded amused, but reluctantly did let go of Xander's hip.

"Good." Xander stuck out his tongue and swiveled away, grabbing a bowl, and headed toward the deck, where he kept his herb planters. There he gathered rosemary, basil, parsley, and oregano. Damon watched from the sliding glass door.

"I can grow those for you," Damon offered.

"I sure hope so," Xander said as he tossed the bundles on his massive wooden cutting board and began to mince them.

"Can you text me the varieties you like?" Damon asked. "I *did* actually swing by to show you something. I've got a meeting in town in about twenty." He made a face. "As much as I'd like to stay."

"Oh, right." Xander had forgotten about the reason why Damon had supposedly stopped by. He'd secretly hoped there hadn't really been an excuse at all, and the thing Damon wanted to show him was actually his dick. Again.

Damon pulled his phone out of his pocket, and flipped through a few screens. "Here," he said, extending it toward Xander. "I got the first drafts on the logo for the restaurant."

Glancing over, Xander looked through the different choices the graphic designer had provided. "That one," he said, pointing with a flour-dusted finger. It was a combination of a swirly, elegant font and rough-looking letters that seemed inspired by the wood that the Barrel House was named for.

"I like that one too." Damon stared at the screen. "But I think I have a few notes for Carol. I'll email them over and as soon as she sends me the final, I'll text it to you."

Since the night Damon had come to Terroir, determined to woo Xander into working for him, he hadn't known how this was supposed to work. How their professional and personal relationships—both so new and so different from anything either of them had experienced before—could co-exist.

This morning, for the very first time, Xander glimpsed a future that looked very much like today had. And to Xander, it was one of the best things he'd ever seen. Instead of feeling dread that they might fuck one or both of their relationships up, he could see it working. One of the facets of their partnership encouraging and nurturing the other and vice versa.

This might not end in a fiery disaster; this could really *work*. Nobody was more surprised than Xander, who tried hard to keep both a level head and also a realistic, pragmatic view of the future. He rarely let himself get carried away, but he threw both arms around Damon, smudging his plaid shirt with flour and leaving the scent of herbs behind.

"It's just a logo," Damon said, laughing.

But it wasn't just a logo. It was the combination of both their visions, it was their two selves melding and merging and becoming more powerful together than they were individually.

"Sorry," Xander said, but he was laughing too. "I got a bit carried away." He brushed as much of the flour off as he could, but they were both smiling. As good as last night had been, it felt like this morning was even better.

Wasn't the morning after supposed to be awkward and difficult? Maybe they were running on a high of sexual endorphins and potential professional success and maybe they were eventually going to come back to earth, but Xander didn't want to think about that.

So he didn't. He brushed a kiss over Damon's cheek, fingers still lingering on the waist of Damon's jeans, and sending him off with a bright smile and a promise he'd bring some of the focaccia over tomorrow morning.

"I can't stop looking at you this morning," Xander said. He'd had the thought the moment he'd climbed out of the car, dawn rising over the Napa Valley hills, and Damon's dark hair and eyes matching the muted colors of the plaid he wore today. "You're gorgeous."

Damon looked up and smiled, only a little self-consciously. "I am?"

Xander nodded emphatically. He didn't always say this sort of thing—he was far more likely to spit out, bluntly and clearly, all the things he didn't like, than to let anything pass his lips that was overly demonstrative.

He was still afraid of falling harder, of being the one left holding what was left of their relationship after Damon moved on. *If* Damon moved on, Xander told himself firmly. There were zero indications he had any intention of doing that, but it was still hard for Xander to trust completely.

So he usually kept comments like, *I can't stop looking at you this morning*, to himself, but the few he'd let out recently had produced such a beautiful effect on Damon that he'd started *wanting* to relax his own self-imposed rules.

And really, it was silly to let a little fear get in the way of Damon's gorgeous blush whenever Xander complimented him.

"You don't look so bad yourself," Damon said, pulling Xander in and planting a firm kiss on his mouth. "But I always think you're handsome."

Xander usually got the *you're so cute* moniker, so being told he was handsome was surprisingly electrifying. Or maybe that was just the hot look in Damon's eyes as he said it, his gaze sweeping down Xander's white t-shirt and black running shorts.

"You don't have to suck up," Xander teased. "I brought treats."

Damon looked just about as excited to taste the focaccia samples as he had to see Xander pull into the driveway.

"Should we go in the house?" Damon asked, glancing around. He'd been checking on some of the plants, as he did most mornings before David arrived to work on the Barrel House building. They were starting refinishing the flooring soon, and Damon had complained at length at what a nasty, dirty, smelly job it was.

"It's so nice out here," Xander pointed out.

"My hands are dirty." Damon lifted his palms and they were streaked with mud.

"That's okay. I'll feed you and you can tell me what you and David have planned for today."

"We're going to expand the front door, add in a few more windows and add the back door," Damon said, eyes glued to the container in Xander's hands as he popped the lid open.

Immediately the air smelled of fresh baked bread, herbs, citrus, and garlic—and not just the morning dew over the freshly tilled earth.

"I have three kinds for you to try," Xander said. He picked up a piece and held it toward Damon's lips.

"Lemon basil," Xander said, as Damon took a quick, neat bite.

"Mmmm," Damon hummed as he chewed. "That's really, really good."

"I know," Xander said, and he couldn't help but sound smug. He'd already sampled these all himself. In fact, these were the second and third versions of his original idea—or Kian's original idea. He'd perfected them since then, and he'd been hard-pressed to keep himself, Kian, and Nate out of the Tupperware container long enough for Damon to try them.

"What's the next one?" Damon asked.

"Sun-dried tomato with rosemary and orange zest."

Damon made a face. "Orange zest?"

"Trust me," Xander said, as he pulled the piece out of the container and held it up toward Damon's mouth.

He chewed longer on this piece, his thoughts clearly whirring as he let each unique taste roll off his tongue.

"That was . . . incredibly interesting and shockingly good," Damon finally pronounced. "I wasn't sure about the orange zest, but it . . . worked?"

"Unusual flavor combos aren't usually my sort of thing," Xander confessed. "But that came to me in a dream when I was napping yesterday, and it totally worked. To my own surprise."

"You weren't surprised," Damon scoffed. "You're brilliant and you know it."

Xander grinned. "True." He pulled the last piece out of the container. "Last one. Garlic herb. A more generic combination. Safe maybe, but still delicious."

Damon chewed this piece just as thoughtfully as the last two.

"Is it weird," he asked in a conspiratorial tone, like maybe Bastian Aquino was watching this whole taste test go down from outside the fence, "that I liked the orange and sun-dried tomato one best?"

"No, not at all. It's really good." Xander was still surprised that Damon had picked it. It was definitely a little outside the box, and he hadn't been sure if Damon's palate would like it or hate it.

"We'll do a rotating focaccia," Xander continued. "So we'll have options for the less adventurous. But the sun-dried tomato-orange will be featured every day."

"So you've decided to go with the rustic Italian spin on farm-to-table?" Damon asked.

Xander sighed.

"I love the idea, I really do. Mostly because it's what you love, and I'm a firm believer that you should always do what you love."

"It's not that simple."

"It's exactly that simple," Damon argued. "I'm not asking you to be Mario Batali, I'm telling you to cook the food you love—because that love is *always* reflected in the finished product. A happy chef is usually a successful chef. And I want both."

Mario *fucking* Batali. Xander tried to grasp at the peace and contentment he'd felt just a few minutes ago, watching the sunrise gleam on Damon's dark hair and admiring how strong and capable he looked in one of his ubiquitous plaid shirts with the sleeves rolled up.

"I'm definitely not going to be Mario Batali. I don't want to be *that guy* that started an Italian restaurant."

"Why not?" Damon still sounded mystified, and Xander wasn't sure he was even capable of explaining.

"Because in high-end restaurants, you typically can't point to one single inspiration or culture."

"And high-end matters to you?" Damon asked. Even though Xander told himself he was imagining things, he could hear the hurt edge in his voice.

And *yeah*, he hadn't been intending to be a high-end establishment trying for Michelin stars. Definitely nothing like Terroir. But he didn't want to be laughed at either, and despite being completely confident in his own abilities, somehow this was the one tender spot in his ego.

"What other people think of our restaurant matters," Xander snapped.

"Impressing people is good, even if we're not going for Michelin stars." Damon seemed to mentally digest this. "I'm sorry. I guess I thought we'd be impressing people with our great food. No matter what country inspired it."

Panic clawed up from the bottom of Xander's stomach, where he felt slightly sick. Like he'd eaten too much focaccia with too much olive oil over the last twenty-four hours.

"That's not it. No. Don't be sorry." Xander reached out and grasped Damon's bare forearms, his fingers curling around them. His skin was warm even though the sun had barely come up. "I'm the one who's sorry. This is . . . this is all me. My insecurity. I'm going to it figure out."

"I wish you'd let me help," Damon said softly.

"I wish you could," Xander said with reluctance. "But this is something I've got to come to terms with."

"I was going to suggest we could take a little trip—maybe a bit of research thrown in," Damon said ruefully. "We need to go to San Francisco to pick out the major equipment you need. I thought we could stay at the family townhouse while we're there. Do a little fine dining. Get away while David refinishes the floors."

Xander raised an eyebrow. "While David refinishes the floors?"

"That's all you got from that?" Damon scoffed. "That David is going to be stuck refinishing the floors by himself?"

"No . . ." Xander drew out, trying to hide his smile as long as possible. The fight didn't last longer than a few seconds. The grin bloomed across his face. "It actually sounds incredible. You have a family townhouse in San Francisco? You want me to pick out equipment? When can we leave?"

Damon laughed, and pulled him the rest of the way into his arms, hugging him close. "You're adorable."

"Seriously, when are we leaving?" Xander asked. "I've got lists to put together."

"Lists?"

"Restaurants we have to go to. Food suppliers I want to visit. Equipment I need. Clothes I'll have to pack."

"Few days?" Damon hesitated. "I promised David some sort of help, and I have to find the help first before we escape."

"I suppose I can wait that long," Xander told him with an exaggerated sigh. He rose to his tiptoes and kissed Damon on the cheek. "I'll let you get to that. I've got more recipes to test today. A variation on scampi. I bought the store out of bay scallops."

⁂

Watching Xander walk back to his car, Damon wondered how much the scallops had cost, but as soon as he had the thought, he dismissed it. It didn't matter. He had the money, and he wanted to give Xander whatever he needed to be successful—whether that was a crate of bay scallops, high-end equipment or a confidence boost.

The San Francisco trip was sort of unnecessary and entirely unplanned, but Damon knew what it felt like when the unique pressure of the expectations Napa held started to creep in. He was seeing it in Xander right now. But it was a good time to get away—Damon would be happy to hire someone to help David finish the floors, and he hadn't really had time to spoil Xander yet.

Taking him to the city and staying in the condo would be a chance to do that.

Which left Damon one last action to take. It just happened to be something he really didn't want to do. He dialed the number reluctantly, but with determination.

"Hi, Nancy," he said when his father's secretary answered the phone. "It's Damon. Can I talk to him?"

Damon wasn't sure who was more surprised that he was calling—him or Nancy. If it wasn't for Xander, and that haunted look in his eyes, he wouldn't be making this call at all.

"Sure, of course," Nancy said, fumbling a bit. "Let me transfer you in."

A click, a single dial, and then his father's rich voice answering, "Nathan Hess."

So Nancy hadn't told him who was calling. Damon took a single deep breath. "It's me."

"Damon!" Nathan sounded surprised. And pleased. Never a good combination. "I wasn't expecting your call."

"I need a favor," Damon managed to say.

"Of course. What do you need? Wine for the new restaurant? You should really go through our distributor, but I don't think anyone would be surprised if I sold to you directly. You're a Hess, after all."

Yes. He was a Hess, and he was always going to be a Hess. Damon gritted his teeth. "No. I'm going to the city for a few days. I need to use the condo."

"Oh." His disappointment was clear. "Naturally. I'll have Nancy email you the codes. It's not in use currently."

"I thought as much," Damon said stiffly. "And it seemed silly to stay in a hotel when it was empty."

"Right. Naturally."

"Thank you," Damon said, and this was even harder than asking for the favor in the first place. "I'll look for the email."

"I'll tell Nancy to send it right over."

"Bye." As Damon clicked off the call, he realized that he and his father, who had never really known how to talk to each other, had spent that entire conversation talking about other people.

For a brief moment, he wondered if he should have told his father that Xander was coming with him, but no, that was a terrible idea. Nathan knew abstractly about his son's sexuality, but had never actually been confronted by it. Damon didn't know what he would say—or do—if he was confronted by it now.

Better, much much better, to play it safe when it came to Xander.

Chapter Eleven

"Fucking hell," Xander said, pushing his sunglasses up and staring at the townhouse through the windshield of Damon's car. "This is yours?"

"Well, it's not *mine*," Damon pointed out, more than a little subconsciously. How had he forgotten how Xander initially had reacted to the fact that he was a Hess? Was it so wrong he wanted to show Xander some of the nicer perks of being part of the family? "Technically, it's my father's."

Xander's gaze swiveled over to him only for a split second. Then it was right back to the white stucco edifice with its lake blue shutters. "You're going to inherit it one day, though."

He really wasn't sure that was true. Yes, he was his father's only child, but after what he'd done with his grandfather's legacy, Damon really wasn't certain he was even still in the will. But that touched on all sorts of issues that 1) Damon did not want to discuss right now and 2) Damon did not want to discuss ever. Even with Xander. *Especially* with Xander, if he was being truly honest with himself.

So he changed the subject.

"If you think the outside is gorgeous, wait until you see the inside," Damon said, turning off his Jeep and opening the driver's door. "I usually hate houses designed by interior decorators, but the one my dad hired really did a good job. It doesn't feel look a showpiece, more like a real home."

The sad part was that Damon had partially grown up in this house and while it might have *looked* like a real home, it had never really felt like one.

But that was another thing he didn't need to tell Xander. Damon knew from personal experience that the poor-little-rich-boy act got old for everyone after awhile, if it didn't start out that way.

"What's the kitchen like?" Xander asked, and this time his voice was eager, not hidden behind shock or dismissal. "Wait, no. Don't tell me. I want to be surprised."

Damon pulled their bags from the trunk and shut the hatch. "Well, let's go inside," he teased. "I don't want to keep you waiting."

Following him up the stairs, Damon repeated the entry code his father's assistant had sent over and Xander carefully typed it in.

"What happens if I enter this wrong?" Xander asked in a hushed, almost reverent tone. "Will there be cops? Firemen? Will they arrest me?"

"If the cops are hot, they can definitely put me in handcuffs," Damon joked as Xander swung the door open. No alarms went off. "But the truth is, yeah, my father pays for a security system for this place, but I just asked him for the code so I know it's good."

The entry was a narrow, arched passageway they passed through, emerging into an open rotunda, complete with a circular staircase, edged with a gleaming curved wood banister.

"Hooooly shit," Xander exhaled. He seemed transfixed by the handblown glass chandelier at the top of the rotunda. Then he turned back toward Damon, his eyes narrowing. "You just asked him for the code? I thought you sort of grew up here."

Damon sort of had, which had been part of his explanation when Xander had asked questions about it on their drive from Napa.

"As you might have guessed," Damon finally admitted wryly, "we haven't been close in some time. Well, more like *ever*, but yes, I did used to spend a lot of time here. My dad is a workaholic and the city was where he did a lot of his work. He came, so I came too."

"Where was your mom?" Xander asked.

"Traveling back then, doing marketing and publicity for the winery. She didn't want to hire it out because she thought she could do it better herself. Then, dead from a stroke." Damon knew people believed that if you sped through bad news like it was rote and routine, then it made the terrible shit less terrible.

Damon didn't believe that worked at all.

"God, I'm sorry," Xander said, voice low. "I . . . I realized we didn't know much about each other. Our families, that is."

"And now you just realized why I don't talk about them?" Damon laughed without humor. "Sorry."

"Why don't you give me the full tour?" Xander asked, turning on a determined and brightly sunny smile. Damon appreciated the effort, but he wanted to tell him that if it had ever been that easy to leave his family and their demons behind, he wouldn't have ended up so dependent on the bottle.

"This way is the living room," Damon said, reaching out and taking Xander's hand. The touch of his skin wasn't quite enough to dismiss his bad mood, but it helped. The sweet wry look Xander shot him helped too. That Damon had epic plans to fully corrupt every single room of this damn townhouse really helped.

Maybe they could start in the living room.

"Wow," Xander said, turning toward the big picture window that looked out on the San Francisco marina. "This view just doesn't quit."

"When this townhouse came up for sale, my father bought it sight unseen," Damon said. He'd told himself he wouldn't mention any other Hesses for the rest of the trip, but being back in this place made it impossible. The memories—good and bad and every other shade in between—were hiding in the corners like ghosts. "He told the realtor to make the offer based on the address alone. When she asked him if he wanted to see the pictures, he told her that if he didn't like it, he'd tear it down and build something else."

Xander squeezed his hand. "It must have sucked growing up with someone who thought he could buy anything."

When he'd thought of, and told, that story, Damon hadn't been thinking of that bad habit of Nathan's. He'd only been thinking it was one of the few stories he could think of that he found vaguely amusing.

But that had always been Nathan Hess' problem. He'd worked hard and believed that every interaction was transactional. And Damon had never had anything his father had valued enough to trade with.

"Yeah," Damon said shortly, regretting that he'd told the story. He'd always believed Xander was an intuitive person who was better at reading people than you'd expect someone who'd locked themselves away in a kitchen for a career could. From the first moment, staring at each other in the pouring rain, Damon had felt like Xander knew him.

Now it felt like he saw right through him, and Damon wasn't sure if he liked it or if it scared the ever-living shit out of him. There were dark corners and cobwebs he didn't want anyone—especially someone he could love—to see.

There was a Casset hanging above the fireplace, the only color shining bright on a simple white wall. Xander let go of his hand and went closer, eyes taking in every brushstroke. He didn't ask if it was real—and Damon was grateful because then he didn't have to answer.

They went through the dining room, with a spiky modern chandelier that Damon didn't recognize. It looked like a trendy piece of destructive art. Perfect for murder in the middle of a dinner party.

Damon imagined what his father would look like with the spikes buried in his chest, and then abruptly swept the image away. He didn't want his father dead; he wanted his father to have never existed at all.

The kitchen, which was a major part of why they'd come to the townhouse and not some random hotel in San Francisco, elicited a large enough gasp from Xander that Damon believed coming here was worth it.

The space was cavernous, bordering on nearly obscene, with acres of shining wood floors and rows of lake blue cabinets that perfectly matched the shutters outside. The blue was beautiful outside, but it was startling inside a kitchen, and even more startling was the fact that all the high-end professional appliances had been custom ordered in the exact same shade of blue.

Nathan had once told Damon that the color was the same tone as his mother's eyes, but he'd always believed that was more of his father's bullshit. Now he looked and he wasn't quite sure.

"I know we're going out to dinner a lot," Xander said, fingers a death grip on Damon's hand, "but I've got to cook in here. Please. Just one night."

"Anything you want to do," Damon said. "It's all up to you."

Xander reluctantly let Damon guide him out of the kitchen and upstairs. There were a series of bedrooms, each more luxe than the last, but culminating in the master with its textured blue walls and *chinoserie* hand-painted ceiling.

"This color," Xander stated hesitantly, turning around the massive room, "it's used a lot in this house."

"The blue?" Damon repeated stupidly.

Xander's frank look was a clear direction to cut the bull-shit. But Damon wanted the bullshit; it was a lot easier to stomach than the truth.

"It was my mom's favorite color," Damon said softly. Which was one hundred percent true, no Nathan Hess bull-shit needed to embellish it.

"It also looks a little like your eyes," Xander replied.

It was impossible to miss the flash of guilt on Xander's face, and no matter how painful some of this felt—dredging up so many old wounds that Damon kept hoping had healed finally—he'd come here for a reason. He'd wanted to share the best of his family with him, and he wanted to try to tell him some of what he'd come from. The good and the bad and the horrendous.

Xander was the kind of guy who wouldn't take some of him. He'd want it all, when he figured out that's where the two of them were headed, and Damon would have to give him as much as he demanded.

Some of it wasn't going to feel good or cathartic. Some of it was just going to suck.

"Don't feel bad," Damon said, reaching out and pulling Xander flush against him. Xander's head tucked under his chin, and a hand stroked up and down his back.

"I don't feel bad," Xander said in a muffled voice. "I want to fucking kill them for not giving a shit about you."

Damon managed to laugh through the lump in his throat. "Thank you."

"Is it . . . would it be okay if we stayed in here?" Xander asked with hesitancy.

Damon hadn't had any intention of doing so, even though it had never really felt like his parents' room, but he found himself nodding anyway. He'd never imagined that some things were better with the right person beside you, and just having Xander here helped. It hurt too, but Damon was beginning to believe it was the sort of catharsis he needed to grow. Even after therapy, he'd dragged all this baggage around with him—every inch of this house and the others he'd grown up in—but it was impossible to really move past it without ever looking at it.

"Are you sure?"

Damon sighed. "I don't talk about this stuff, because part of how I've been sober is by pretending it didn't happen. But it happened, and I can't keep ignoring it forever."

Reaching up, Xander's hands cupped his cheeks, staring right into his eyes. "If you didn't ever want to talk about it, that's your prerogative. I don't know everything you've been through, but figuring out how to stay sober makes you the bravest person I know. So yeah, you can ignore it as long as you fucking want to."

It was impossible not to laugh at Xander's indignant tone. He wasn't going to let anyone judge Damon—even himself.

Damon pulled him close, hugging him tight. "You're so great. How did I get this lucky?" he murmured into Xander's shoulder. He wasn't sure he wanted him to hear how he felt just yet, but it was also impossible not to say anything.

The honesty in Xander's dark eyes was stark and bright. "I think that all the time."

"You want to go to the Wharf? Stop by Ghirardelli?" Damon asked after a long moment where they just held each other. He'd never expected to have anyone again, not with his emotional baggage and his alcoholism, and Xander was so miraculous, he just wanted to bask in him. But they'd come to the city for a reason. "Tomorrow we've got some appointments to look at equipment."

Xander slid away, right out of Damon's grip. They weren't perfect. Sometimes he still pulled away when Damon held him too tight. Another reason why he hadn't confessed all his feelings yet.

"Appointments?" Xander lifted an eyebrow questioning-ly.

"The family name has a reputation people see coming from a long way off. I might not be my father, but being a Hess carries weight."

"Right." Xander, while really enjoying this house, didn't seem to know how to accept that there were a lot of different facets of being a Hess. This house was definitely a benefit, but the expectations and strings attached could be a real bitch.

"The Wharf sounds great," Xander said after a long pause. "We could swing by Boudin for lunch."

Xander didn't know why he'd suggested such a godawful tourist trap for lunch, but he'd sort of been feeling out this new Damon who'd emerged since they had arrived in San Francisco.

He was a Hess no matter where he was geographically, but standing in that elegant, insanely expensive townhouse, looking like he belonged even with his worn blue button-up and jeans, still bits of mud on the heel of his boots, had thrown Xander for a loop. He wanted the Damon he knew back—this newer, richer, darker Damon wasn't someone he quite recognized and he definitely didn't know how to deal with him.

It was even harder to convince himself that this Damon would happily publicly date someone like Xander. Someone who up until a few weeks ago had gotten his hands dirty on the regular in a kitchen. Someone who worked for an hourly wage.

Damon acted like it didn't matter, but it mattered. At least to Xander. In his experience, only rich people thought money didn't matter.

"Wow, it's packed in here," Damon said in a dismayed voice as he surveyed the packed Boudin café.

"It's right by the Wharf," Xander scoffed. "What were you expecting?"

"I don't know," Damon said, as they shuffled in the available next few feet, adding themselves to the winding line that went up to the bank of order stations. "It's been years since I've been here."

"Packed, but good bread," Xander said. "Ready to carb load?"

Damon grinned, a spark of the man Xander had started falling for emerging. "Would I ever turn a good carb down?"

Xander had never seen him hesitate over anything he ate, but he also worked hard, and there were lots of instances where Damon mentioned hitting the weights. And Xander had definitely seen evidence that he didn't need to worry about carbs. Not with Damon's flat, muscular stomach, and rippling biceps and thighs. A spike of arousal echoed through Xander as he thought of what they were probably going to do in that gigantic raft of a bed later tonight.

He'd wanted them to go slow at first, but now that they'd started, Xander had discovered he wasn't just hungry, he was starving.

"I'm going to get the chowder bread bowl *and* the roast beef sandwich," Xander announced, making his position on carbs very clear.

Damon nodded, and as they finally got up to the ordering counter, he listed off a similar order, and after Xander ordered, whipped out his credit card.

When Xander shot him a look, Damon shrugged and mouthed, "tax deduction," in his direction.

Xander didn't think the IRS was going to necessarily approve of a tax-deductible trip in which they hopefully took advantage of that incredible townhouse to have sex on every single surface available. But he guessed if they produced enough receipts for the restaurant it wouldn't matter.

Besides, a Hess would have a skilled and aggressive accountant on their payroll, Xander told himself as he went to find a table.

He finally located one in the faraway corner of the busy café, and they ate quickly without much conversation.

"You want to do the Wharf or Ghirardelli?" Damon asked as they walked back outside.

"You pick," Xander said. He was full from lunch, but he could always make room for chocolate.

"I haven't ever really done all this tourist stuff," Damon confessed. "My father would have hated it."

"Wharf it is," Xander said. It hadn't escaped his notice that Damon had mentioned his father more in the last twelve hours than he had during the whole time they'd known each other. He considered bringing it up, but he also didn't want to push Damon. He was trying to open up, and he didn't need to be pried open, all his bloody, dark insides spilling out. He'd tell Xander when he was ready.

Damon reached out and gripped his hand, nearly stopping Xander in his tracks and definitely vetoing any questions about his dad. "Is this okay?" he asked, a little self-consciously.

"Of course it's okay," Xander said. He didn't ask if it was okay for Damon, because he'd been the one to reach out. But then Xander had made it very damn clear that he wasn't into dating someone who he couldn't take out in public.

He'd done that once before, and gotten burned, and he wasn't into repeating the experience. Especially not with someone he could really care about like Damon.

"I know we're not the most traditional of couples," Damon said, and he still sounded nervous. His palm was warm and a little damp. Nerves? Xander wasn't sure. "But I think this is nice sometimes."

Xander spent a lot of time trying to pretend he didn't need this sort of wooing—hand-holding, extravagant trips to the city, fancy dinners, expensive kitchen equipment—but that was a total lie. He liked it. He liked the certainty it gave him that he was who Damon wanted.

"I like it," he admitted to Damon.

"So I shouldn't stop?" he teased back. "You're not gonna get sick of me?"

Never. But that was too soon to say, much too serious much too soon. "I'll make sure to let you know if I do," Xander retorted lightly.

But he felt all sorts of light and bright as they walked down along the bay to the Wharf.

He bought an ugly nautical-themed magnet, claiming he was going to stick it on one of the industrial-sized fridges they were buying this weekend. Even when Damon let go of his hand in one of the more crowded touristy stores, his hand lingered on the small of his back, leading him without being asshole-ish or obtrusive about it.

And Xander couldn't help it. He kept seeing the future, laid out before them like a beautifully varied Persian carpet, dotted with milestones and the good and a little bit of the bad, but with love woven through it consistently and constantly. The more he imagined it, the more real it became, and the harder he continued to fall.

By the time they returned to the townhouse, a little sunburned and stuffed full of Ghirardelli's ice cream sundaes, Xander was searching for some balance. Something to prevent the other shoe from dropping quite so hard.

It made perfect sense to drop their bags in the master bedroom, and for Xander to tackle Damon, somewhat successfully, to the bed.

"What are you doing?" Damon asked with a laugh as Xander settled over his big, muscular thighs. Thighs he definitely intended to get between very, very soon. Like *right now* soon.

"What," Xander said, dipping down to plant a kiss on Damon's lips, "do," he repeated the action, feeling Damon smile under his mouth, "you think I'm doing?"

"I have a few theories," Damon drawled as Xander propped himself back up with a palm to his lover's chest.

"Oh?" Xander used that hand to start popping open the buttons on Damon's shirt, slowly revealing the worn, thin white tank that he was wearing underneath. "Jesus," he exclaimed in a hushed tone, reverently stroking up and down the fabric that left very little to the imagination. Shirtless Damon was a revelation—there was no question of that—but with the dips and shadows outlined in the tight, nearly transparent cotton, he left Xander's mouth dry.

"Like what you see?" Damon's lips quirked up at the expression on Xander's face. Though it probably wasn't just at how turned on he definitely looked. Xander experimentally rocked his denim-clad cock against Damon's taut, flat abdomen, and felt his muscles flex in response.

"You know I do," Xander retorted, and there was heat, but it lacked his normal teasing edge. He was done teasing—both Damon and himself.

"Come up here and kiss me," Damon pleaded, and it was impossible to deny him. Xander leaned out full length on Damon's broad chest and kissed him. They'd both been thinking about this for days, and the kiss turned wild almost instantly, Xander's tongue slipping inside Damon's mouth, curling around his lover's.

Damon's hands clamped over his hips, and ground Xander and his cock into his stomach in a slow rhythmic motion that left him seeing stars. "Stop," Xander finally had to say, tearing his mouth from Damon's. "If you keep this up this is going to be over way too quick."

"So? We have all night. I made dinner reservations, but I'd much rather stay here, with you."

"No argument here," Xander said, still gasping a little as Damon's hands continued tormenting him.

"What do you want?" Damon asked then, a hint of hesitancy in his tone. He tried to act like this wasn't all new to him, but it was. Xander didn't always like taking the upper hand, but while Damon was still figuring sex with guys out, he was perfectly happy to lead the way. He shimmied down Damon's body, dislodging his hands as he settled between his thighs. His fingers opened the button of his jeans and slid the zipper down.

"I want this," Xander said, sliding his jeans down and ghosting his palm over Damon's cock. "Are you going to let me have it?"

Damon's pupils were blown wide, his expression wavering between ecstatic and disbelieving. He nodded, swallowing hard, his Adam's apple bobbing.

Xander took that as a green light, slid his jeans off the rest of the way, followed by his socks and then his boxer briefs. "I'm going to suck your cock now," he said, remembering how he'd promised himself that he'd continue the dirty talk that Damon had enjoyed so much last time. It was a little more difficult to do that with his mouth full of dick, but he could do his best.

His eyes grew bigger, tracking every movement of Xander's without blinking.

He was fully hard, curving a little toward his stomach, the tip damp with pre-come. Xander leaned down and licked up the underside, tongue curling around the tip.

"Holy fuck," Damon exhaled.

Xander was under no illusions that this was the first blowjob Damon had ever received, but he was determined it would be one of the best ones.

He gave his cock a shallow suck and let go with a *pop*. "You have a really gorgeous cock," Xander said, hand reaching up to stroke the length experimentally. "I've been wanting to do this for a long time."

Damon gave a short, humorless bark of laughter, and the thigh muscles under Xander twitched. "What was stopping you?"

It was clear it was a theoretical question, and Xander just smiled. "Nothing stopping me now."

Damon's hand reached down, cupping the back of his head, and Xander let his mouth be guided right back to his dick. Xander figured that was Damon's way of saying there was enough time to do all sorts of dirty talk later, and that he wanted Xander's mouth to be doing something other than talking.

Xander got the hint, and went to work, bobbing his mouth up and down in earnest, hand resting low to cup Damon's balls. He must have been doing a good job, because Damon kept groaning like he was killing him, and way too soon, he tugged hard on Xander's hair. He glanced up and Damon was sweating, breaths coming in short pants.

"I'm too close," Damon said. Xander gave his cock a little flick of his tongue, and watched his head fall back to the bed, and he groaned loudly again.

It was just a few more strokes to finish him off, Xander letting his come pump onto his tongue. He swallowed and crawled up Damon's chest. For a split second he forgot that Damon hadn't done this before, and started to lean down so they could kiss.

Then he remembered, realizing that Damon might not be comfortable tasting his own come in Xander's mouth. He hesitated, nearly pulling back, but Damon's big hand returned to the back of his head and pulled him in the rest of the way.

They kissed for long minutes, Xander rocking almost subconsciously against Damon's stomach, pleasure spiking through his veins. If the kissing bothered him, Damon didn't show it once, instead he dove in, hands wrapping around Xander's waist, sliding down toward his ass.

Finally Xander pulled up, knowing he needed some sort of relief. Just the thought of Damon's hand wrapping around him again made him almost come in his pants.

"Can I try that too?" Damon asked, surprising the hell out of Xander.

"If you want to," Xander said, trying to be casual. "It's not required."

"I want to," Damon said stubbornly. "I'm not going to be very good, probably, but I still want to try it."

Xander gave a short laugh. "Truthfully, it's hard to give a bad blowjob."

Rolling them over, Damon pulled off his tank, the way his abs flexed leaving Xander a little short of breath. He reached out, stroking them. "You're so gorgeous."

Damon smiled. "If you think so, I'm not going to argue. But you . . ." he was just finishing pulling off the rest of Xander's clothes, "are so fucking hot."

Leaning back on the headboard, Xander grinned. "Do your worst."

Damon hesitated, just staring at Xander's cock. There wasn't much blood in his brain at the moment, which was probably why Xander had forgotten how he'd dirty-talked/coached him through the hand job the other night.

He could definitely do that again. It was hot as fuck, and they'd both enjoyed it.

"Lick the tip," Xander said, and his eyes fluttered close as the pleasure radiated through him. "Yeah, just like that. Fuck, that feels good."

Damon did it again, curling his mouth around the head, just the way Xander had. He didn't know whether to be pleased or annoyed that Damon had been coherent enough to take mental notes. But it felt so damn good, any annoyance he did feel faded almost immediately.

"Slide it in your mouth," Xander directed. "Just as much as you feel comfortable. Use your hand for the rest." It shouldn't have felt so good and so hot to have Damon doing exactly what he was telling him to do—somehow the anticipation should have been less, since he knew what would happen—but somehow the pleasure doubled, tripled, multiplied beyond anything Xander had ever experienced before.

Damon was undeniably cautious as he took Xander's cock in his mouth, curling his tongue right around the underside, and Xander's vision whited out.

How could he have been disappointed in Damon not lasting longer, if he was liable to come much faster?

"God damn," Xander exhaled slowly. "Do it again."

Damon hadn't even needed the direction, because he already was, taking Xander further, taking him down so good that it was hard to imagine that he hadn't done this before.

Xander felt his orgasm building. He made the mistake to glance down to check on Damon, but all that did was give him the ball-busting image of Damon sucking his cock, blissful expression on his face, like this was all he had ever wanted. And suddenly the oncoming orgasm wasn't just a possibility but a certainty, roaring down the line like an out-of-control freight train.

"Damon," Xander was barely able to squawk out to warn him. But Damon kept his mouth on his cock, clearly determined to duplicate Xander's actions.

And then Xander couldn't think at all, because the orgasm was blasting through him, the pleasure digging in with claws.

When he finally opened his eyes again, Damon was wiping his mouth, but he was smiling so brightly that Xander's heart gave an agonized beat in his chest.

How could he keep reminding himself that eventually Damon would tire of his interlude when he seemed so god damned happy to be doing it? It was hard bordering on impossible.

Chapter Twelve

It was almost impossible to not feel smug after Damon settled back on the bed next to Xander. He hadn't made any moves to put clothes on, and if he wanted to sit here naked with Damon, he certainly wasn't going to do anything to dissuade him—like put his own clothes back on.

The smugness probably came from the fact that Xander kept sighing happily and murmuring at how good it had been. Damon was under no illusions that he had any blowjob skills. Yes, he'd taken one for the team and watched quite a bit of porn to try to get a better idea of what he was doing, but there was nothing for learning like practical experience, and before today, he hadn't had any.

Still, Xander wasn't exactly complaining.

"If you liked it," Damon offered, trying and failing to keep a cocky edge out of his voice, "I'm happy to try it again."

Xander raised his eyebrow, shooting him a dubious glance. Damon adored that questioning look of his—like he was trying to front by pretending he wasn't one thousand percent on board with that idea, and it was Damon's job to break down his pseudo-skepticism. And Damon *really* enjoyed digging his way right behind the façade to find the truth beneath. There was something very satisfying about proving to both of them that Xander was equally vulnerable.

"Soon," Damon added with a grin. "Real soon."

"Or we could try something else," Xander offered slyly.

Damon felt his stomach tighten with something hot and nervy. He had a feeling he knew what Xander was suggesting, and it wasn't that he wasn't interested. He definitely was—but it felt like Xander had shot him straight to the heart with adrenaline. He was maybe a little too interested.

He'd definitely watched too much porn this week, fantasizing the whole time that the men on screen were him and Xander.

Xander placed the palm of his hand on Damon's chest, probably feeling just how fast his heart was suddenly racing. "Just to be clear," he added, "I want you to fuck me."

As if the first adrenaline shot hadn't been enough, Xander gave him another. "Yeah? Is that what you want?" Damon wasn't a young guy anymore, but he could already feel himself getting hard. Like he'd been granted his number one fantasy, and his cock was going to make sure it didn't let him down.

Glancing down, Xander smiled so smugly that he grew harder with just the look. Clearly it wasn't just *his* fantasy.

"Yeah, and it's what *you* want too," Xander pointed out. He reached down, and gave Damon's cock an experimental little stroke.

"Well, I was the one to suggest we stay in bed instead of going to dinner," Damon said. But it was impossible to pretend he wasn't dying for it. It felt like all his previous orgasm had done was take the very edge off his hunger, and afterwards, he still felt insatiable.

Xander grinned at him knowingly as he stroked a little harder, making Damon moan. "I'll be right back," he said.

He scrambled off the bed, went over to his bag on the dresser, and pulled out a tube and a whole string of condoms. Damon gave himself a very firm warning that he wasn't going to come early; he was going to make sure they both fully enjoyed this.

Giving him a very frank stare, Xander set the lube and condoms on the bedside table. "I think it's going to be easier if you let me take the lead here."

Like Damon hadn't been letting him take the lead every single time so far. But he nodded anyway, because his practical experience wasn't just lacking, it was literally nothing.

Xander settled back on the bed, but this time closer to the edge and within easy reach of the supplies. "Why don't you come over here and kiss me first?" he asked, and as Damon scooted over, he was definitely gratified to see that Xander was already half-hard too. He wanted this just as badly as Damon did.

This time, Damon didn't hold back, he leaned over and kissed Xander greedily, taking his mouth the same way he intended to take his body. When Xander reached over and began to stroke his dick again, Damon followed suit, mimicking his actions. It only took a minute or two, and they were both breathless.

"Stay right there," Xander said, his voice low and gravelly, shooting another dose of arousal through Damon's body. "Don't move."

Damon had no intention of disobeying.

Grabbing the tube, Xander wet his fingers, and rising to his knees, slipped his fingers behind himself. "Watch me," he demanded.

"Oh fuck," Damon swore, once he realized what he was doing. "Fuck, fuck, fuck."

"If I blow you," Xander asked, his voice even deeper, "are you going to come?"

Damon shook his head sharply, reins tight on his self-control as he did what Xander asked and watched him prep himself.

"Good," Xander said, groaning a bit on the end of the word. He leaned forward and there was no teasing this time, he just slid Damon's cock into his mouth. He moaned around it, and the vibrations shot right through Damon's veins, lighting him on fire. Gripping the sheets with his fists, he reminded himself that they were both going to enjoy this and he had to control himself to make sure that happened.

But it was too hard to watch and not surrender, his eyes flickering shut of their own accord. Xander must have glanced up and seen because almost immediately his warm, wet mouth was gone, and his other hand was gripping the base of Damon's cock tightly.

"Don't come," he warned. "And open your god damned eyes."

Damon did, and swore as he watched Xander moving up and down on his own fingers. "I'm almost ready," Xander said. "Are you ready?"

Damon thought he could have prepared for this for a hundred years, and he never would have been ready, but he nodded anyway.

He was definitely not ready for Xander to pull his fingers from his body and climb over him again, grabbing a condom on his way, ripping the wrapper viciously and eagerly with his teeth. He positioned Damon's cock where he was wet and ready, sliding that hand up and down a few times after he'd sheathed Damon's dick with the condom.

Like he wasn't already rock hard and eager to go, Damon thought desperately as he tried to hang onto the last shreds of his restraint.

"Don't you fucking move," Xander warned, and suddenly he was sliding down very slowly, hands braced on Damon's chest.

It was different than fucking a woman—somehow tighter and hotter—and Damon let out a long exhale as he forced himself to stay perfectly still. The last thing he wanted to do was hurt Xander, but it was tough to ignore every instinct of his body.

"Fuck," Xander moaned. "You're so god damned big."

Damon got the impression this was both a good thing and a bad thing, but he wasn't about to apologize, because he couldn't even figure out how to voice anything, let alone an apology when it felt so incredible. He could only hope that it would feel that good for Xander after he adjusted.

Finally, Xander settled his thighs on top of Damon's and froze there for a moment, his wide eyes staring right into Damon's.

"You haven't moved," Xander said, face relaxing a bit.

"You told me not to," Damon panted.

Xander's hands curled into Damon's chest, each fingernail leaving a divot. Damon couldn't complain because the pain grounded him, and helped him regain a grip on his urge to move.

"That doesn't mean you wouldn't," Xander said, and Damon couldn't help but think he was far too coherent right now. Damon was one big bundle of exposed nerves, all blind instinct and emotion, and he needed Xander to be in the exact same place.

But then he finally moved, shifting up and then sliding back down, and from the way his face crumpled, Damon realized that his coherency of even a moment ago had been one big act.

"Does that feel good?" Damon asked, remembering how much Xander had liked the talking before. It didn't come as naturally to Damon but he didn't mind making an effort. Especially not if Xander enjoyed it as much as he had.

"Fuck yes," Xander swore. "I can feel you everywhere."

"That's right," Damon encouraged him. "Take what you want, baby."

Xander moaned again, and the sound echoed right through Damon, tapping right into the source of his pleasure and magnifying it even more. He sped up and Damon bit down on his tongue, tasting the blood in his mouth as he tried to hold on, wanting Xander to enjoy this as much as he was.

"Touch me," Xander gasped. Damon didn't need any further instruction, he reached up and wrapped his hand around Xander's leaking cock, and twisted it in his grip, repeating the motion with the same rhythm Xander was using to ride him.

It only took a few more pulls of his cock, and Xander let out a strangled scream, tensing up and throbbing tightly around Damon's dick. He hadn't expected that—had never felt anything so good in his entire life—and as Xander began to paint his chest with stripes of his come, Damon couldn't hold on any longer.

❧❦

Xander woke up alone, stomach grumbling and heart wondering why the other half of the bed was empty.

They'd ordered a pizza late, devouring it like they were starving, and then had fallen back into bed, talking and giggling until late.

He couldn't quite remember falling asleep but he was pretty sure he'd had Damon wrapped around him when he had.

Getting up, he went to the bathroom, and smiled wide when he saw a note propped up on the tile vanity counter. *Went to grab coffee and breakfast,* it read, with a big *D* scrawled across the bottom. He did his business, and decided that if Damon was going to bring him breakfast in bed, he'd better do his part to make that happen. He settled back into the nest of sheets and leaned back against the headboard, feeling lighter and freer than he could ever remember feeling before. As far as he was concerned, the other shoe wasn't going to drop. As far as he was concerned, after last night, the shoe didn't even exist.

It was a really fucking amazing feeling.

It was only then that he heard the voice echoing through the townhouse, coming from down the stairs. And it wasn't Damon, because Damon didn't have a voice that feminine. Xander grabbed the sheets and pulled them up further. He didn't know where his briefs had gone last night, and he wasn't about to get rid of his cotton shield to go find them either. The voice came closer.

"Damon? Are you here?"

Whoever she was, she must have the access code, because he heard her make a confused noise and then start up the staircase.

For a split second, his heart beating wildly, Xander considered hiding. Maybe in the massive walk-in closet? No, it was totally empty, and if she even stuck her head in, she'd see him—and his bare ass—in a second.

"Damnit," Xander swore under his breath. Every option he desperately flipped through seemed worse than the last. Which was, of course, to let her come into this room and catch him here, minus Damon and with the lube on the side table and a whole string of condoms on the floor, it wasn't going to be a state secret what they'd been doing all night.

Stupidly, he flattened his hair, trying to arrange it into something that looked less like they'd been fucking all night, though he knew that ship had already sailed. He yanked up the sheet practically to his chin, and that was all he had time to do before a young woman poked her head into the master bedroom.

She saw him instantly, and he wasn't sure who went redder.

"I'm sorry," she said. It wasn't much of a consolation, but she sounded at least a fraction as humiliated as he felt. "I didn't know . . . I thought Damon was here."

Xander smiled wryly. "He was. He went to get breakfast."

"Oh." She hesitated, and he knew that was when she took in the long strip of condoms on the floor. He'd loved bringing them, and pulling them out to Damon's obvious delight. The whole night had been so perfect, and now it was crashing down around his ears. "*Oh.*"

He watched her try to regroup. She was pretty, with light brown hair curling around her shoulders, and kind eyes.

"I guess, um, I guess I'll wait downstairs for Damon."

Xander said *fuck it* and scooted out of bed, trailing bedsheet as he went. "Let me get some clothes on." He paused. "How did you even get in here?"

Burying her head in her hands, she definitely looked as embarrassed as he felt. Maybe even more. "I'm Rachel. Damon's ex-wife. His father told me he was in town for a few days, and gave me the entry code. It never . . . I never imagined that he would bring someone."

The woman's humiliation was beginning to make more and more sense. This was Damon's wife. Xander froze, and couldn't help but wonder if she had even known if he was bisexual. Xander wanted to believe she had, because Damon didn't seem like the type to keep that kind of secret from someone he loved, but then Xander kept waiting for Damon to make their relationship public, and that hadn't happened yet.

"I'm his new head chef," Xander said flatly. "I'll see you downstairs." He definitely wasn't going to drop his bedsheet in front of her now that he knew who she was.

She turned and fled. Though he'd had hope that she would just leave, the embarrassment overwhelming her, after he found his clothes and ventured downstairs, he found her in the empty kitchen, leaning over the counter.

"I'm so sorry," she said again. "I should have known Nathan wouldn't have good intentions."

"He didn't know," Xander said flatly. "Damon didn't tell him he was bringing me." His hands reached out and he gripped the edge of the marble tightly. Like maybe he could keep himself from falling apart. The last person he wanted to do that in front of was Damon's ex-wife.

"So you're the chef for Damon's new restaurant?" she asked, clearly trying to change the subject, and he might have appreciated that, but he couldn't find it in himself to appreciate anything about her. It wasn't fair and it wasn't right, and he knew absolutely fucking nothing about her, but he *hated* her.

"I am," he said shortly.

"And you're . . ." she hesitated, "you're involved with Damon."

"I am," he repeated. "We're together."

That seemed to throw her a little, but she recovered quickly enough that it was obvious she'd known that Damon was interested in both men and women.

"I'm happy he has someone," she said, surprising the hell out of Xander. He'd half-expected a jealous tantrum, but instead she looked pleased. It shouldn't have really surprised him because she had such kind eyes, but he wasn't doing his best thinking right now. She reached out with a hand. "I'm Rachel. It's really nice to meet you."

The petty, nasty part of Xander did not want to shake her hand or introduce himself. But if Damon came home and found them in a catfight in his kitchen, it wasn't exactly going to reflect well.

He shook her hand briefly. "I'm Xander Bridges."

Rachel gave him an appraising look and Xander fought not to squirm at her careful perusal. He began to wish he'd taken time to put something on other than an old pair of running shorts and a loose tank. "You're the chef who just left Terroir, aren't you?"

Damon had barely mentioned his ex, only a few times in passing, and frankly that had been a few times too many for Xander so he'd never asked about her. His confusion must have showed, because she laughed.

"I'm a restaurant consultant, here in San Francisco," she explained. "You're now the third person to leave Aquino in the last eight months. Word starts to get around."

"People leave all the time," Xander defended.

"Yeah, but not someone with your skill level, and not when he promised you *chef de cuisine*, and you left anyway. Now it makes sense. You wanted to be in charge of your own restaurant."

She paused. "*And* I suppose working for Damon seemed like a pretty good gig. He's a good guy."

It was petty and stupid jealousy, but Xander didn't want to listen to his ex-wife talk about how great Damon was. He already knew, thank you very much.

"It does make sense why he'd come to the townhouse," she continued. "He wouldn't come here at all when we were married, and when Nathan called me to say he was staying here, I was a little shocked. That's really why I stopped by. I wanted to make sure he was okay and not like . . . punishing himself somehow by coming back here."

Curiosity overcame his reservations about talking to Rachel. "He wouldn't come here *at all*?"

"I don't know what he's told you," Rachel said, her voice dropping, "but Damon has a really difficult relationship with his father."

"He's told me," Xander said dryly. "It would be tough to miss if you were paying attention. And I am."

Rachel smiled. "I really meant it, you know? I *am* glad he has someone and he's happy. We were good for a little while, but we were two kids struggling with something we didn't understand."

"His drinking?" Xander guessed.

"I wanted to help him so badly," she said with a heavy sigh, "but I didn't know what the hell I was doing. He needed an adult, a support system, and I was so young, I couldn't be what he needed. I hoped for so long that it wouldn't mean that he didn't date again." She smiled wryly. "It was selfish, but I didn't want that on my conscience."

"I do think he worries about it sometimes," Xander admitted. "Not because of you. But because he's afraid he's not worth the risk."

"And you obviously know that's bullshit."

"Obviously," Xander retorted.

"Do you mind if I wait for him?" she asked. "I haven't seen him in so long, and it would be good, to see him happy." Her smile had a bittersweet edge, and Xander realized that their marriage hadn't been a particularly happy one. Why was he jealous of it? It hit him like a lightning bolt that his jealousy wasn't about Rachel or Damon—it was his own past rearing its ugly head. He wanted so badly for Damon to admit to the people around them that they were together. If he did that, maybe Xander could finally stop worrying that it wouldn't ever happen.

"Of course not." He gave her a lopsided grin. "It's only awkward if we make it awkward, right?"

She laughed. "I knew he was bisexual, just in case you weren't sure."

"I figured you must have. You were more surprised that there was someone in his bed than the fact that it was a man. Do you think . . ." Xander hesitated. "Would you imagine he'd have trouble telling anyone?"

She shook her head emphatically. "He made zero secret of it when we were together. We'd check out hot guys together, honestly. I really wouldn't worry about it."

But her words only made him actually worry more. The niggling fear in the back of his head expanded with her confession. If he had no issue with it, and had been unapologetic about it years ago, why would he continue to hold back? Was he ashamed of Xander? Was the problem not that Xander was a man, but that Xander was *Xander*?

That didn't seem possible after last night but with the cold light of day and Rachel's admission, it was hard to trust any other explanation. But before he could question Rachel further, he heard the front door open and then close.

Xander stepped into the foyer, the soaring ceiling above them. Damon was carrying a paper bag and a coffee carrier with a few cups in it.

"You're up," Damon said, sounding disappointed. "I was hoping to surprise you."

Xander took a few steps closer, until Damon could hear him with a low murmur. "Rachel is here. In the kitchen."

Damon couldn't look more surprised than if he'd told him Bastian Aquino had just asked them for a threesome. "What?"

Xander just shrugged. "I guess your dad told her you were here."

"Shit," Damon hissed. "Was it as bad as I think it was?"

"No. I mean, *yes*, but we're both adults, and she doesn't seem too jealous."

"She wouldn't be," Damon admitted wryly. "She remarried a year and a half ago."

Xander hadn't bothered checking out her ring finger, but it made sense, considering everything Rachel had said this morning. She hadn't come here to get Damon back, or to even see if he was interested. She'd come here to do exactly what she said; to make sure he was okay.

"Do you want me to tell her to leave?" Xander asked. "You don't have to talk to her."

"Nonsense," Damon said firmly. "We're friends, sort of."

It shouldn't bother him for Damon to walk into the kitchen without a second thought, leaving Xander behind, but it sort of did. He wanted answers to all the questions swirling through his head, and he wanted to sit Damon down and force him to explain. But the truth was, Xander just wasn't brave enough to hear the truth—if it was what he suspected.

Still, he put a brave face on, and followed Damon into the kitchen. He shouldn't have flinched when he saw Damon hugging her, but he couldn't quite help it.

It wasn't jealousy exactly; it was something more like envy that he'd had zero issue standing up in front of all his friends and family and marrying Rachel. They weren't ready for that by a mile, not even close, but Xander suddenly wasn't sure that if they made it that far in their relationship that Damon would do the same with him.

And that *hurt*.

"It's so good to see you," Damon said. "You look good."

"So do you," she retorted, giving him a little smack to the shoulder. "*Happy*."

Damon flushed, like he'd been caught in some sort of secret. "I am."

"And you're starting a restaurant. You should have called me."

"I wanted to do it on my own," Damon said dryly. "And I have someone with plenty of experience." He glanced back, right at Xander, and smiled broadly. "No offense to your skills, Rach, but it'd be overkill."

"Understood. But I'd better get an invite to opening night," she insisted.

Damon glanced back again, like he was making sure it was okay with Xander. And Xander wasn't stupid; he knew his envy or jealousy or whatever the fuck it was, wasn't attractive.

He nodded, adding, "Of course."

Her face lit up. "Oh, that's so great. I can't wait."

"We're actually here to scope out equipment and furniture," Damon said, glancing down at his watch. "And we'd actually better be going. We have appointments starting in an hour."

Xander took that as his cue to leave. He reached out, took Rachel's hand, and he could say, almost without a lie, "It was really good to meet you."

She beamed, like she totally agreed, and it made his statement even less a lie. "Ditto."

Xander was in the shower when Damon came in to bathroom, leaning a hip against the vanity counter. "Thank you for not freaking out when she showed up," he said.

"It's fine," Xander said. It wasn't quite fine, but he didn't know how to tell Damon the things that were bothering him without word vomiting it all up.

"I love that you're so chill," Damon said earnestly.

Personally, Xander didn't think he was chill at all, but he was willing to agree with Damon. "It's no problem. She's nice."

"We were young and stupid when we got married," Damon said, which was basically a version of what Rachel had told him earlier. "I think she was relieved when we got a divorce. She met someone more her style and married him not long after."

"It sounds like you're both happier now," Xander offered cautiously.

"Definitely." Damon's smile made it clear that was true. If only his smile could banish all Xander's new worries.

"We have a couple of restaurant supply stores to hit," Damon said, "and then dinner tonight at Michael Mina. Is that okay?"

"It sounds great," Xander said, flipping the water off, and he realized that despite this whole debacle, he meant it.

Chapter Thirteen

It was tough to wrap his head around it, but Damon was about to open a restaurant, and after coming back to Napa, the reality of it hit hard. During their San Francisco trip, they'd ordered the restaurant equipment Xander had picked out, and had purchased the rest of the tables, chairs, and other miscellaneous furniture they'd need for the dining room.

As an extra bonus, he'd taken Xander to Michael Mina, where they'd definitely enjoyed the food, but more than that, Damon had loved the glint of determination that had emerged in his lover and head chef's eye. Xander might have felt like his rustic Italian food couldn't find a place in high-end dining, but after eating Michelin-starred Michael Mina's rustic Greek food, he'd been converted.

It could be done, and it could be done well—and Damon knew Xander was just the person to do it.

David had texted him to let him know the refinished floors were done, and that both the new addition for the kitchen and the bathrooms were now roughed in. He gave the project another few weeks, and after reading his text, Damon had sat down heavily. It wasn't hard to feel overwhelmed. Opening a restaurant involved so many decisions, and a to-do list that was frighteningly long.

Still, as the week post-San Francisco ticked by, he and Xander were able to cross off a good portion of it.

The logo was finalized and Damon ordered the signage, and tonight, Xander was cooking him the rest of the dishes he'd yet to taste. If everything was delicious as Damon knew it would be, the menu would be finalized too. Of course, it was seasonal, so the menu development wouldn't ever truly be finished, but getting that first one locked in was vital.

"I'm nervous," Xander said as Damon sat at the dining room table in Xander's rental house, watching as he wrung his hands.

"You shouldn't be," Damon reasoned.

Xander shot him a glare. Damon found it sexier than he probably should have. That was the problem since they'd started sleeping together; everything Xander did, conscious and unconscious, seemed to turn him on. He'd been celibate a long time, and he'd forgotten what it was like to be completely, head over heels attracted to someone.

He lifted his fork and tried to ignore the clanging voice in his head that told him that he wasn't just head over heels attracted—he was head over heels *in love*.

He'd felt it before they went to San Francisco, but afterwards, there was no pulling back or rescaling the cliff. Jumping off it had felt as natural as breathing, and it was undeniable, even if he wasn't even close to being ready to admit it to Xander. Though that probably had more to do with Xander than Damon's own feelings.

"You take me to Michael Mina," Xander said, starting to pace, "and then you came back and expect me to be *satisfied* with mediocrity. I can't be. I *won't* be."

"Your food isn't mediocre." Damon had discovered in the last few weeks that his boyfriend—because that fact was also undeniable even if they hadn't exactly discussed the label itself—had a secret dramatic side that only emerged when he was stressed.

Xander was absolutely, one hundred percent stressed right now. He threw his hands up and muttered. Probably something unpleasant about Damon's father in Italian. Again, probably way sexier than it should have been.

Whenever Xander got a little worked up, it was so easy to distract him by kissing him or touching him or offering a convenient method to work off his extra energy. But tonight, they *had* to finalize the menu; Damon had promised to send it to the printers in the morning. They couldn't get distracted with sex, no matter how much Damon might want to.

"It sure feels that way right now," Xander grumbled.

"Well, why don't you serve me some of it, and I'll give you my honest opinion. I promise."

Xander raised an eyebrow and shot him a very dubious look. "You promise to be honest?"

Like Damon hadn't been honest, as honest as he could be anyway, for their entire partnership and relationship. Besides, if they could make it through his ex-wife showing up while Xander was still lounging around in bed, a whole chain of condoms on the floor, they could make it through anything.

Though Rachel, after Xander had gone upstairs, had smacked him in the shoulder then given him a high five. "He's nice and really cute and a real catch," she'd murmured to him while she was hugging him goodbye. "Don't let him go."

He hadn't exactly let Rachel go, but in the end, it boiled down to that. How could he have asked her to stick around when the love between them had slowly been suffocating, strangled by Damon's demons?

Still, he agreed with her. There was no way he was ever letting Xander go, even when it still sort of felt like he was getting away with the better end of the deal.

Stressed-out drama queen episodes and all.

Damon rose up out of his chair at the dining room table and crossed toward the kitchen, stopping right in front of Xander. "You," he said, reaching out and taking his hands in his own, "are special. Talented. But even more than that, I know you can do this because you used to do this every single damn night. Bastian might have been the seed of Terroir, but by the time you came around, he was just a supervisor. You and the rest of the kitchen staff earned him his stars every year. I know you can do this because you've already done it."

Xander stared at Damon like the thought had never occurred to him.

"How many nights did you turn out his tired dishes, reinventing them without ever changing the recipe? Making sure they were flawless? And how many nights," Damon demanded, "did you stand there and wish you could make something else? Something *better*?"

Xander glanced away, like he didn't want Damon to see the look in his eyes. The truth of what Damon was forcibly revealing to him.

"Every night," he finally murmured. "I thought it every single fucking night."

"This is your time," Damon said, squeezing his hands. "This is your chance to do just that. I know you're not going to blow it because there's never been anybody less inclined to blow things."

A laugh bubbled out of Xander's throat, and Damon gave himself a mental pat on the back. He looked marginally calmer than he had a few moments ago, and he was laughing, relaxing a second at a time.

"I'd say I'm pretty inclined to blow things," Xander pointed out with an amused voice.

Damon pulled him into a quick, tight hug, then lingered because each day they grew closer, and each day, he was less inclined to let him go.

"Hold that thought," Damon said when he finally did. "Now, are you going to feed me or not?"

There was a new resolve in Xander's expression and Damon wanted to believe that he'd helped put it there—but truthfully, Xander had a stockpile of steely reserve and all Damon had done was show him where it was.

Returning to his chair, he watched as Xander cooked the halibut, gently lifting it out of the pan with a thin metal spatula, arranging it on the prepared plate just so. He walked over and placed it in front of Damon.

"Halibut with lemon and a fresh tomato gastrique," Xander said.

Damon lifted his fork. "Are you not eating?"

Xander let out a rueful laugh. "I've eaten this about ten times in the last five days. I think I'm good."

The halibut was buttery on his tongue, with just the sour, yet impossibly sweet, tang of the lemon. The burst of tomato and fresh mint finished off the bite. It was glorious, and while Damon knew his expression said it all, he couldn't help but add a single word. "Wow," he said. "Just . . . wow."

"It's simple but it's a perfect simplicity," Xander said and he sounded justifiably smug.

It should have occurred to Damon long before this. After all, he'd sought out Xander in the first place, determined to make him his partner in the restaurant and any other way he was willing to be. Still, somehow the realization took Damon entirely by surprise.

Maybe it was the stray thought that he wanted to see that smug expression of Xander's for years. For forever, if he had his way. He'd never tire of seeing the man he loved acknowledge just how brilliant and talented he was.

Because he did love him. Had started falling in love with him a long time ago, maybe even that night a year ago, and he'd simply never stopped falling. Until now, when his heart fell right at Xander's feet. And Xander just stood there, smiling away, thinking that this was all about a perfect piece of halibut, when the truth was it was so much more.

"You really like it," Xander stated, not even questioning it. Knowing it. *Believing* it.

"I love it," Damon said honestly.

"I thought you might."

Damon reached up a hand. He might not be ready yet to tell Xander—he still wasn't a hundred percent sure he was even doing the right thing, involving Xander in his life, burdening him with his problems—but he could show him.

He grasped Xander's hand in his and tugged him down, pulling him down to sit in his lap. "You really need to try this," he said.

Xander made a face, but he was also smiling and looking undeniably pleased. As well as settling right into Damon's lap like it was a throne made just for him. And as far as Damon was concerned, *it was*.

"I suppose you could tempt me with a bite," Xander said.

Loading up the perfect bite on his fork, with a little bit of everything, Damon guided it gently to Xander's lips. He chewed and swallowed, a pensive expression on his face. "It is pretty good," he admitted, the smugness melting into a boyish, bashful pleasure at the taste.

Damon fell hard again. He had a feeling he would be falling many times a day for as long as his relationship with Xander continued. Possibly even after it ended. There was a terrifyingly beautiful complexity within this man—his certainty and his honesty tempered with his sweetness and his kindness and his loyalty. The way he'd look right before he sucked Damon's cock, combined with this look right here.

"I am so glad you came into my vineyard a year ago," Damon whispered. He wasn't sure if he even wanted Xander to hear him, but he also couldn't swallow the words back anymore. They just spilled right out. "And I'm so glad I went looking for you again."

"I am too," Xander replied with a grin, laying a big smacking kiss on Damon's cheek before hopping off his lap. "I hope you're hungry because I have two more dishes I want you to try."

Damon watched him go. It was impossible not to look at him with the overly romanticized goggles of someone in love, but they still felt tempered—and maybe even tainted—with too much reality.

If the restaurant wasn't a success. If their partnership didn't work out. If he relapsed and lost his fight with sobriety.

There were so many potential pitfalls between them it was impossible to just throw everything to the wind and trust it would work out. But at the same time, he knew he'd come too far, both personally and professionally, to let Xander go now.

"Are you coming to the interviews tomorrow?" Xander asked as he threw some thinly sliced carrots into a sauté pan.

"Interviews?" Damon, lost in thought, couldn't remember what was happening tomorrow.

"Remember, I'm picking staff tomorrow," Xander said patiently. "Well, not *picking* per se, because I already know who I want to work with. It's sort of a formality but I still want you there to meet them."

"Oh, right. Yeah, I think I can make it." Damon didn't even bother to check his calendar; if Xander wanted him there, he'd make sure he was available.

"David texted me to tell me the equipment was all hooked up too," Xander said excitedly. "I'm going to have everyone cook a recipe. Maybe I'll have them try the halibut."

Damon didn't mention that he'd had a long walk through the restaurant with David just this afternoon, going over a thousand tiny details, and when David had told him the kitchen hookups were all done, he'd been the one to encourage him to tell Xander.

David had looked at him strangely, and asked if maybe Xander wouldn't want to hear it from Damon himself. Even though he'd known David forever, and he *knew* David wouldn't give two shits about Damon being involved with Xander personally, he'd still shied away from the implication. Tried to act like it was all just professional between them.

It wasn't shame or guilt or his inability to claim his own sexuality. He just didn't want Xander's life and career torpedoed by association with someone like Damon. Someone who was still a ticking time bomb.

Damon knew it was all Xander's choice. He was a grown man, with an intelligent and analytical mind, who could make his own informed decisions. But Xander had only ever seen the sober and controlled Damon; he'd never met drunk Damon. Never experienced any of drunk Damon's terrible choices.

It wasn't like Damon was going to go out and get drunk to prove a point, simply to show Xander what *could* happen if he lost control, but Damon couldn't seem to get his lingering concern to dissipate completely.

"I can't wait for tomorrow," Xander said, happily babbling away, a complete one-eighty from Damon's darker thoughts.

He dragged himself back to the present, forced himself to sit here, in this moment, with the man he loved who was cooking food they'd soon be serving to their patrons. It was a crowning achievement, and he should enjoy it.

"It's going to be great," Damon enthused. "I can't wait either." It wasn't faking it, he reasoned with himself, it was re-focusing himself into the place he needed to be. The place he *should* be.

⁂

"This is the full menu," Xander said, distributing a single sheet to each potential staff member that stood around him in a loose semicircle. "We'll be creating seasonal menus and specials based on what's fresh and in season. The majority of the vegetables will be coming straight from the garden outside the door."

Billy, the ex-Terroir line cook who had grown up in the last two years, and who Xander really wanted to be *sous*, raised a tentative hand. "Can I see the wine list?" he asked. Xander knew he had ambitions to be a chef/sommelier, and in Napa that wasn't even that unusual. But he had a feeling that Damon's no-alcohol policy might dissuade Billy from taking this job. Xander just hoped that Billy could see the other benefits of working here.

"There isn't a wine list." Xander met Billy's eyes like he held a fraction of Damon's conviction but the truth was he liked wine. He liked drinking it, he liked the taste, and he'd liked the way he used to unwind after a long day with a glass. He wouldn't go as far as to say he *missed* it, but he sort of did. But he'd known the score when he took this job with Damon, and he'd known it was non-negotiable. That hadn't stopped Xander from wondering if he should bring it up about half a dozen times. A Napa restaurant that didn't serve wine was an aberration, and while sometimes unusual things stood out, Xander was afraid Damon's policy would sink them before they could even begin changing people's minds.

"No wine list?" Billy sounded disbelieving. "The restaurant is called the Barrel House."

"It's called that because of the history of this building. Damon Hess feels the name is representative of the heritage of this land, while he's recreated it in a new image."

"You mean he tore out all those vines." Billy's voice was flat.

"Yes."

"So you won't be serving any alcohol," Susie, who he really wanted to steal from the French Laundry, piped up. "Seriously?"

Xander didn't like all these questions. He also didn't like that all these questions echoed so many of the concerns he'd had about this. He knew Damon's feelings, but maybe he should bring it up anyway. It was worth a try; Damon was a reasonable and logical person who wanted this place to be a success.

"Let's move onto the first dish," Xander said, hating that he was actively copying one of Bastian's voices—the one he used when he didn't want a single voice of dissent. He didn't like the feeling that Damon had put him in this position.

No. What he really hated was that he hadn't even considered the position existed before now. Usually Xander was thinking a dozen steps ahead, and his feelings for Damon had blinded him to reality.

But he'd also hated it when they went to Michael Mina, and the glorious wine list—one of the very best in the Bay Area—went untouched on the side of the table. He'd told himself that he didn't resent Damon for this one rule and that he didn't need booze to be happy—both of which were true, but it also turned out that he couldn't keep everything as black and white as that.

Xander knew he was beginning to slip into a gray area, and he wasn't sure there was nothing he could do about it.

Damon chose that moment to poke his head into the kitchen. Xander held back the frown. He'd told Damon to be here ten minutes ago, so he could meet everyone, but he'd been surprisingly late.

"This is Damon Hess, the owner," Xander said, introducing Damon, who only gave a brief, distracted wave while mostly looking down at his phone.

That was bullshit because this was *his* staff, too. Xander reached out a hand and possessively wrapped it right around a plaid-covered bicep. "Damon is responsible for the incredible garden you see outside. He also has real plans to make improvements. Even an orchard, at some point."

"I definitely have the land and the space," Damon responded, still distracted and now wiggling right out of Xander's grasp and walking over to stand in the corner.

It was definitely weird, and Xander couldn't figure it out.

He stood there, surrounded by the men and women he'd asked to come to the new restaurant for an interview and "audition" and Damon couldn't seem more distant or fidgety.

Had they taken things too far in San Francisco a week ago? Were they moving too fast? Was Xander alone in falling in love? He didn't know, but the thought scared the shit out of him.

Xander tried not to consider the possibility that seeing Rachel again had shaken Damon. He'd insisted he'd moved past her and that their relationship hadn't been healthy on either side, but the niggling thought remained in the back of Xander's uncooperative brain.

He went through the motions of describing how the sauce was made, and then demonstrated how to construct the plating. Terroir had been famous for its beautiful plating, and Xander had always enjoyed the intricacies of making each dish a work of art.

"Now we sauté the halibut," Xander said, and while he heated the pan, couldn't help but wish that Damon was a little more consistent. Sometimes Damon was incredibly supportive and attentive, like last night, when he'd never been sweeter, but then sometimes he was also like he was today. Distant. Removed. Cold.

Xander didn't understand how those two halves could belong to the same damn person.

"We add the butter near the end of the cooking," he continued, hands moving on autopilot, like he'd done this dozens of times, which he actually had.

He'd been so excited to share this part of the process with Damon; introducing him to the small, hand-picked kitchen team he'd assembled, and part of Xander was definitely peeved that he was acting like he wasn't involved with this at all. Damon's money was paying for these people, at least at the beginning, just like it had paid for the renovation of this building and the glass and the tables and chairs in the dining room and the high-end gas stove he was currently sautéing on.

It had even paid for this pan and the spatula in his hand.

He'd also been counting on Damon to help Xander make a strong case for why the staff should leave their current employment and take a chance on a Napa-area restaurant that didn't serve wine. Xander decided right then that he was done letting him skate by.

"When I made this dish the other night for Damon," Xander said, "he nearly fell to his knees and begged me for more." He shot a sharp look in Damon's direction, and when he looked up, he definitely looked skewered. His dark brows furrowed and he didn't look too pleased either.

"I'd like everyone to try the recipe," Xander finally said, after he lifted out the fish and deposited it on the already prepared plate. Fish last, as it was the crowning piece, and also because the halibut's cooking time was both short and incredibly precise.

He turned to Damon and placing an insistent hand on his bicep, practically dragged him out of the kitchen and into the dining room where nobody could hear them.

"What is your deal today?" he demanded.

Damon shrugged, which was even worse. "Sorry, I guess I'm just distracted. Didn't sleep well."

Xander had slept next to him, and knew he'd slept just fine, so that was just bullshit. He was about to say so when Damon continued.

"Do you think you should be so . . . friendly in front of our employees?" Damon finally asked, dropping his voice down until even Xander could barely hear him.

"Friendly?" Xander crossed his arms over his chest.

"You were practically caressing my arm when you were introducing me to them," Damon said.

Xander couldn't believe it. Actually, *scratch that*. He could. He could totally believe it because it had happened to him once before, and he had sworn to himself—an ironclad promise he'd never had any intention of breaking no matter how soulful Damon's dark eyes were or how ripped his arms or how when he looked at Xander it felt like he was seeing (and loving) his whole complete self—that it would absolutely never happen again.

And now, it was happening again. "You don't want *your* employees to know we're dating." He said it flatly, without emotion, like somehow that could contain the sudden hurricane whipping up inside him.

"No. *No*." Damon said it clearly. "I don't want . . . I guess I want to make sure we stay professional."

"Explain," Xander said. He was holding himself back from judgement—barely.

"We want to maintain high standards, we want to have a professional work environment, right? I think that starts with us. If you're going to be flirting with me, talking about me on my knees begging for you, that doesn't exactly scream professional. You worked for Bastian Aquino. I know you want something different than Terroir. Maybe Aquino wasn't alluding to his sex life, but he was a shitty boss. I want to be something better, and I want that for you too."

Xander took a deep breath, and let it out slowly. Trying to calm himself down. "So if I told everyone in there that we were dating but we're going to be keeping that part of our lives at home, you wouldn't care?"

"I told you," Damon said, patiently. "I don't care if people know if we're together. I care if it affects the Barrel House. We've both put a lot into this. Let's make it a success."

Xander wanted to believe him. He really did. He *almost* did, but not quite. There was still that voice whispering in the back of his mind that this was just like Dustin had been. Dustin had been full of excuses too, and in the beginning some of them had been good ones. Convincing enough that Xander had agreed easily to let the matter of their relationship being public slide.

And, he added, further trying to silence that voice, it wasn't like Damon wasn't willing for people to know. He just didn't want it encroaching in the workplace. He didn't want it affecting the restaurant he'd poured all his money and his dreams into. Xander couldn't blame him for that.

He nearly retorted that if Damon wanted to make the Barrel House a success, then he should hire a sommelier and have them pick a wine selection, but he held back. That wasn't this fight. This was a whole different fight.

"Okay," Xander said, cautiously. "But you should know why I'm concerned." He hesitated. He had never intended to tell Damon about his high school boyfriend, and how he'd left him. *Left* wasn't even the right term. Dustin had drifted away further and further, no matter how tightly Xander had tried to hold onto him, no matter how desperately he tried to convince Dustin to come out.

"Tell me," Damon encouraged, and that helped. It always seemed just as Xander was about to get truly fed up, Damon managed to dig himself out of the hole.

"My boyfriend in high school. He wanted all the convenience of a boyfriend. In secret. I couldn't get him to be honest about me. I just made myself a promise after going through that heartbreak that I wouldn't let it ever happen again."

"And you're afraid it's going to happen again," Damon answered.

"Maybe a little, yes."

Damon pressed a swift kiss to Xander's lips. "I'll take out an ad in the paper and tell every single person I meet. I'm not ashamed of you. I'm not ashamed you're a guy. I just want to keep it professional here."

Xander already knew he was going to make the conscious decision to trust Damon. After all, Damon had given him no reason to doubt him before this. Sure, he hadn't told his father about bringing Xander to San Francisco, but based on the comments Rachel had made, Damon didn't typically share anything with his father.

All he needed to really reassure him was to remember those few days in the city. Damon had been so attentive and wonderful. *Loving*, Xander could even say. And now this.

That was the kicker, here, Xander thought ruefully. He loved Damon, and he wanted Damon to love him back. Wanted it so much that he was even willing to believe him despite his own ugly history.

He leaned in to brush a kiss across Damon's cheek. "The rest will have to wait 'til we get home," Xander said cheekily, purposefully trying to lighten the mood. "I'd better get back in there before they destroy something."

Damon raised an eyebrow. "Is that a possibility?"

Xander laughed. It felt like the unsettled ground they'd been walking across for the last day or two had solidified. Everything was fine, they were going to be fine.

"God, I hope not," Xander confided. "Else I should have hired other people."

"Can you spare one more moment?" Damon asked, sounding so hopeful that it was hard for Xander to deny him, so he nodded his agreement. It would be good to test the new staff's focus and dedication. Damon *was* right about that; he did not want to be another Bastian Aquino, micromanaging everyone within an inch of their lives.

"Come with me," Damon hissed with a naughty grin, and grabbed his hand, dragging him off toward the nearly finished bathrooms David had just put in.

He pulled Xander inside one of them, and locked the door behind him. "What are you doing?" Xander asked, mystified.

"This," Damon said. He crowded Xander against the door and, without any warning, leaned in and kissed him hard and fast, one hand reaching up to cup his cheek and the other slid down toward his hip, gripping it tightly.

It took Xander a single moment to catch up. For someone who didn't like PDA at work, Damon was pretty amenable to sneaking off to the bathrooms to make out. But then Damon changed the angle on the kiss and it went from merely passionate to straight-up dirty, and Xander was reminded of how busy they'd been and how much he wanted another marathon night of sex.

"That," Damon said, breaking away breathless, "was an apology. I'm so sorry. I was an ass. It won't happen again. Especially now that I know how much it hurt you."

"It's okay," Xander said, curling his hands into his pants so he wouldn't reach out and run his fingers up Damon's obvious hard-on. "I know you're not an asshole."

"We good?"

This time Xander felt confident in his answer when he nodded. "We're good."

"I'd tell you good luck," Damon said, "but I know you don't need it. You've got this." He looked like he believed one hundred and ten percent in what he was saying. And someone who looked like that might finally love Xander the way he'd been waiting for.

Xander put a hand over Damon's heart, just resting it there. He was silent a long moment. Maybe he shouldn't say it. He'd known it was true for a long time, but maybe it was too soon. Maybe it would scare Damon away. But, he reasoned, Damon should know. Maybe Damon even *needed* to know. Xander thought he'd been pretty clear that he wasn't in this to fuck around, but maybe he needed to be even clearer.

"I love you, you know," he said, and he got the words out with only a tiny waver of uncertainty. And nobody could blame him for that.

"I know," Damon said, a smile breaking over his face like a particularly spectacular sunrise. "I love you too."

Xander grinned back giddily, his heart beating madly in his chest, matching Damon's beat for beat. "I should get back."

"You should," Damon said. But he didn't move either.

"It seems like neither of us is pretty good at this profession-al-at-work thing," Damon added after a long moment. He was still smiling.

"It's okay, I forgive you," Xander said with another brief kiss to Damon's cheek. "I'll see you tonight." He reached around, unlocked the door and slipped out, feeling like a new man as he headed back into the kitchen.

Damon *did* love him, he hadn't been imagining that. And someone who loved him the way Damon seemed to wouldn't fuck this up, Xander reasoned. He just wouldn't.

Chapter Fourteen

"I heard a crazy rumor today," Kian said, walking into the kitchen. Xander almost did a double take, but then remembered that today was Kian's one day off every two weeks.

"That you didn't actually have to work?" Xander asked, not looking up from the focaccia dough he was kneading.

"It's actually a two-parter," Kian said, pulling out the orange juice carton from the fridge and a glass from the cupboard. "One, you've decided to become a baker. Two, you're not serving booze at your new place."

Xander punched the rising dough down a bit harder than he probably needed to. "It's not a rumor," he said.

It was Kian's turn for the double take. In fact, Xander was pretty certain he almost spit his juice out. "Billy was actually telling the truth?"

"He was." Xander punched the dough down again as he remembered Billy's email response to the job offer he'd sent. It had been polite enough, but there'd been a whiff of incredulity between the lines, like he couldn't believe Xander was going along with this. Still, he'd agreed to take the position—but only if Xander was able to talk Damon into serving a limited wine menu. Billy even volunteered to help create the list himself.

"I know you care about him," Kian said, "but that doesn't mean you have to go along with every crazy scheme he comes up with."

Xander knew Kian wasn't talking about Billy.

"That's rich, coming from you," he nearly sneered.

"I think it's worth at least having the conversation. I know Hess has money but you want to be at least commercially viable, you know? How long can his trust hold out if he's paying to keep you afloat?"

Xander knew. He kneaded the dough instead of answering, each turn and punch down more vicious than the last. He was never going to be able to bake this—the waste of flour and oil and yeast serving Xander's frustration instead of his stomach—but it felt good to use to hands.

"Being involved should make it easier to talk," Kian continued.

"Supposedly, yet I don't see you doing it," he pointed out darkly.

Kian crossed his arms over his chest, his juice long forgotten. "I don't see why you keep dragging me into this. We're talking about you and Hess. Or *I'm* trying, at any rate."

"There's nothing to talk about. Damon has a . . . difficult history with alcohol. He doesn't want it around. He doesn't want to serve it."

Kian's face did soften a little. He reached out and put a hand on Xander's shoulder, and he slumped at the touch. "You still need to talk to him. This is your life, too."

"I had two ideas," Xander said after a long silence. "I thought about making a menu of non-alcoholic cocktails to divide the focus from alcohol."

"That's good. And what's the second?"

"Donate profits from any alcoholic sales to a substance abuse charity." Xander stared at the dough. He'd been awake most of the night thinking about the quandary, and he, just like Kian, had known he needed to talk to Damon about it. It was at least worth a conversation.

"So you *are* going to talk to him," Kian said.

"It's the only logical thing to do." Xander had just been trying to come up with something else to do instead, and had come up with exactly nothing.

"He coming over tonight?" Kian asked, and Xander nodded.

"I'll make myself scarce then." Kian put an arm around his shoulders and pulled him into a quick hug. "You're doing the right thing."

After Kian disappeared, Xander dumped his overworked focaccia dough in the trash and after cleaning out the bowl, started re-assembling a new batch with fresh ingredients.

The truth was Xander didn't know if bringing it up with Damon *was* the right thing. Why did they have to serve booze anyway? People could get booze anywhere. Why did they have to get a drink with their dinner at the Barrel House?

Logically, Xander knew they didn't. But people were creatures of habit and expectation, and at higher-end restaurants in the Napa Valley, there was always wine.

Maybe someday they could flout the trend, and do whatever the fuck they wanted, but you had to establish yourself before you broke the rules. Especially when you were expecting customers to help pay for your continued existence.

He spent the rest of the afternoon lost in the familiar and reassuring rhythm of baking. Even though preview night was in two days and the opening was the day after that, none of this would keep. At least it wouldn't be as fresh as Xander demanded it be.

Xander collapsed on his bed after a quick shower, hair dripping onto his bare chest. He shouldn't feel so worried about this conversation. He and Damon loved each other, and Kian was right; this was exactly the sort of thing they should be able to talk about with that level of emotional commitment. But Damon had always shied away from discussing his alcoholism, like somehow it tainted him and therefore Xander by comparison. Instead he locked it away, behind walls that he hadn't let Xander see behind yet.

"Now, that's a sight I could get used to."

He glanced up and saw Damon in the doorway, smirk on his face. Seeing Damon and knowing they loved each other was still a rush that Xander wasn't quite used to. He grabbed the towel around his waist and started to stand up, but Damon took the few steps to the bed and put a hand on his shoulder, holding him in place.

"Stay," Damon said quietly. His dark eyes were intent on Xander, filled with longing and lust and need and desperation and a thousand different shades in between.

Xander raised an eyebrow, questioning Damon's request, and was rewarded with another flash of bone-melting desire in his lover's gaze. For some reason, Damon adored it when Xander challenged him in bed; it was guaranteed to stoke Damon's blood so much hotter and this time wasn't an exception.

"Brat," Damon said, affection and hunger layered equally together in his voice as he lowered himself to his knees in front of Xander. He licked his lips in anticipation and that alone would have turned Xander's knees to jelly even if he wasn't already sitting down.

Damon peeled back the towel, not in any huge hurry, which definitely meant that he was going to tease and take his time.

"Suck my cock," Xander said, surprising even himself at how breathy his voice was. "I know you want to."

Laying a reverent hand on Xander's bare thigh, Damon leaned in, breath warm on his skin.

"Fucking tease," Xander swore impatiently as Damon's tongue reached out and licked right up the underside of his cock.

"You love it." Damon's voice was rough and wild, and his hands clamped around his thighs, dragging them open wider.

For someone with zero practical experience when they'd started dating, Damon had taken to blowjobs like a fish discovering how to swim for the first time. He was gentle yet demanding, both of Xander and of himself. Like he desperately wanted to prove to both of them that he wanted it—that he wanted *Xander*.

"You love this too," Damon said, one of his hands sliding higher, cupping around his quivering thigh, curling downward, brushing his balls and then lower. He gave Xander's hole a brief touch, then another. His fingers were damp, maybe even wet, though Xander couldn't remember seeing any lube when Damon came in.

Maybe he was a magician. Frankly, with the way his fingers and his mouth were teasing him, quick little tantalizing touches that seemed to drive him higher and higher until he was mindless with how much he wanted Damon's cock inside him, that made sense. Because nobody had ever made him feel this way before—out of control and yet completely grounded with how much Xander trusted him.

It took too long for Damon to even slide a whole finger inside him, and like he sensed Xander's desperation, he didn't make him wait nearly as long for the second. By then, the towel was gone, Damon's shirt was off, his biceps bunching and flexing as he slowly fucked Xander thoroughly with his fingers. The first time they'd done this, Damon had been more hesitant, but now he knew Xander, and he knew what he liked.

"Good?" Damon asked, voice nearly a growl as he practically slid Xander across the bed with his thrusts. "You want more?"

Xander knew he said words. He knew they were probably something pleading, but he wasn't entirely sure of what he was saying. Sweat dripped into his hair, into his eyes as he held onto the edge of the mattress, moaning as Damon finally began to slide his cock inside him.

"Tell me how it feels," Damon insisted, a hand smoothing down Xander's back, burying itself in his hair. He wasn't rough though. Every touch felt touched with love, with adoration. "Tell me," he repeated when Xander uttered some sort of complete gibberish.

"Big. Full. Close," Xander gasped. "So close."

Damon draped his big body over Xander's and began to work his hips in and out, in the same driving insistent rhythm he'd fucked him with his fingers. "Yeah, I'm close. I'm in you, and you're in me," he murmured into Xander's damp hair. "God, I love you."

"So much," Xander managed to say as he wrapped a hand around his own cock, getting in one long stroke before his orgasm roared through him. Damon gave one last deep thrust before throwing back his head and groaning in pleasure.

They slumped to the bed together, the sheets and blankets shoved to one side. "I like being able to reduce you to single-syllable words," Damon finally said drowsily, stroking up and down Xander's back. "Makes me feel like I'm giving you exactly what you need. Not just what you want."

Xander sighed, the buzz of pleasurable contentment warring with his anxiousness of earlier. The sex had helped take him out of his head a bit, but the residual worry hadn't dissipated. He knew they still needed to talk.

After Damon slipped out and grabbed a cloth, cleaning them both off, he came back to bed, resuming his earlier position, a gentle hand on Xander's back. It was easier, Xander discovered, to ask if he wasn't looking at him. So he gathered his courage and leapt.

"I want you to talk to me about everything," Xander said quietly. "I love you, and sometimes I think you want to save me from the bad stuff. The stuff you've been through. I want to know. I want to help you bear it."

The hand stroking his back hesitated for a split second, then continued its lulling rhythm. "I don't tell you because it's ugly. And you don't need that ugliness touching you," Damon said. Xander didn't miss the undercurrent of iron beneath his words. He didn't want to share, and somehow Xander was going to have to convince him.

"It's not ugly. It can't be when it's *you*. All it does is prove to me how brave and strong you are," Xander argued. At first it had seemed easier not to look in Damon's eyes when he asked these questions, but now it suddenly seemed impossible to say any of this if he *wasn't*. He turned over and immediately saw the doubt clouding Damon's expression. "I love you. No matter what."

Damon rolled to his back and sighed heavily. "People are telling you that you're stupid for hitching yourself to a guy who won't even serve alcohol at his restaurant, right?"

It was not fun getting caught, but Xander reached out anyway, grasping his upper arm, then sliding his hand toward where his heart beat steadily in his chest. "It's not stupid. But I still want to talk about it."

"It was inevitable." Damon sounded close to tears, like he'd been dreading this moment for their whole relationship and now it was finally happening.

Xander reached up and cupped his cheek, tilting his head down so Damon could see his face. "We can't pretend like it doesn't exist. I wish we could, too, but that's not real life. I want this love to be real, and to be real, it has to exist in the real world."

This time Damon didn't look away and Xander recognized the look brewing in his eyes as resolve.

"I don't remember when I started drinking," Damon said quietly. "I . . . I always did. Always. I remember holidays, Christmas or Thanksgiving or probably even the Fourth of fucking July, my dad leaning over and letting me sip from his glass. Usually it was wine. Sometimes it was a beer. Occasionally a glass of whiskey or a gin and tonic. I got used to it, I liked it. I liked the way it made me feel when I got older, and it felt so *normal*, like it was something I'd been around forever, like it was a part of the family."

He took a deep breath, pausing, and Xander laid a hand on his bicep, squeezing gently. "It was a part of your family because of who your family is," he replied gently.

"I know alcohol isn't evil. I know some people, *lots* of people enjoy it and it doesn't ruin their lives. They don't start using it because it's a better parent than their father or because their mom is never around. I know that. Logically, I do get it." Damon's fists flexed once, then again. "But sometimes, some things aren't logical."

Xander didn't know what to say, other than a desperate need to apologize. For the shitty childhood Damon had experienced? Because occasionally Xander wanted to enjoy a glass of wine? Because he wanted to serve alcohol at the Barrel House?

Because while Xander now understood Damon's relationship with alcohol better, he still selfishly wanted to serve it.

"It's the point of the thing," Damon admitted. "It's not that I don't see a lot of value in any argument you might make, but when I ripped those vines up, I knew exactly what I was doing, exactly what I was throwing away, exactly what those vines were worth—I was doing it because I was done with alcohol completely. I was sober, had been sober for years, but it still haunted me."

Xander looked at the man he loved frankly. "Do you really believe that ripping up those vines meant you aren't ever going to want a drink again?"

Looking away, Damon shook his head slightly.

"I'm not the person who has to tell you what to believe, and what to discard. I'm not you, and I can't make decisions about what's important and what has meaning. But the physical manifestation is gone; it's still here, inside you, and it's going to be there until the day you die." Xander pressed his palm to Damon's chest, right where his heart beat. "Even if you never take another drink, it's going to be part of you. I can accept that—I want to accept all of you—but can you?"

Damon turned further away, and Xander's heart ached. Maybe he shouldn't have been so honest; but he couldn't be in this relationship and be any other way. He'd always prized truth and he couldn't become another person for Damon. No matter how much it fucking hurt.

"I don't know," Damon mumbled, turning his face into his arm. Xander thought if he lifted it away he might find damp skin. "I don't think I know anything."

"You know lots of things. You've conquered your demons. But locking them away doesn't mean they *go* away." He slid off the bed and went around to the other side, crouching by where Damon's face lay against his arm. And as he'd imagined,

Damon's eyes were red and wet. "Let me ask you something. If we serve wine, let's say, at the Barrel House, are you going to want to have a drink any more than you normally want one?"

Damon shook his head emphatically.

"If you ever feel that's true," Xander said with quiet determination, "then this isn't a conversation. It's a decision, solid and final. But I don't think you're really tempted anymore."

"I hate it. I'm envious of it. I'm jealous as hell of anyone who can just have one glass of wine with dinner and call it good," Damon finally admitted.

"The final decision is yours," Xander said. "I'll respect whatever you decide. It's your restaurant, it's your land, it was even your idea. And it's your disease. I'm willing to do whatever you want. Would I like to serve wine at the restaurant? Yes, because sometimes I like to have a glass of wine with dinner, and I know other people do too—especially people who come to Napa. But I'll abide by your decision and we don't ever have to talk about it again."

Xander kept his word. He let Damon have some time alone in his room as he showered again, and when he was done, he went into the living room and flipped on the TV.

Damon heard him calling for Chinese, putting in an order for sweet and sour pork and Damon's regular order, Kung Pao chicken, and some fried rice and potstickers. He heard the delivery guy at the door, and heard the door shut again, even smelt the spicy aroma of dinner in the air, but he didn't come out of the bedroom.

He considered leaving and going back to his lonely house. It had always been lonely, since his grandfather had died and left it to him and he'd moved back to Napa, but ever since he'd met Xander, being alone there had grown claws. Now, he found it nearly unbearable.

Sometimes he wondered if he'd decided on building a restaurant because that meant he'd always be surrounded by lots of people on his land.

Maybe that was what this was really about; not the booze at all.

No, Damon thought grimly, it was really always about the booze. He was a Hess, living in Napa; that much was inescapable. He'd left here briefly but he still came back home. He belonged here, whether he wanted to be here or not, whether he resented that fact or not.

Xander was a great believer in the truth, and Damon knew, as he dragged himself upright and wiped his eyes, that he meant everything he'd just said. But that didn't mean he didn't mean what he *hadn't* said—and what Xander hadn't said was that he didn't think the restaurant could be a success without serving wine.

What it boiled down to was that he didn't think the restaurant could be successful with Damon involved. Because Damon and wine did not mix, no matter how Xander tried to justify his opinion. An alcoholic shouldn't be around alcohol, that much seemed pretty obvious, at least to Damon.

Rachel was happening again. Exactly what had prevented Damon from even dreaming about love was happening again.

Damon gingerly leveraged himself up and walked to the bathroom, shutting the door with a quiet click and staring at himself in the mirror. Red eyes, tight mouth, hopeless expression. He recognized the man in the mirror a little too well.

As devastating as the divorce had been, Damon knew he loved Xander more completely and more fully—more *maturely*—than he'd ever loved Rachel. They'd been kids; he was a man now and so was Xander. Losing him was going to destroy Damon all over again, except it was going to be much worse this time around, because Damon wasn't going to be able to run away to lick his wounds.

Xander was going to be right there, right in front of him, every day, and it was going to hurt like hell. It was a good thing, then, Damon thought darkly, that he wasn't a stranger to pain.

He dressed and went into the living room. Xander had an old episode of *Kitchen Wars* on, Landon Patton and Quentin Maxwell bantering over a lazy Susan contraption, berries flying everywhere, and every molecule in Damon's body ached at the normalcy he was never going to be able to have.

Xander flipped the sound off, and looked up at Damon, concern written all over his face. "Are you okay?" he asked. "I . . . I . . . maybe I shouldn't have made you talk about it."

"No. No, I'm glad you did." He took a deep breath. "You're right. What you said is right. We should serve wine."

"You think we should serve wine?" Xander asked cautiously.

"No, I really don't. But what I want doesn't really matter. It hasn't mattered in a long time. Ever, probably." Damon sighed. "Eat your dinner. You have training tomorrow and you need your strength. I'm going home."

Xander raised his eyebrow and it didn't do anything for Damon. Nothing like what it normally did. He felt beaten and numb instead. Like he'd fought his battles all over again, but this time he'd lost.

He loved Xander. He was talented and smart and bright and deserved a restaurant that would showcase him to his best advantage; a jewel in the proper setting. Damon knew, with his issues and his darkness, that he couldn't really be a part of that. Not really. Xander would figure it out sooner or later, the same way Damon just had.

Xander belonged to the shiny, bright world of people who could have a glass of wine with dinner or a beer on a warm afternoon and it didn't mean anything. People who didn't have a difficult and complex reaction to a drink menu on a patio table. Damon had known this from the very beginning, he'd understood it was fundamentally true almost from the first moment, but he'd tried to push the inevitability aside, and then he'd straight-up begun living in a fantasy world where it didn't exist at all.

Earlier tonight, Xander said he wanted a real love. This was a real love, in a real world.

He got up and put his arms around Damon, pressing a kiss to his cheek. "I'll talk to you tomorrow, okay?"

Not talking wasn't going to happen. Breaking up wasn't going to happen. Not with the restaurant opening on the horizon, only a few days away. The best Damon could do was to pull gradually away until Xander realized the same thing he just had. They were better off as friends and business partners.

"Yeah, of course," Damon said, ignoring the lump in his throat.

"Night. I love you." Xander pressed another kiss in, deeper, firmer this time. Like he could permanently brand his lips there. Damon wanted to tell him that it didn't matter, he was going to feel his mouth against his skin forever—there was no erasing it now.

"I love you too," Damon said, and meant it just as much, if not more, tonight, than he ever had.

Xander just didn't realize that those three little words also meant goodbye.

The second the door closed behind Damon and he heard his car start up in the driveway, Xander dialed his phone in a blind panic.

"Wyatt," he said desperately, "I think I just really fucked things up."

"What did you do?" Wyatt asked. "Did you over-whip the marshmallows again?"

"Have you been talking to Miles again?" Xander demanded.

"Of course I talk to Miles. We live in the same freaking city," Wyatt drawled. "Stop changing the subject. What's got you sounding so panicked?"

"I told Damon we should serve wine at the Barrel House."

Wyatt was silent for a long moment. "Didn't you tell me last month that he was a recovering alcoholic?"

"Yes," Xander said miserably. "He is."

Xander didn't know what he'd been thinking—actually, scratch that, he knew *exactly* what he'd been thinking. He'd been thinking with his ego, hyper-aware of what people were saying about him, worried that nobody would give the restaurant a chance because of the lack of booze.

He'd let his fear get in the way of . . . Xander hesitated, unsure how much he'd really fucked up, then realized he'd let his fear jeopardize *everything*. The restaurant. His relationship with Damon. His future and Damon's future, seemingly so bright only a few days ago, suddenly dimmed because he'd been dumb enough to listen to Billy and Kian. And his own fucking ego.

"Listen, opening a restaurant is a crazy thing to do. It's absolute insanity before it happens. People say stuff all the time when they're stressed. Chalk it up to that and move on."

The last time they'd talked, Xander had given Wyatt a very vague idea that he and Damon were just sort of screwing around, nothing serious. Why had he done that, when Wyatt was going to find out the very first time he saw him and Damon together? Especially when that particular event was going to be happening shortly with the restaurant opening?

Plain and simple, Xander hadn't wanted to be the new Kian. Involved with his boss and his partner, potentially screwing up his own future.

The worst part of this whole thing was that he hadn't even needed Wyatt or Miles to warn him. He'd done it all on his own, with zero help from anyone else.

"I don't think he's going to move on that easily," Xander admitted.

"Why not?" Wyatt sounded distracted and he suddenly heard the roar of a crowd in the background. Flipping to ESPN, Xander sat down heavily and watched as Wyatt's boyfriend Ryan hit a solid stand-up double in front of a packed Dodger Stadium.

"You're at Ryan's game, aren't you?" Xander asked flatly.

"Yes, but as I'm discovering, the baseball season is 162 games long. I think I can talk to you for five minutes to keep you off the cliff *and* be a supportive partner.

"You really care about him, don't you?" Wyatt persisted when Xander didn't respond.

Xander was quiet still, but Wyatt could be damn stubborn when he wanted to be and he wasn't letting him off the hook now.

"I love him, okay?" Xander finally said, voice cracking. "I really love him, and I fucked it all up."

"You're going to apologize, and he's going to forgive you. It's gonna be fine." Wyatt's voice was almost drowned out by more crowd noise. "I'm sorry, I really do have to go now. But I'm coming up tomorrow, and I'm bringing Miles with me."

Xander almost told Wyatt not to bring Miles, because somehow it was worse that Miles was going to be front and center to him totally screwing up his life. Wyatt was chill; Wyatt also always understood. Miles was a little pricklier.

But he didn't, because in the process of epically fucking up, he'd realized just how much he needed his friends here. Even Kian, who he kept trying to be pissed at. Maybe if Kian hadn't brought up the rumors and his concerns hadn't so closely echoed Xander's own. That was bullshit though, and Xander knew it. It wasn't Kian's fault he'd selfishly mouthed off, suggesting that his recovering boyfriend serve booze at their restaurant. That was all on Xander, and he wasn't being pessimistic when he knew he'd be paying for it.

Chapter Fifteen

Xander woke up to a text message from Miles the next morning, demonstrating very clearly that yes, he and Wyatt definitely talked. **Apologize**, was all it said, and Xander wished it was just that easy.

There was nothing on his phone from Damon, which was unusual even with how busy they'd gotten with the preview night tomorrow and the real opening the day after that. Damon still got up early to tend the gardens, though he'd been talking about hiring some gardeners to help him out, and he liked to send something Xander would wake up to.

Sometimes it was silly like, **you know, you were drooling all over my chest last night while you were sleeping** or sometimes a picture of the sunrise. Lately he'd been sending simple, **I love you**s.

It was difficult to not read something into the fact that Damon not only hadn't sent that particular message, but that he hadn't sent anything at all.

His heart was aching and his stomach was in his shoes, but Xander was still a god damned professional, and he dragged himself into his chef whites, pulling back his hair with one of his favorite chili pepper bandanas and drove to Damon's.

He didn't even bother detouring toward the house. Instead, he met with one of his food distributors, set up a delivery schedule, and received orders from his other distributors. After everything was meticulously labeled and put away, his new employees started showing up.

Billy shot him a little smirk, and Xander gave him a cold stare, daring him to ask if he'd brought the wine issue up with Damon. But Billy must have been smarter than he assumed, because he didn't say a word. Maybe the fight was written all over his face. Xander didn't know, and he wasn't sure he *wanted* to.

The morning was devoted to organizing the kitchen, putting all the tools and equipment away and establishing the processes by which Xander expected every single member of his team to do their jobs. This might not be Terroir, but he'd learned there that organization was next to cleanliness and godliness.

Noon rolled around without Damon showing up at the restaurant, and Xander let everyone take a break. He ran down to the corner store and grabbed two sandwiches and some bottled water, walking into the back door of Damon's house without even a knock.

Xander set the food on the counter, the quietness of the house unsettling him. He wasn't even sure Damon was here, and after a thorough check of the rooms, realized that he'd been right. Damon wasn't even around today, the first full day of training and only a day before the preview night.

The Barrel House was ready: the dining room stood pristine, the furniture arranged, the plates stacked in the kitchen waiting to be filled, the massive refrigerators already beginning to fill up. The crates of vegetables from the garden had been sitting on one of the stainless steel counters this morning, like Damon had left them early and then departed, not even bothering to wait for Xander.

The concern that a simple apology might not be enough began to swell inside of him. He pulled his phone out and sat down heavily at one of the barstools, staring at the screen. But instead of dialing Damon's number, he called Miles.

"When are you guys going to be here?" he asked before Miles could even ask if he'd apologized.

He would have—he *wanted* to—but Damon wasn't here to apologize to. And Xander couldn't help the bad feeling lingering that Damon had arranged it that way on purpose.

"Soon," Miles promised. "We're about two hours away." He paused, and Xander gave him full brownie points for waiting more than twenty seconds before asking. "Did you apologize?"

"I haven't been able to," Xander said. "I wanted to. I came to his house, with lunch as a peace offering, and he's not even here."

It was obvious from the whispered consultation that Wyatt and Miles were having in the car that neither of them believed this boded well for Xander. The knowledge he'd really, truly, *epically* fucked this up, continued to gnaw at him.

"Did you call him?" Miles asked.

"Yeah," Wyatt chimed in, Miles clearly having put him on speakerphone, "you should call him. It's only two days until opening. He's probably running a thousand errands."

Except Xander had seen Damon's ever-evolving to-do list for the opening, and he'd whittled it down to just a few items. They'd worked it together, crossing off item after item, and that had helped make it a lot more doable. Not for the first time, Xander regretted forgetting, even for a split second, that they were always better together, working as a united front.

"Okay, I'll call him," Xander said, and not really because Miles and Wyatt thought he should. He knew he should.

"Okay, we'll see you tonight," Miles said, and Wyatt chimed in, adding his goodbye.

Xander hung up and stared at the screen, working up the courage to dial Damon's number. It probably should have been tougher, but then Xander imagined life without him, a life where they were professional partners and nothing else, and his fingers flew across the screen.

Damon answered on the final ring. "Hey," he said, sounding distracted. "Everything okay?"

"I'm in your house, eating a sandwich, and you're not here." Xander wasn't going to buy that faux casual tone of his. Everything wasn't okay, and no matter what Damon pretended, he couldn't believe otherwise.

"I had stuff to do today," Damon said. "Besides, I thought you'd have your hands full with training. How's it going?"

"I do, and it's going well. But I wanted to talk to you."

It must have been clear from Xander's voice what he wanted to talk about because Damon went silent.

"I didn't want to do it over the phone, but you're not here." He knew he was supposed to be apologizing, but frustration still leaked into his tone.

"If this is about the conversation from last night, we've both said enough, don't you think?" Damon asked snidely, and it cut Xander to the bone.

"No . . . yes . . . I mean, I wanted to apologize."

Damon sighed heavily on the other line, and Xander felt his unease begin to ratchet into a full-blown panic.

"You were being honest, why would you need to apologize?"

Xander didn't miss that Damon had answered all his questions with questions of his own.

He gritted his teeth. He'd fucked up; he'd not imagined that apologizing and forcing Damon to hear it and accept it would be easy, but this was turning out to be far trickier. "I was insensitive and tone-deaf. It's your restaurant, and you told me straight off how you were planning to run it. It's not fair that I come tromping in at the last moment and demand you change your mind."

"You were right; if I want to be commercially viable, I'm going to have to make some changes."

Xander didn't want Damon to accept what he'd said as legitimate. He didn't want him to be quietly, mildly agreeing to his argument; he wanted him to be pissed as hell. As pissed as Xander was at himself.

"You shouldn't make any changes, not because of what I said," Xander argued.

"But you just made the case last night," Damon said, and he sounded perplexed. "It was a good argument."

"It was not," Xander retorted. "It was insensitive and insecure and cruel. Not to mention quite a bit selfish. I love you. We are going to make this work no matter what we serve. That much I'm confident about."

"Okay," Damon said, but it was absolutely clear that he wasn't agreeing with anything. Xander's fingers tightened over his phone, and even though he might be grumpy and tactless sometimes, he didn't generally have a temper. It was flaring now, and he was struck with a sudden inexplicable desire to demand Damon's location, storm over to where he was, and express his feelings. Strongly.

The worst part was that he knew he was still attempting to apologize.

"I don't think you get it," Xander said, barely hanging onto the reins of his anger, "I fucked up. Badly. I said a lot of shit that I shouldn't have, and you going and accepting it is not good. It's not okay. It's not what I want, at all."

"It's what you asked for, Xander," Damon said quietly. "I've got to go. I'll see you later."

Later, Xander realized after, he'd said *later*. Not tonight, not tomorrow, not the day after. Not in the kitchen during the preview or during their triumphant opening. Non-specific, so

Xander wouldn't know if he could depend on him, or wouldn't know for sure if he turned around one day if he'd see his quiet, steady smile.

The phone left his hand before he could even help himself. It shattered into about a hundred pieces against Damon's hardwood floors—reclaimed wood, Damon had told him once—and at the time all Xander had wanted was to reclaim *him*. He still wanted that, he'd have to be dead not to want it, but right now, all he wanted was to burst into tears and imagine that after his crying jag ended, everything was going to be okay.

But he couldn't help but wonder that nothing was going to be okay again.

"You broke your phone," Wyatt said, edge of his mouth quirking up, like he was really trying to tamp down a smile. It wasn't funny, but maybe in a thousand years, after this restaurant opened successfully, and Damon had forgiven him, Xander thought he might find it amusing too.

But right now, he wanted to punch Wyatt in his perfect face.

"I broke my phone," Xander muttered back.

"I'm guessing that apology didn't go so well," Miles said gently.

Miles never did anything gently, especially when it came to Xander, and that was another blow to his aching heart and his rapidly fading belief that this might all fix itself.

"He wasn't even mad!" Xander yelled. It was pretty ironic that the only one mad here was him, when Damon deserved to be really pissed over what he'd said.

That was the worst realization of all; Damon wasn't angry because he believed what Xander had said was the truth. Had probably worried about it for awhile, had carried that concern in the back of his head, and then Xander had gone and given it to him on a silver platter.

Xander resumed pacing back and forth in the living room, ignoring that Miles and Wyatt were exchanging looks of concern.

"Did he say he'd be back for tomorrow?" Wyatt asked. Tomorrow was the preview, and while everything was set, it was something that Damon should be there for. *Deserved* to be there for. This was his restaurant and had been his dream long before Xander was even involved.

"No," Xander muttered, stopping in front of the sofa and collapsing on it, the old springs squeaking. "No, he was deliberately vague."

Xander ignored more concerned looks. He didn't need them to be worried; he was worried enough for all of them, a constant gnawing at the base of his stomach.

He stared at his hands as the silence dragged out. Wyatt and Miles didn't even know what to say, because what *was* there to say? They'd both miraculously ended up with healthy and happy relationships, but of course, that wasn't in the cards for Xander. Of course he was going to fuck it up. That was inevitable. He should have held onto that bone-deep pessimism he'd cultivated for so long, but instead he'd let it get swept away by Damon's magnetism and the mind-blowing happiness Xander felt whenever he was around.

A wine glass was set down on the coffee table in front of him with a click. Xander glanced up and saw Miles standing there, a glass of his own, filled with ruby red liquid, in his hand.

"Really?" Xander demanded. "You really think this is the best time to have a drink?"

Miles shrugged. "Have you had a drink since you met him?"

Xander remembered one; the night he'd been wild to kiss Damon, and had come home and had kissed Nate instead, believing that he could convince his mind and his heart and his body that anyone would do.

"See, that's not really healthy either," Miles said firmly. "You can't stop being who you are for him. I know you probably could have been more diplomatic with what you said the other night, that much I will agree with completely, because subtlety has never been your strong suit, but you had a point."

Reaching out, Xander picked up the glass. Stared at it. It was a beautiful color, clearly one of Nate's better bottles that Miles had just stolen.

"Booze isn't a crutch for you," Wyatt agreed quietly. "You need to be able to enjoy a glass if you want to. You can't change for him, and he can't change for you. Yeah, you might be better and stronger together than you are apart, but you still need to be yourselves."

Xander took a sip. He had been a little carried away by Damon's dream and his ambition and his entire self; it had been hard not to since so much of those things were reflected in Xander himself. But he had resented a little his self-imposed sobriety. He'd never asked, but then Damon had never clarified either, and back then, when they were still figuring their relationship out, Xander hadn't wanted to give him any reason to walk away.

The wine was rich and dark on his tongue. This was definitely one of Nate's better bottles. "This is good," he said. "Nate is going to kill you."

Miles waved a hand, clearly unconcerned. "That guy is weak. I could take him in my sleep."

Wyatt chuckled, almost definitely amused because at one time, a very long time ago, Nate had been his boyfriend.

"This is what we're going to do," Miles said, and he suddenly sounded like he *could* take Nate, or just about anyone else for that matter. "We're going to go get you a new phone. We're going to get some more wine. We're going to go over tomorrow's arrangements. And the preview *will* kick ass, I promise."

It was impossible not to voice the secret, dreaded fear that was lodged in the base of his throat and in his stomach, and weighing down all his limbs. "What if he doesn't show?"

"Then he's a fucking idiot," Wyatt said, reaching over to give Xander a reassuring shoulder squeeze. "I know it's not the same, but we're going to be there, and we're going to get through this. I promise."

Xander didn't sleep.

Lying awake, it was impossible not to notice that the cotton of the sheets still smelled like Damon. It had only been a few days, but it felt like an eternity.

His new phone sat on the nightstand charging, its silence damning Xander to another sleepless night, taunting him endlessly. Finally, he picked it up and stared at it. Found the number he'd dug up this afternoon when Miles and Wyatt had left him alone for five minutes and he'd realized that Damon wasn't going to answer or reply to any of his voicemails or texts.

It was late—after midnight—but Xander hoped she would forgive him for calling, but he didn't know where else to turn and he just couldn't take it anymore. The phone rang twice, then three times, and just when he thought she wasn't going to pick up, a breathless female voice answered.

"Who is this?" she asked, sounding annoyed.

"It's Xander. Xander Bridges. We met once . . ." He trailed off. Suddenly what had seemed like such a good idea, felt like a terrible mistake. He shouldn't be calling Rachel. She wasn't involved with Damon anymore. She didn't know him anymore; that was why people got divorced, right? They'd lost sight of who the other person in the marriage was.

"We did," Rachel confirmed, her tone hushed, but no longer angry. "Is everything okay?"

Xander's throat constricted. He pushed the tears back. "No."

She was quiet for a long moment.

"I wouldn't call you," he finally said, "I wouldn't do it unless I knew what else to do."

She laughed, a little wry and a little wet around the edges. Like she was crying too. "He's not an easy person. He likes to run when he's afraid."

"He won't listen to me," Xander admitted.

"And you think he'll listen to me?" Rachel asked.

"It was the last thing I thought I could try," Xander said. "The preview is tomorrow. Well, today, actually, and I can't . . . I don't *want* to do it alone. I wasn't supposed to be alone."

"I can come," Rachel said. "And I can call him, if you want me to. But it's not going to make a bit of difference."

"Can you just . . . tell him, for me? He's not answering my calls anymore. Won't talk to me, anymore."

"Once, he disappeared for a week straight. We'd been married for three months," Rachel said. "He did come back, but he wasn't the same. He carries his demons with him, and they're always trying to get to him. Sometimes they win." She sounded resigned to it, but Xander wasn't. He wanted to fight, fight *with* Damon, if only he would let him. Let him *in*.

"I'll call him," Rachel said finally. "I'll let you know if I get ahold of him. Try to get some sleep. You're going to need it for tomorrow."

Xander didn't want to tell her that it was going to be impossible, but in the end, he must have finally fallen asleep in the early morning, because the next thing he remembered, he was opening his eyes up and listening to a hushed argument happening right outside his bedroom door.

It was painful dragging himself out of bed, but he did it because the only thing Miles and Wyatt had to argue about was *him*, and he wasn't going to let them discuss him when he wasn't even present.

Sure enough, when he wrenched his bedroom door open, Wyatt and Miles were caught red-handed, their conversation stuttering to an abrupt, awkward halt.

"What's going on?" Xander demanded.

They both looked at him, both attempting innocence, and neither one pulling it off. Finally Wyatt sighed and said, "For the record, I think this is a bad idea."

"What's a bad idea?" Xander really hoped that they hadn't heard him call Rachel.

"Come on," Miles said reassuringly, reaching out and taking his hand. "Let's go have some coffee and I'll show you."

In the kitchen, Wyatt poured him a mug of coffee, adding in half a spoon of sugar, just the way he liked. He took a sip. If Wyatt thought coffee was enough to distract him, he was sorely mistaken. "What did you want to show me?"

Miles moved away from the opposite counter, revealing a plain white box tied with white ribbon. "It was sitting on the front porch this morning," he explained. "There's a tag. It's for you. It's from Damon."

Xander hesitated, his grip tightening on the mug. The truth was, he wanted to throw that too, but when they'd taken him to get a new phone, Wyatt had pulled him aside and made him promise he'd stop throwing things. "I know you're pissed, I know you're confused, and you have every right to be," he'd said, "but you can't let that turn you into Bastian. Because I know that's the last thing you want."

He didn't want to end up like Bastian; sad and lonely and isolated, too emotionally scarred and too much of an asshole to even see something good right in front of him. He didn't want to be a jackass, he didn't want to make his employees worry that one day he'd snap and toss a plate at their head.

He didn't want to be that guy or that boss or that friend; he'd always aspired to be better than that. But with the fallout from Damon disappearing, Xander was beginning to realize just how slippery the slope into becoming that man was. A few more doses of distrust and bitterness, Xander knew, and he and Bastian might practically be clones.

He didn't want that, but he also didn't know what to do with all this anger boiling away inside him. He kept trying to keep the noxious steam inside him—absorb the fumes and not let it spread to everyone else—but it was tough.

The truth was there was a part of Xander that was dying to act out, to spread it far and wide until everyone was just as poisoned as he was.

"You don't have to open it," Wyatt said, reaching over and gripping his elbow. "We can just leave it here, we can put it away in a closet, and you don't have to face it until you're ready."

But Xander shrugged. "I'm not ever going to be ready to face it. And whatever's in that box, it can't be worse than going to the restaurant today and not seeing him, knowing he's not going to show up."

It should have hurt worse to undo the ribbon, feel the silk slide under his fingertips as he set it aside and opened the lid. Maybe he was just numb; frozen so he didn't have to feel all the pain slipping through him like water.

Under the lid was tissue paper, which he pulled aside to reveal a pristine white chef's coat. Above the left breast pocket was the embroidered Barrel House logo, and underneath it, his name, and "Executive Chef." Xander traced his finger across the blue threads, remembering nights in a room this exact same color.

Was it better or worse that Damon remembered? Xander didn't know, all he knew anymore was that it hurt and he just wanted the agony to end.

"You've worked a long time for that title," Wyatt said softly.

"I'm sure he ordered this weeks ago," Xander said, even though that didn't help at all. "He just wanted to make sure I had it." That was all he could surmise, because there was no note, no last-minute expression of good luck, no promise that he would be there tonight, ready to watch Xander's triumph.

"It's going to be okay," Miles said, and even he didn't sound convinced that it would be anymore.

You're not going to cry, Xander told himself sternly, reaching inside and finding that steel that had always seen him through the worst of Bastian's days back at Terroir. *You're not going to let anyone see*, he promised himself, *you're going to walk in proud and head high, and nobody is going to know you're dying inside.*

By the time he was out of the shower and they were getting ready to head into the restaurant, Xander couldn't decide which was worse: that Damon believed the worst about himself or that he had decided it was okay for this day, which was supposed to be one of the best of Xander's life, to devolve into an agonizing exercise in emotional containment.

He was a bomb, waiting to go off, and maybe if he just kept going, putting one foot in front of the other, not thinking, not remembering, not *wishing*, he might not explode. Even for Xander, there were a lot of *maybes* and *mights* in that sentence.

***

"I knew I would find you here."

Damon glanced up in surprise. Nobody else knew he liked to come here, way up on the hills of Mount Veeder, only accessible by a dirt road, and never used except for once a year by the land surveyors hired by Hess.

Someday, his father would develop this land. But not now, not until all other options were exhausted, because it was a trek.

And today, Rachel had made the trek up here.

"Xander must have called you," he said morosely, staring at his feet, picking at a loose thread on the hem of his jeans.

"He did. He didn't know what else to do, because you just ghosted on him." There was definitely a reprimand in his ex-wife's voice. "I thought I told you not to fuck it up."

She sat down beside him, put a hand on his knee. "What are you doing here?" she asked. "You're supposed to be down in the Valley, helping him. Being there for him. Running your new restaurant, not up here, pretending like you're not good enough for any of those things."

"It's not pretending," he insisted roughly.

"I told him that you're always fighting your own self, and sometimes you win. You need to figure out how to lose." Rachel's voice was soft, but he couldn't look at her.

"I let you down. I *left* you. I fucking abandoned you for booze. I don't think that's winning."

She laughed, shocking him enough that he glanced up at her. There was a wry expression on her face and tears in her eyes. "You never left me. We left each other because we weren't happy. Did the alcohol help? Of course not. But you can't take all the blame for the disintegration of our marriage, Damon. It was already over. It was nearly over before it even began. And now you've met someone you can really love, who loves you back—loves you so much he's willing to throw his own pride to the wind just to help you. *Fix this.*"

Damon stared out over the Valley. The cause of so much of his pain, and now the cause of so much of his hope. "I can't."

Rachel sat up, and dusted off her legs. Blocked the harsh rays of the sun as she stared down at him. "Then you don't deserve him."

It was a sentiment that Damon had spent the last two days trying to believe, but with Rachel's pronouncement, he had to admit it didn't sound quite right.

He still didn't believe that. At least not enough to stay away entirely.

⁘

After arriving at the restaurant and the initial painful realization that *no*, Damon was not here, Xander discovered there was so much to do, it was impossible to think of anything but the task in front of him, and the fifty million tasks left to do. That helped; not quite enough, but it was enough to make him functional.

He thought about calling Rachel again and asking if she'd gotten anywhere, but the gaping hole left by Damon's continued absence answered every question he would have asked her.

Xander started the team prepping. Miles assisted Monica, the part-time pastry chef, not even saying a word about how menial the tasks were, just chipping in and wordlessly assisting, and when Monica looked over at him like she wanted to say something about Evan or his show, he'd simply shook his head.

He wasn't Miles of *Pastry by Miles* today, he was Xander's friend. It helped shore up Xander's defenses a little, and when Wyatt wordlessly volunteered to manage the front of the house—a job that Damon had given himself—it helped a little more.

At five, Xander went into his tiny private office, tucked behind the kitchen, something he'd claimed not to need when he and Damon had first discussed the remodel, and Damon had insisted on anyway. He pulled off his old stained jacket, and just stared at the new bright white one sitting on his desk.

It fit perfectly, and Xander didn't want to know *how* Damon had known, even though he already knew how. Too many nights with Damon's mouth and hands skating across his shoulders and chest and stomach, becoming intimately familiar with every ridge and curve of him.

The door opened before Xander could dwell any further, saving him from a headlong tumble into misery. He did up the buttons as Wyatt looked at him steadily.

"It's time," he said and all Xander could do was nod wordlessly. It was a good thing his staff, while not yet completely familiar in his recipes, were already impeccably trained and knew every single responsibility. He didn't need to say a word and he probably wasn't going to be able to.

He just had to get through the next four hours.

Wyatt pulled him into a quick, tight hug and whispered into his ear, "We can do this. *You* can do this."

One hour down, and Miles had gone out to assist Wyatt with seating. He reported back that diners were cleaning their plates, all with joyful smiles on their faces. One of the new wait staff reported offhandedly to Xander, while he was standing at the pass-through, inspecting plates bound for tables, that diners were having difficulty even selecting their meal for the night, because "everything sounded amazing."

So far there hadn't been any complaints regarding alcohol, or if there was, Miles and Wyatt were keeping him perfectly, completely isolated from it, and he'd never been more grateful. If even one person walked up to him and demanded a glass of wine, Xander was probably, almost certainly, going to punch them in the face.

Two hours down, a plate came back to the kitchen for the first time. Xander stared at it, the perfect presentation slightly jumbled, and finally looked up wordlessly at the waiter.

"Too much red pepper flakes," he said apologetically. "Could she get it remade with less? She's particularly sensitive to spice."

Xander wanted to retort that if she was sensitive to spice, she shouldn't order something with *pomodoro* in the title, but he took the plate, dumped it in the garbage, sent it down to Chris, his dishwasher, and began to remake the food himself.

Hour three, the kitchen and the dining room were humming along so seamlessly that Xander took a piece of focaccia and a glass of water to his office and tried to force something down.

It didn't work.

He should be the happiest man on the planet right now. His restaurant was a success. People were happily buying his food and claiming they couldn't wait to return. But it all felt empty without Damon here.

Four hours into the preview, they were winding down. Miles came into the kitchen and told him he should hire Monica, the pastry chef, full time, and that he needed another line chef because they were going to end up being busy. Xander made a note on his to-do list and tried to give his friend a genuine smile, but instead it felt fake and plastic. Like someone else was happy and smiling for him. There just wasn't any joy inside of him, and there definitely wasn't enough for a real smile. Miles hugged him and told him he'd stay the rest of the week.

Hour five, and as the staff cleaned and Miles and Wyatt bickered over the tally for the evening and closed out the register, Xander went outside to try to clear his head.

It felt like a fog had overtaken him, the price of having to go through this all while feeling abject despair and abandonment.

He was just leaning against the back of the building, gulping in air and trying to clear his mind, when he spotted a dark figure in the distance, standing in between the rows of vegetables.

Heart thumping painfully, he pushed away from the building and started walking toward him. He knew who it was; he never could have left him alone for this night. After all, this had always been *Damon's* idea, first and foremost. He'd even been the one to convince Xander that the plan had merit. He never could have left him alone tonight.

He started jogging, then he ran, breath coming in harsh pants as he reached the man he loved.

Damon looked over at him, almost in surprise. Almost as if he hadn't expected to get caught or if he had expected it, that Xander wouldn't have even come over.

And fuck that, Xander was in love with him. He'd said some stupid shit, sure, and he'd not understood entirely where Damon was coming from, but he still loved him, and he still wanted this. If he was being honest with himself, he wanted it even more than he had before, because now he knew what it was like to do it without Damon.

"You got it," Damon said first, before Xander could even figure out where to start. What to say first. Should he hug him? Kiss him? Punch him? He didn't know, but in the end it didn't matter.

"I got what?" Xander demanded incredulously.

"Your jacket," Damon said, reaching out like he was going to touch the embroidery right over his heart, but then his hand jerked back, like he hadn't ever intended to touch him. "You needed it, and I couldn't let you go without. Not tonight."

"Then you should have brought it to me yourself," Xander said. He was trying to stay calm, but it was really fucking difficult.

"I couldn't. You know that. I . . . I never should have done this." Damon said this with a small shake of his head, like he couldn't believe he'd ever imagined he could, and that just added more fuel to Xander's anger.

"We *were* doing this!" he yelled. "As far as I was concerned, two nights ago, it was actively happening. I know I fucked up, I know I wasn't as understanding as I needed to be. But I can be better. We can fix this. You can't just walk away and not let me fix it."

Damon's eyes were sad in the moonlight as he stared at him. "I knew after I divorced Rachel that involving myself with anyone ever again was a huge risk. I'm a burden, Xander, and I don't need you to say it for me to know it's true."

"You have baggage. You're an alcoholic. I know. I get that. I don't think less of you, and I don't think you're going to destroy me if you are. You didn't even destroy Rachel. She's moved on, she's happy, she's got a husband and a job and a life. Your demons aren't going to torpedo anyone—even *you*." Xander felt desperate, like his chance was slipping away. He wasn't sure if Damon would believe him, now or ever. He certainly didn't *look* like he believed him.

"They run deep," Damon said with regret in his eyes and his voice. "Sometimes I don't even know how deep they run."

"Then we'll figure it out together," Xander said, and he knew he was pleading. He wasn't even above begging. "Just don't vanish. Don't shut me out." He hesitated, anger swelling again when he thought of what he'd endured today. "Don't fucking take what was supposed to be the best day of my life and make it impossible to get through. I can't do this again. This is not what was supposed to happen."

"It's what needs to happen," Damon said gently, and when Xander tried to reach over, to touch him, to remind him of what they'd shared, of what they'd been through already, he pulled away.

"You can't do this," Xander said blankly. "You can't do this."

"I know it doesn't seem that way now, but this is better for everyone. Including you."

Xander snapped. "You're fucking right it doesn't seem that way. You don't get to make these choices! You don't get to decide that you're too fucked up to be with me. You're the best man I've ever met. The strongest, the bravest, but right now you're acting like a fucking coward and it isn't a good look."

"You're right, it's not. But then you've always been right about a lot of things," Damon said, and Xander wasn't stupid, he knew what a goodbye sounded like.

"Wait," he said when Damon started to turn to walk away. "You can't do this. We're supposed to be a team. We're supposed to do this together."

"It's your restaurant now. You run it. You're going to make it shine. I have faith."

Xander didn't want to tell him he didn't have faith in himself. He didn't want to tell him that running it alone hadn't been what Damon promised. But it was too late to say anything he didn't want to say, because Damon was walking away, and it seemed that even apologies weren't enough to save this.

Alone, in the middle of the garden where they'd first met over a year ago, Xander finally started to cry.

Chapter Sixteen

Damon sat in the car, eyes on the lights of the restaurant and on the solitary figure in the dark field, and cried. There were a hundred things he was thinking, but one particular frustration stood out above all the rest.

Why? Why him?

One of the first things he'd demanded after showing up in rehab was *why*. Why did he rely so heavily on alcohol? Why did having one drink make him want ten more? Why did life only exist in technicolor when he had a drink in his hand?

Grant, his sober coach, had looked at him frankly during one of their first sessions and had told him that there wasn't an answer to any of his questions, and that Damon was going to have to find a path to sobriety a different way.

That had pissed him off, and subsequently, he'd spent the last four years pissed off that he didn't know *why*. He'd gotten sober anyway, with determination and with Grant's support, but the whole time the questions had burned away inside him.

The questions were why he'd been out in the pouring rain, ripping up the vines in the first place. The questions were why, after Rachel, he'd been determined to stay single so that he wouldn't ruin any other lives besides his own.

For a little while, falling in love with Xander had brought happiness and joy and hope to his life, wrenching it from his boring black-and-white existence, and transporting it into technicolor reality for the first time since rehab.

It had been hard enough to find his way to sobriety and leave all that brightness behind when booze had been responsible, but love was a lot tougher to turn his back on. What he wanted was something he had no right to demand, but he couldn't seem to stop himself.

Xander didn't even know why Damon had walked away; it wasn't because he "fucked up" and said some stuff he wanted to take back. It was because the stuff he'd said brought all Damon's fears into the forefront.

There was a part of him that wanted to go see his father and demand an explanation, or maybe even apology. But he'd covered that after rehab. Nathan Hess took zero responsibility and had zero fucks to give that his son was an alcoholic. No amount of ranting or threats or tears were going to change his mind. Damon had stopped looking for answers from his father a long time ago because there were never any to find.

He glanced down at the phone in his hand and realized his fingers were trembling. He couldn't remember the last time he'd seen them shake like this—then it hit him. The last time, he'd wanted a drink so badly he could nearly taste the wine pooling on his tongue. Or the beer. Or the whiskey. He hadn't particularly cared what it was, only that it promised oblivion from feeling like this.

He couldn't pinpoint the time or the day, or even the month. It had become part of him, a background haze that he could ignore now because he wanted to be better more than he wanted the emptiness alcohol brought. But today?

Today and the fight with Xander had just reminded him of how easy it was.

Damon knew what he had to do. He called the person who had seen him at his worst and had still never judged him.

"It's been a long time, Damon," Grant answered, only letting it ring twice. "Is everything okay?"

Right after the two months Damon had spent in rehab, he and Grant had talked every day—sometimes multiple times a day. He'd supported Damon going to collect his vineyard inheritance when nobody else did. Grant's phone calls and texts and emails had gotten Damon through a lot of bleak nights, but in the year since first meeting Xander, they'd dwindled, especially as Damon became more confident in his sobriety.

By the time he hired Xander, he and Grant were only exchanging emails once or twice a month. And before, that was perfectly okay. Damon was fine, he didn't need Grant's help. The last email from Grant had mentioned that sometimes there were other, uncovered issues that stemmed from alcoholism, and he'd encouraged Damon to find a regular therapist.

Damon had thought Grant was full of shit until now. But clearly he had issues, or else why would he have left the man he loved to deal with the restaurant opening by himself? Why else would he have walked away tonight, even though it had hurt like hell to do it?

"No," Damon answered truthfully. "No, it's not okay. I'm not okay."

"Are you drinking?" Grant asked, his voice careful. "Do I need to come get you?"

"I'm sober." He took a deep breath. "In love. But sober. I just don't know how to deal with it. Sobriety I know, love is a complete fucking mystery."

Damon felt Grant's knowing smile over the phone line. "We talked about this. What happened with Rachel wasn't entirely your fault. Marrying so young, you'd already begun to drift apart by the time you started drinking more heavily."

"I know," Damon said, but he wasn't sure he really believed his own words.

"It doesn't matter if you have an addiction, Damon. You still deserve good things. Like finding someone to love."

Damon's voice was barely above a whisper. "How do I believe that?"

"Probably a lot of therapy, but I'll get you started since you called me first. Does this person love you back?"

Damon thought of Xander's destroyed face as he'd walked away. "I think so, yeah."

"Do you think they're a smart person? Intelligent? Thoughtful? Do you think they value their own happiness?"

"Of course I do," Damon snapped. He never would have fallen in love with Xander otherwise.

"Do you think they'd fall in love with someone who wasn't worthy of their love?"

"I know what you're doing." Damon knew the leash on his temper was short tonight; it was almost definitely because it had nearly killed him to walk away from Xander. Staying away completely had been impossible. He'd come because he couldn't be anywhere else. He'd stood in the garden for hours, watching the lights and the customers pour in, and then pour back out, happy and grinning, full from Xander's creations. Anger and envy had surged inside him, nearly bringing him to his knees, but what had actually done it was Xander showing up. Yes, he'd come here, but he'd never actually expected Xander to catch him.

"Then you know what I'm going to say," Grant said, always so painfully reasonable. "If the person you love sees something worthwhile and worth loving in you, then it must exist. You don't have to believe me. You just need to believe in them."

"I do," Damon whispered. He'd believed in Xander from the first moment they'd ever met, rain dripping relentlessly through his dark hair.

"Then you have your answer. You just have to *choose* to believe it."

"You make it sound so easy."

"It is that easy. You can do this, I have faith that you can. Now, tomorrow morning call one of the therapists I sent you."

"I almost called my dad, and I'm so glad I didn't," Damon confessed. "I'm glad I called you instead."

"I'm glad too," Grant said. "He's a waste of your time. You're never going to get a worthwhile answer out of him. You already know that. But this person you love, that's a different story. They deserve better; they deserve your best." He hesitated. "And don't tell me you're not capable of your best because you're an addict. We both know that's not true."

For the first time in days, Damon felt a spark of what Grant was describing.

"Yeah," he said. "Yeah, you're probably right."

Grant laughed. "I'm totally right. Now go fix this."

"I'm going to," Damon said. "There's just something I need to do first."

The security code to the vault was unchanged. Damon supposed he should be surprised, because of the hundreds of dollars of wine stored here, but his father was a creature of habit, and also egotistically believed that nobody would ever dare steal from him.

He looked up at the camera in the corner, and gave his father, who would be watching the security footage hours from now, a one-finger salute.

Nathan was damn lucky that the only thing Damon intended to steal from him was some alone time.

Pulling the door open, hearing the hiss of the pressure release, Damon stepped into the vault, and let the particular smell of wine barrels and dust wash over him. Even though he'd wondered if it might, it didn't make him desperate to pull a bottle from the shelf and drain it dry.

Maybe he was never going to get answers from Nathan Hess. Maybe he was never going to get answers at all, but he could still let go of his poisonous anger—and all the frustration that Nathan was never going to apologize. Not for being a shitty father, not for giving him booze at such a young age, not for making it seem like a perfectly normal part of every single day.

He walked around the vault, pulling out a bottle here, examining the label of another. The wooden racks didn't just hold the cream of the Hess collection, but also housed Nathan's personal wine collection. Even though Damon had been out of this lifestyle for years now, he could still recognize and appreciate the value of some of the bottles he was looking at.

An idea was beginning to form in his head. He didn't know initially why he'd come here—it had seemed like a good plan to go back to the beginning, and this had always felt like the start of it all. He'd been watching his father come in here for years, ever since he was a little boy, to pick out a bottle for a special occasion or even for a normal Tuesday night. He knew this place like the back of his hand. And maybe he'd been wondering if coming here, to the beginning of his own obsession with alcohol, would make it tougher to resist the draw of the oblivion so close at hand.

But all he felt was a vague disgust. He didn't want to be that man anymore, holding onto old, ancient baggage, with all its anger and its hostility and its uncertainty. He knew he wasn't going to drink anymore; Xander had been right about that.

"I don't want a drink," Damon said out loud, feeling a little lame, but also hoping that his father had installed sound with the sophisticated security system. "I really could give a damn if these are worth thousands."

He thought coming here would absolve him of all the guilt and the frustration, but all it showed him was that he'd absolved himself of it a long time ago, he just hadn't realized it. He'd already moved on; he just hadn't caught up with the fulfilling, happy life he was already living.

If he hadn't conquered the thrall of his addiction, he never could have dreamt of starting something of his own. He never would have built a new future for himself. And he sure as fuck wouldn't have fallen head over heels for Xander.

There were only two things he needed to do now before he went to Xander.

The first would have to wait until morning, but the second he could take care of right now. He looked right up at the other camera, smiled broadly, gave his father the second middle finger of the night and sauntered off.

"There's a lot of stuff about last night that we can celebrate," Miles pointed out, pouring another cup of coffee. They were sitting on the outdoor porch of one of their favorite brunch places, conducting a complete rundown of last night's preview success.

Xander knew they were trying to cheer him up, but it wasn't exactly working. Not after the way Damon had turned and walked away last night. The very worst was Xander knew how much it had hurt him, and he'd known just how much it was hurting Xander. And he'd done it anyway. Xander didn't know whether to be pissed as hell at Damon for attempting to ruin them, or leaving him on what was supposed to be the greatest night of his life—or for Damon believing that he didn't deserve Xander's love and support.

"You're not even listening to me," Miles said with a frown.

"I can't imagine why," Xander retorted back.

"We're just trying to . . . cheer you up," Wyatt said with one of his more optimistic, sunny smiles plastered to his face. "And if that fails, then distract you."

Xander reached for his glass and took a big sip of his peach mimosa. "Then distract me."

"You should be hydrating," Miles said with a frown at his glass. "You drank a lot of wine last night."

Yes, he had. He hadn't only done it to forget; he'd also done it as sort of a petty *fuck you* to Damon. Except he'd woken up this morning with a bottomless pit in his stomach, the victory from last night long since faded.

Xander switched his champagne flute for the water glass, and glared over the rim at Miles.

"Well, if you really want to be distracted," Wyatt said. "We can talk about what didn't go well last night."

He switched his glare from Miles to Wyatt. "What?" Wyatt exclaimed. "You need to know, since you're the general manager now."

"Speaking of that," Miles said. "You need to hire a front of the house manager. As awesome as it is for Wyatt and me to be handling that side of things, if Damon's not coming back, you're going to need someone."

Xander took a deep breath. Was he ready to face the possibility that Damon might not ever come back to the Barrel House? Not really, but he wasn't sure he had a choice.

Except the idea of doing it alone, without Damon being that steady and certain force behind him, was a nightmare. Xander wanted to bury his head in his hands and wail that he couldn't do it. Instead he finished the rest of his mimosa and set the glass aside with a decisive click.

"Do you think we could cancel the reservations tonight?" he asked.

"What?" Wyatt and Miles bellowed at exactly the same moment.

"I know I said there was stuff to work on," Wyatt continued. "But it's small stuff. For a preview, last night went so smooth. There's no reason to cancel the reservations."

Xander set his elbows on the table and leaned forward. "There is, if I never intend to open. I'm not doing this alone. I didn't sign on to do this alone."

There was total silence at the table.

"Are you kidding?" Miles burst out finally. "You can't do this, not now! Not when you're so close!"

"Miles is right," Wyatt said seriously.

"I should record this," Xander said. "I don't think you've ever said Miles was right, *ever*."

"Well, he's right *now*," Wyatt countered. "You've worked so damn hard to get to this place. Just think of how many shitty shifts you endured to be offered head chef. How many times did Aquino yell at you? Throw a plate at you? Are you really going to give up after you've finally gotten out from under him?"

"This isn't me giving up," Xander tried to tell them.

"It sure as fuck looks like it," Miles pointed out.

Xander glared but neither of them backed down.

"I just can't believe you're willing to throw this opportunity away because Damon let you down," Wyatt said with a shake of his head.

"He didn't just let me down, he broke my fucking heart," Xander burst out.

"We know," Miles said, reaching over and squeezing Xander's hand. "And I wish he hadn't. I want to go find him and chop his balls off, and shove them down his throat. But this isn't about him, Xander. This is about *you*. You're the strongest person I've ever met. The most driven. The most determined. You shouldn't let one guy's shitty behavior change that."

"You quit before you've even started, and you've let him win," Wyatt added.

Xander's gaze narrowed. "You know, you're a real asshole."

"What, me?" Wyatt asked with a faux innocent tone and a hearty laugh.

"You know me too well," Xander retorted. "You know exactly what will get me to the Barrel House tonight."

Miles shrugged. "To get you there, we're willing to play dirty. You've sacrificed too much to just give up now, and we love you too much to let you."

"Don't make me cry," Xander drawled, but inside he was feeling all warm and fuzzy. Who made it through life without friends like Wyatt and Miles? He might even consider adding Kian to the list, even though sometimes he wanted to twist his neck in frustration.

"We'll be there tonight," Wyatt said. "And we'll be there as long as you need."

"Next Friday, we'll be here until next Friday," Miles inserted with a grin. "And then you either have to pay us or hire someone else."

"Fine," Xander grumbled. "Now let's hear about the issues that need cleared up for tonight."

"You're going to need another mimosa," Miles said and flagged the waitress down.

"Chef," Miles said, his voice respectful, but his eyes glittering with amusement. "I need to talk to you for a minute."

Xander glanced up. They were two hours into dinner service, and even though there were a few moments where he wanted to set down his pan and walk right out, sticking his best chef's knife in Damon's door for good measure, things were going even smoother than they had during the preview.

But Miles didn't just look amused, Xander realized as they walked toward the back, to the long prep tables by the refrigerators. The problem with having a large glass wall in between the kitchen and the dining room was that everyone saw everything. Xander typically didn't have anything to hide, except when his heart was broken and Miles was making *that* face.

"Everything okay?" he asked, dreading the answer.

"Do you want the bad news or the really bad news?"

Xander raised an eyebrow. "Really bad news first."

Miles still didn't say anything. "Okay," Xander corrected testily, "I guess I'll take the bad news first."

"Bastian Aquino is here. He wants a table."

"I don't care about that asshole," Xander said. "If he's decided to lower himself by eating at my humble establishment, you might as well give him a damn table."

"Damon is also here," Miles said, before Xander could really prepare himself. He'd sort of expected what Miles was about to say, but maybe there wasn't anything he could do *to* prepare himself.

"I can't talk to him right now. We're in the middle of service," Xander complained.

"Which is what I told him," Miles soothed, reaching up to put a hand on Xander's shoulder.

"But he's not going to continue to take no for an answer and you don't want him to cause a scene," Xander finished wryly. "Fine, tell him I can give him thirty seconds."

"You want me to bring him back here?"

"He decides to bail," Xander said firmly, "and he comes to confront me in the middle of opening night, when Aquino just walked in? He can say whatever he's come to say in front of God and everybody. I'll be in the kitchen."

Miles looked mildly impressed. The hand on his shoulder squeezed reassuringly. "You've got this," was all he said before he walked back out toward the front of the restaurant.

Xander was focusing on the food at the pass-through, making sure every single plate was picture perfect before the waiter picked it up to take it to the table.

"Xander," Damon said roughly, and Xander's fingers hesitated on a lacy nest of microgreens decorating the top of his eggplant parmesan. He didn't look up; suddenly he wasn't sure he could. Why had he thought this was a good idea? That speech of Wyatt and Miles' from earlier this morning, when they'd talked up how brave and hardcore he was, that's why. Xander mentally cursed them both.

"You have fifteen seconds," Xander said, his voice thankfully steady, but he still didn't look up. He was painfully aware that the whole kitchen had slowed down and all his employees were focusing more on the confrontation in front of them than their own tasks. But could he really blame them? Hell, *he* certainly wasn't focusing on his own tasks right now.

"Miles said I'd have thirty," Damon said, and the flippant edge to his voice just pissed Xander off. He did not get to waltz in here, no matter how shitty the things Xander had said were, and make jokes.

Xander glanced up and he knew his expression was hard as steel. "You got docked fifteen seconds because it turns out you're not the good guy here. You're an asshole."

Damon's eyes were bloodshot and he looked tired. Something uncomfortable bloomed in Xander's stomach. Was Damon drinking again? Had their fight pushed him away from his sobriety? As pissed as Xander was, he didn't ever want that for him. He loved him—still, always, *forever*—no matter what Damon had done. Even if Damon was an asshole.

"No," Damon said wryly, answering the question Xander hadn't asked. "No, I'm not drinking again, even if I look like shit. Apparently not sleeping for multiple nights in a row does that to you."

"I'm still waiting," Xander inserted testily. "I've got a job to do, a job you fucking hired me for."

"I know, and I'll leave you alone after this, to do it and do it brilliantly. I saw Bastian come in when I did, please make sure you knock his fucking socks off."

"Well?" Xander asked again. "I'm still waiting."

"I just didn't want you to go through tonight without you knowing. I love you." Damon said the words clearly and loudly, definitely loud enough for every interested party in the dining room to hear.

It shouldn't have mattered, not after his behavior of the last few days, but Xander felt his eyes fill. For so long this was exactly what he'd wanted—someone to love him with zero shame or embarrassment, and he'd finally found that.

Except that Damon had still massively fucked up the last few days, and Xander wasn't ready just yet to accept such a bad non-apology.

"I know," Xander said calmly. "I know you do."

"And I need to apologize?" Damon guessed with a heavy sigh. "I know I do. We'll talk after dinner, and I'll apologize the right way. I just wanted you to know I love you before you do this."

"We'll see if it's the right sort of apology first," Xander challenged.

Damon's face broke into a bright grin. "Oh, it's gonna be good."

Xander's hands stilled on the microgreens. "It better fucking be."

Turning around, Damon sauntered out of the kitchen and to Xander's surprise, he saw him walk over to where Miles was greeting guests at the host stand. They exchanged a few words, and Miles *left*, like he intended to give Damon the job he'd so callously forfeited.

"Chef," Billy said, suddenly right next to him. "Chef?"

Xander's gaze snapped over to him. He was still replaying watching Damon greet guests in a snazzy, sharp sport coat and jeans, one of his nicer plaid shirts underneath, smiling and shaking hands like he felt a real sense of pride in the Barrel House.

The pride that Xander had been convinced after the last few days that he'd felt alone.

Maybe things weren't quite as they seemed.

"What?" Xander barked.

"Nothing," Billy stammered. "I just . . . didn't realize you were involved with the owner."

Xander rounded on him. Was it nice that Damon had made that particular confession in front of everyone, so there was zero confusion about where he stood? *Yes*, but he also had zero intention of letting his staff turn into a bunch of gossipy grannies on shift.

"Right now," Xander bit off, raising his voice so every single employee could hear him, including Chris who washed the dishes, "Bastian Aquino is sitting in our dining room. You might have heard of him. He's the head chef at Terroir, he has Michelin stars, he's my old boss, and he's affectionately known as the Bastard. Just in case you thought your distraction was going to slide for one millisecond. Now, let's get to work."

"Yes, Chef," they replied in chorus.

"Damn right you will," Xander said, and did something he hadn't in two full days—he smiled.

⁂

It had been a really great night, Xander realized as he rolled his shoulders and cracked his neck, releasing all the tension from so many hours bent over stoves and plates. Tonight, Bastian had proved there were rare exceptions to his Bastard nickname by even sending compliments back to the chef. He'd also said that he could tell Miles was working on his desserts, and his regular pastry chef better be up to Miles' level, or the quality was going to suffer when he went back to his real job and his real life.

But Xander had been in such a good mood that he'd just laughed. Bastian wasn't saying anything he didn't already know, and if he hadn't offered *any* criticism, then Xander would have believed he'd been taken over by the pod people.

The kitchen had been scrubbed clean, and the staff had slowly been departing, even Billy high-fiving Xander on his way out. He had a feeling that Billy wasn't going to quit if they never put wine on the menu. He'd bought in, and even though the waitstaff had reported a few odd looks and comments with no wine list on the tables, he felt like Napa was slowly buying in too.

It wouldn't be easy, but they could build something with a lot of hard work and dedication.

They, Xander realized. He was still thinking about the Barrel House as a joint effort, something he and Damon shared together. To know that for sure going forward, he was going to have to leave the safety of his kitchen and go find him.

He was nervous and apprehensive about it. What if Damon's apology wasn't as kick-ass as he'd promised? What if after hearing it, Xander still felt angry and betrayed? How were they supposed to move forward if he couldn't forgive?

And Xander wanted to move forward and put these two days of hell behind them so badly he could nearly taste it. The only problem was he couldn't do that if he didn't let Damon make his apology first. Besides, there was another apology that Xander still felt honor bound to make.

Whether Damon's reaction was deserved or not, Xander still hadn't had the faith in him that he should have. He'd been selfish and callous, and he needed to make that right.

He walked into the dining room, the lights turned down low, and when he didn't see Damon anywhere, ventured outside. There were lights on in the distance, where Damon's house sat, so he wandered that direction.

When he crested the slight ridge that hid the house from the restaurant parking lot, Xander froze.

There were candles on the table sitting on Damon's patio, the same setup that he'd had the first night Xander had ever cooked for him. The night that Xander had long believed was their first date. But it wasn't just the candles that stopped him, it was the wine bottle sitting on the table, a single empty glass next to it, glittering in the candlelight.

"What are you doing?" Xander nearly yelled, panic overtaking him as he raced down the ridge toward the patio. "You can't drink. Not like this. Not for me. God, please don't do this."

But Damon just smiled. "Don't worry," he said as Xander skidded to a stop next to the table. "I'm not drinking. The wine isn't for me. It's for you."

Xander sat down opposite him with a huff. He looked at the label, recognizing it as one of the most prized Hess vintages. One of the vintages that had helped Nathan Hess rule Napa.

"Where did you even get this?" Xander said, picking it up and reading the label carefully.

"My dad's vault," Damon said casually.

Xander looked up suspiciously. "Is this your really good apology? A thousand-dollar bottle of wine?"

"It's part of it," Damon said. "I know you haven't been drinking around me. I know you enjoy wine, and I want you to know that while what you said probably could have used better delivery, it was all true. I don't really want to drink anymore, not really. I don't want to be that man anymore. I want to be better; you *make* me want to be better. The last thing I want to do is hold you back from things you like doing."

"I never said I enjoyed drinking wine," Xander said. Which was technically true.

Damon laughed. "You never had to, sweetheart. I knew. I saw your face at Michael Mina, when they took the wine list away, and I realized then that I was the one holding you back. Then you tried to convince me, with a very logical argument, by the way, that we should serve alcohol at the Barrel House. And that's when everything I believed, deep down, came back in spades. I never believed that as an alcoholic I deserved happiness and hope and all that. I thought I'd fucked up my life, and nobody should get dragged down with me. Nobody else deserved it."

Xander opened his mouth to say that was complete and total bullshit, but Damon beat him to it.

"I know, that's such asinine crap," Damon said wryly. "I can't believe I took that to heart for so damn long. But I did, and I'm still fighting against it. I also want you to know that it's not going to change overnight, no matter how much I want it to. But I'm going to start seeing a therapist, who's going to work with me on this stuff. I'm going to be better. I *want* to be better."

"Wow," Xander said softly. "This *is* a pretty good apology. Except that you haven't really apologized yet." He shot a quick grin at Damon. "But maybe I can have some wine first?"

Damon poured it without a single tremble in his fingers. Maybe Xander shouldn't have believed him, but he did. He understood how it was so easy to believe that you were worthless and didn't deserve someone to love who loved you back. He'd believed that too, for a long time, and instead of figuring out he was wrong, he'd gotten angry and bitter. That's when Damon had found him—or he'd found Damon.

Xander took a long sip. The aroma was glorious, the flavor unmatched as it slid across his tongue. "This is really good wine," he said. "Is your dad going to kill you?"

Shrugging, Damon didn't seem particularly concerned. "I'm sorry I didn't believe more in myself, and that I didn't believe more in you," he said seriously. "If you give me another chance, I swear you won't regret it."

"I believe you. I believe *in* you," Xander said, either the emotion or the wine making his voice hoarse. "I love you."

"I know," Damon said, and his smirk made Xander's heart soar. "Now come over here so I can kiss you."

Xander wanted to and even got up from his chair because damnit, he wanted to kiss Damon too. It had only been two days but it had felt like an eternity. But then he looked over at his glass. He'd been drinking. He didn't know what Damon's tolerances were or what the rules *really* were.

"Oh, get over here," Damon said with the brightest laugh. "I poured it for you, didn't I? Do you trust me?"

"Forever," Xander said, coming over and settling on Damon's broad thighs. He linked his hands around his neck, pulled him close and kissed him.

Epilogue

Twelve months later

"How are you feeling?"

Damon leaned back on his therapist's couch and discarded the initial, defensive response because that wasn't going to get him anywhere. He'd learned from his weekly sessions that the sarcasm he was picking up from Xander did him zero favors with Amy.

"I'm good," Damon said.

Amy's eyes narrowed. He liked her because she didn't take any of his bullshit, and always said exactly what she meant. "Tell me more," she said, tapping her pen insistently on the yellow pad resting on her lap.

It was one of his therapist's favorite sayings, and Damon narrowly avoided gritting his teeth together. "Well," he said, "tonight is the big celebration dinner. We've been open a year, and haven't managed to kill each other yet."

"And?" Amy asked.

"And my father is coming because I invited him." Damon frowned at a stain on the rug in front of him. "I'm trying to figure out if I regret that yet."

"Why don't you tell me why you invited him?" she suggested. If he didn't know better, he'd think she enjoyed watching him squirm a little under her microscope of honesty.

"You know why I invited him," Damon retorted. "We discussed it for weeks."

"Tell me like I don't already know. Tell me like I'm a stranger."

"I want him to see what Xander and I have built together, and I want him to meet my boyfriend."

"If he doesn't appreciate what you built, and doesn't like Xander, will the evening be a disaster?" she asked.

Damon's mouth twisted into a wry smile. "I try not to let him ruin anything anymore. I guess if he comes and is his normal asshole self, I won't be very surprised, but I also won't be disappointed."

Amy smiled. Damon still found it a little terrifying, but he'd learned to trust it over the last year. Learned to trust *her*. "Does that help answer your question?"

He was never sure whether he loved or hated that every time he wasn't sure about something, she'd ask a handful of questions and his answers would always guide him to his own conclusion.

Damon shook his head. "How do you do that?"

"Practice. Now what else is going on?"

"Xander and I are still talking about selling alcohol," Damon admitted. "Neither of us can make a decision that sticks. Every time I bring it up, saying I'm good with it, he tells me that we don't need it. And vice versa."

"It actually sounds like you've found your decision," Amy said.

"I . . . I . . . guess so?" He hesitated. Considering how long they'd been discussing it, it seemed like the final answer to the question would have been more obvious, but this *was* a subject filled with a lot of personal baggage, and they were both wary of that baggage. But then, if a year had gone by and they still weren't serving alcohol, Amy was probably right. That *was* the answer.

"I know so," Damon finally said with a lot more certainty.

Amy nodded approvingly. "You've come a long way from the first time we met."

The first time they'd met, Damon had been a tsunami of guilt and low self-esteem, endlessly grateful that Xander still loved him and was willing to accept his apology, but not entirely sure how to move forward with that, and to be better for both of them.

"I can feel the confidence radiating out of you," Amy pointed out. "It's a whole different vibe. But the real question is, how do *you* feel?"

"I don't know that I feel all that different," Damon admitted. "I feel less guilty. I feel less like I'm going to fuck Xander's life up. I still look at him sometimes and think *god, I'm lucky*, but there isn't that fear with it that someday he'll figure out he's too good for me."

Damon thought for a moment. "Now it just feels like we're good for each other."

"The first time I met him, I thought that too," Amy said. "And I think you knew it. You just had to discover it for yourself."

"You really like to do that, don't you?" Damon asked with a long-suffering tone of voice, even though he would readily acknowledge to just about anybody else how amazing Amy was and how much of a difference she'd made in his life.

She laughed. "You know it."

Their session length usually varied. Sometimes, if the subject was difficult or hard to talk about, they'd only talk for half an hour. Occasionally Damon couldn't shut up, and they'd chat away for the full hour. Today was a shorter session, which despite discussing Nathan briefly, hadn't been particularly difficult emotionally.

As Amy walked him to the door, she put a hand on his shoulder. "I think you should consider going to every other week, despite how much I enjoy our weekly sessions," she said.

Damon glanced up in surprise. "Really?"

"You're doing great," Amy said. "And don't say you're not fixed, because you know from rehab that fixed and better aren't the same thing."

"I know," Damon agreed seriously.

She pulled him into a quick hug. "Come back in a few weeks."

Damon didn't always leave therapy feeling like a load of crap, but today he felt light and happy and like over the last year, he'd finally found the road he needed to walk on—and the person he wanted to walk on it with.

⁂

"You're smiling," Xander said as soon as Damon walked into the Barrel House. "I thought you were seeing Amy this morning." He walked down from where he was laying place settings at the gigantic table that ran the whole length of the dining room. Setting a table wasn't normally something Xander's staff let him do, but he'd forbidden anyone from coming into work today, insisting that this dinner—the Barrel House's one-year anniversary and also a celebration of the restaurant's unbelievable success—was something he wanted to do himself. Or at least with Damon's help.

The dinner was also a temporary goodbye as the staff went on a three-week paid sabbatical while David oversaw an expansion of the dining room and added a pizza kitchen which included an enormous wood-fired oven Damon had shipped from Italy.

As for Xander, he had demanded a vacation, and he and Damon were headed to southern Italy for a heavy dose of sun and great food, with a lighter dose of work scoping out new suppliers.

"I was," Damon said, and grinned even harder.

Xander raised an eyebrow. "Usually she makes you think too hard and I need to give you a wide berth." That was one of the reasons he hadn't liked the idea of Damon going to therapy today, because the truth was, Xander couldn't do everything, and he needed Damon's help to pull this dinner off. And Damon stuck in his own head was not usually a great helper.

"Not today," Damon said, pulling Xander into a tight embrace, his hands smoothing down the shoulders of his white chef's jacket. "Today was different. She even thinks I can go to every other week instead of every week."

"Really?" Xander couldn't help the surprise in his voice. Some weeks, Damon made it sound like he was still slogging through the worst of his low self-worth and family-inherited baggage. He'd been seeming lighter, and the fact that he'd wanted Nathan to come to this dinner had definitely signaled important change. But Amy thinking he could reduce his therapy sessions was huge.

"You sound happy."

Xander smiled. "I'm so happy that you're happy."

"I was never *not* happy," Damon said seriously. "You've always made me happy. But now when I'm just standing still, even lost in my own head, I'm content."

"Your gray is lighter," Xander pointed out.

"Together we're sort of a light taupe," Damon teased, pulling him even closer. "Now kiss me before I change my mind and we throw everyone out and celebrate just the two of us."

Xander did as requested, pressing his lips to Damon's, and the electrical surge he felt every time they kissed hadn't ever gone away. Even though it had been over a year since the very first time.

"Wait," Xander said wrenching away breathlessly as Damon tried to deepen the kiss while he stepped them backwards, back toward the bathroom. The same bathroom that they'd first told each other they were in love, all those months ago. Damon still had a real nostalgia for that particular bathroom.

Xander had a feeling when he proposed, he was totally going to do it in that bathroom, and he wasn't even going to be disappointed.

"Wait what?" Damon asked innocently, even though the way his dick was poking Xander's hip made it very clear that he had zero virtuous intentions for their trip to the bathroom.

"Did you really want to celebrate with just the two of us?" Xander asked. From the moment a month ago that he'd concocted this plan to throw a celebration dinner, Damon had seemed a hundred and ten percent on board, but he was always partial to anything Xander suggested.

It might be because he was crazy in love with him.

"No way," Damon said. "I fucking lugged in this table from the rental company *and* assembled it. This thing is happening, even if I have to pull people in off the street."

Xander laughed, and the tiny niggling doubt floated away like a cloud in a particularly blue sky. The same place all his doubts, the big ones and the small ones and the medium-sized ones, had all been going for the last year. Just when he thought he couldn't trust or love or adore Damon more, he opened more of himself up to Xander, and he fell just a bit harder.

It might have been annoying if Xander wasn't so damn happy.

"Then we'd better get this table set and then start on dinner," Xander said, reluctantly disentangling himself from Damon's arms before he could make do on all his unspoken promises and actually drag them into the bathroom.

"I guess if we're inviting people to dinner, they're going to need plates and silverware and glasses, and something edible in those," Damon said, definitely sounding disappointed.

"We run a restaurant together. It's been open a year," Xander teased, "and I feel like you're finally learning something about the food business."

"It's only because I have the best teacher," Damon retorted with a broad grin.

Damon surveyed the scene before him: employees and friends and even family—Xander's parents and his own father, deep in discussion at the quieter side of the table—sparkling water bottles and wine bottles intermingled across the surface, and platters holding the remainder of the meal he and Xander had made together.

Surrounded by people he loved—and people he had even learned to tolerate, like his father—he felt an inescapable swelling of rightness. However difficult the path had been to get here, he was here now, and the tougher parts of his life fell into place, giving the greater ones perspective.

He stood, Xander catching his eye from where he was surrounded by Kian, Wyatt, and Miles. Ryan, Wyatt's brand-new husband, was lounging next to them, half-lidded eyes following his lover wherever he went. Evan was there too, making notes on the back of a menu as he talked to Nate. Learning more about wine? Thinking about ideas to incorporate into their hit show, *Pastry by Miles*?

Damon tapped his glass once, then again, gathering everyone's attention.

"The first thing I want to say is welcome, and thank you for coming," he said. He hadn't always loved public speaking—or even tolerated it—but a bonus side effect from his therapy sessions with Amy was that he felt more naturally confident in expressing how he felt and what he wanted.

He definitely knew exactly what he wanted now, and just how he was going to get it.

There was a smattering of applause and Xander kept giving him narrowed looks that all said *what the fuck are you doing?* No, they hadn't planned on making any speeches, and Damon had initially been wanting to do this when they were in Italy, but sometimes the right moment came along. Wasn't it worse if Damon just let it pass them by?

"The second thing I want to say is that the Barrel House wouldn't be what it is today if not for every single person in this room. Xander and I couldn't have done this without you. Billy and everyone in the kitchen, I know you were skeptical at first. Fuck, we were both skeptical at first, too. But what I really wanted was to focus on Xander's brilliance, and you guys made that possible. I can't thank you enough for that."

Xander rose then. "And, somehow without drinking, my boyfriend still manages to be cheesy and a little bit maudlin." He walked over to the head of the table where Damon was standing and slung an arm around his shoulders. "I think what he's trying to say is that he's grateful for everyone sticking with us, especially during the shaky beginning."

"Not so shaky!" Wyatt called out, and he was smiling like crazy.

Xander shot him a look, as always fiercely protective of Damon. Damon couldn't have been more endeared if he was trying.

"We also have to thank Miles and Evan for sneakily mentioning how great the Barrel House is on their show," Xander continued. "If you'd asked for permission to name drop, I would have said no. But luckily for us, you didn't ask."

Miles mimed giving him a fist bump across the length of the table.

Xander turned to Damon, eyes glowing, and he knew this was the moment.

"There's actually a third thing," Damon said, reaching into his pocket and pulling out a small box. "I was going to wait and do this in Italy, but I just discovered that I want to share this with everyone we love."

Among whoops, Damon dropped to one knee and opened the box, revealing a simple platinum band. "I love you, I've loved you from the moment you walked out in the rain and asked me what the fuck I was doing. It turns out what I was doing was waiting for you."

Silence fell as Xander stared down at him, not saying a word. He didn't look unhappy exactly, but he also wasn't saying yes. Or no. Or *let me think about this for a damn second.* Damon's heart skipped a beat, and then another. He didn't move, giving the love of his life a moment to figure out what he wanted to say.

This was Xander, so chances were he had a lot to say.

Finally, he spoke, and instead of heartfelt tears or smiles, all he said was, "Why aren't you proposing in the bathroom?"

There were a lot of things Damon could do in response to that question. But truthfully, there was only one; he roared with laughter.

"The bathroom?" he asked incredulously.

"You love that bathroom," Xander countered, a glimmer of a smile on his face, eyes soft and warm. There wasn't a question of him saying no, it was more the venue that Damon hadn't quite gotten right.

"If you want a proposal in the bathroom, we'll go in there right now."

"You've got it," Xander said, and held out a hand to Damon, helping him up.

They walked past all the incredulous faces, and shut the bathroom door behind them, muting the excited chatter.

"Well?" Xander asked, raising his eyebrow the way Damon adored. "You're not going to get down on one knee again?"

"This is a small bathroom," Damon complained.

"Hasn't ever stopped you before," Xander pointed out cheerfully.

Damon laughed again. "One of the many reasons I love you. You don't let me get away with any bullshit."

"One of the many reasons I love you—you totally give in to *all* my bullshit," Xander retorted, but there were tears in his eyes now, and he pressed Damon against the door, kissing him the way he intended to for the rest of their lives.

A minute later, Damon came up for air, and pinned Xander with a look he'd learned from the source. "So was that a yes?"

"What do you think?" Xander asked, holding up his hand and wiggling a finger, which suddenly seemed to be sporting a silver band. Damon glance down to the box, and discovered he'd been so distracted by their first engaged kiss that he hadn't even noticed Xander take the ring out.

"Yes," Damon said, and pulled him in for another, even deeper kiss—lasting forever or eternity, whichever felt the longest.

Ready to read Kian and Bastian's story? Check out *Indulge Me* on Amazon and Kindle Unlimited.

INTERESTED IN READING MORE OF
BETH'S BOOKS?

CHECK OUT A FULL LIST OF TILES
BY SCANNING THE QR CODE
OR VISITING HER WEBSITE

WWW.BETHBOLDEN.COM/BOOKLIST

WANT TO FOLLOW BETH?

MAKE SURE YOU NEVER
MISS A RELEASE?

SCAN THE QR CODE BELOW
OR VISIT HER WEBSITE
FOR A SOCIAL MEDIA LIST,
NEWSLETTER SIGNUP,
AND SO MUCH MORE!

WWW.BETHBOLDEN.COM/ABOUT

www.ingramcontent.com/pod-product-compliance
Lightning Source LLC
Chambersburg PA
CBHW070404310726
48977CB00003B/554